'This thriller is a read

Claire Frost, *Fab*

'This absorbing mystery also takes a look at police misconduct'

Heat

'I love a police procedural, and this debut ticked a lot of boxes. The tension kept me swiftly turning the pages'

Nina Pottell, *Prima*

'Fun as well as thoughtful, this will be gobbled up by fans of Cara Hunter and the like'

Jake Kerridge, *Daily Telegraph*

ALSO BY CHARLOTTE LANGLEY

The Blame

THE INTRUSION

CHARLOTTE LANGLEY

First published in the UK in 2024 by No Exit Press,
an imprint of Bedford Square Publishers Ltd,
London, UK

noexit.co.uk
@noexitpress
info@bedfordsquarepublishers.co.uk

A CIP catalogue record for this book is available from the British Library.

Authorised EU representative: Mustamäe tee 50, 10621 Tallinn, Estonia

ISBN
978-1-915798-86-2 (Paperback)
978-1-915798-84-8 (Hardback)
978-1-915798-85-5 (eBook)

2 4 6 8 10 9 7 5 3 1

Typeset in Garamond MT Pro by Palimpsest Book Production Limited,
Falkirk, Stirlingshire

Printed in Great Britain by CPI Group (UK) Ltd, Croydon CR0 4YY

PROLOGUE

Thirteen years ago

NO ONE NOTICED HE WAS gone until the fireworks stopped. Every year, Bonfire Night brought an almost frenzied energy to the town of Wakestead. The park near the town centre had been transformed, the usually verdant field trampled into a muddy slurry by the shuffling crowd. Vans serving up burgers and fried doughnuts poured cooking smoke into the freezing night air.

Afterwards, witnesses told the police that the group of boys must have arrived at around 8 o'clock. The boys said they had been drinking at one of their houses before heading to this one event in the town's calendar, the alcohol numbing them to the cold.

The fireworks began shortly after. Children perched on their fathers' shoulders for a better view, mesmerised by the high-pitched shriek of each rocket sailing into the night sky, leaving golden trains in their wake, before exploding and showering back down to earth.

Perhaps the pummelling of the night sky concealed the sound of an argument breaking out between the boys. Whatever it was, something made one of them turn around and abandon their friends, slipping away almost unnoticed. Another followed. A handful of families remembered seeing two figures pushing their way back through the crowd with some effort, wading against the current. But that was the final in-person sighting. No one looked round to see a lanky teenage boy stalking across the field in the direction of the car park. On the busiest night of the year, the town of Wakestead was transfixed on the display.

All the police knew was that, at approximately 9 o'clock, a group of boys turned around to discover two of their party had vanished – one of them forever.

PART I

1

Saturday 21st August

'STILL NOTHING?'

DCI Gregory looked up as DSU Adlington re-entered the observation room, handing him a paper cup of coffee from the machine in the corridor.

'Nothing whatsoever,' Gregory replied.

Together they looked at the woman on the other side of the one-way glass. For ten minutes, she had not moved. Resting her head on her hands, elbows on the table, she stared straight down, a wild mane of black hair shielding her expression as the two detectives who sat in front of her waited with visible frustration for her to cut out this act and finally speak.

Amma Reynolds had not said a single word from the moment of her arrest less than an hour ago.

'I want to remind you that you have every right to request to speak to a solicitor, Amma,' Lewis Jennings said.

No movement. No change in expression. No flicker of comprehension in her face. It was as if Lewis had said nothing at all.

Gregory leant forward until his face was almost touching the glass. He was interested to see how Lewis handled this one. The detective inspector was soft on everyone – colleagues, witnesses and suspects alike. While Lewis's young partner Chris Baldwin sat clenching his jaw, struggling to contain his rage, beside him Lewis watched Amma with concern in his eyes.

'We're in our rights to keep you here for thirty-six hours.

Potentially longer,' Lewis said. 'No one wants that to happen. But we will do it if we have to.'

His eyes implored her to speak. But silently Amma turned her head to the left, in the direction of the observation room. Beneath the sweep of unruly hair, her dark eyes flitted around the one-sided mirror, as if searching her reflection for a chance of escape.

Gregory imagined their eyes connecting through the glass. *Remember me?* he thought.

Another silence, each one seemingly longer than the last.

'Where were you this morning, Amma?' Lewis asked again, for what felt like the tenth time in under an hour.

Amma said nothing.

Watching Amma's listless stare, Gregory let out a sigh of frustration through his nose. Sometimes calmness and patience worked in these situations; sometimes not.

Perhaps he'd made a mistake giving Lewis this one. Too soft, just as he'd thought.

So he felt a deep sense of satisfaction when finally Lewis's partner leant forward across the table and spoke up for the first time in the interview:

'A police officer has been killed, Amma. We need you to start talking.'

2

STEPPING OUT OF THE INTERVIEW room, Lewis noticed a dull pain between his eyes as his vision adjusted to the brighter overhead lights. After a long and fruitless hour with their silent suspect, the cooler air of the corridor was a welcome relief. The moment the door was closed behind them, Chris locked his fingers behind his neck and raised his head to the ceiling, letting out an aggravated groan.

'Fucking. *Cow*.'

At 25, Chris was seven years younger than Lewis but his stocky build made him appear older. Lewis always felt slightly uncomfortable giving orders to the broad-chested young officer with a buzz cut, who looked like he could beat him in just about any test of physical fitness. But now was the time to say what he'd wanted to tell his partner for the duration of the interview.

'I know it's frustrating,' he said, choosing his words carefully, 'but in my experience, when a suspect isn't cooperating, it's better to focus on establishing a connection with them, rather than—'

Chris interrupted him. 'I don't understand how you can be so calm. Surely if she won't say anything, it's because she's done it, right? So why bother establishing a connection? We need to be harder on her.'

Lewis bit the inside of his mouth and said nothing. He had never had to manage anyone in his life until being paired with Chris. Ideally, the super would have given him a shy and self-effacing partner. A nice practice run. It was just his luck to get

Chris instead – who had absolutely no trouble voicing his opinion and seemingly no respect for authority either.

As they headed for the office kitchen in search of a much-needed coffee, Lewis thought of Amma's mournful eyes, fixed constantly on the table. He didn't agree with Chris. Usually suspects said 'no comment' because they either couldn't comprehend the damage they'd done or face up to the consequences. But that wasn't the impression he got from Amma. He got the impression she was simply scared. A terrified 25-year-old woman. Despite what had happened, he pitied her. And he needed to hold onto that pity in order to find out what had happened, and why.

He was jolted out of his thoughts as soon as they entered the main office. The usually bustling space was eerily quiet. Over by the water cooler, a young officer was pink in the face with emotion, talking with obvious distress while Adlington patted him reassuringly on the arm. On one table, a group of officers gathered around one computer, streaming a TV news report. Their expressions were solemn.

The newsreader's calm, well-spoken voice rang coldly around the office:

'This morning, the body of a man was found at Crays Hill in Wakestead, Oxfordshire. A woman in her twenties has been arrested on suspicion of murder. The woman remains in police custody at this time.'

Only then did it start to sink in – the long, painful journey that today's events had set in motion.

3

Earlier That Day

LEWIS PARKED BESIDE THE OTHER police cars at the top of Crays Hill and walked towards the viewpoint.

In their white overalls, the forensic team looked like alien figures drifting across the grassy slopes. Constables flanked the blue-and-white police tape strung between two upright logs that marked the entrance to the top of the hill. He showed one of them his warrant card and stepped over the tape, thinking how strangely calm the scene was. News hadn't reached the local reporters yet. But it was only a matter of time.

As he approached the top of the slope and the ground dipped away beneath his feet, the full scene revealed itself. A tent had been set up near the base of a huge sycamore tree, which stood apart from the blanket of woodland that rolled down the hillside. Behind that wall of trees the town of Wakestead lay sprawled out, the silver thread of the river gleaming in the sunlight, the church spire the tallest discernible point among the cluster of houses.

DS Adlington stood watching the forensics team. The wind up here had blown his grey hair into a crazed steeple on top of his head.

Reaching his side, Lewis said, 'Have we found anything?'

'Nothing yet. No weapon so far.' The older detective's expression was grave.

'It is him, isn't it?' asked Lewis.

Adlington nodded. 'It's DI Mark Stormont.'

It was a dog walker who had found him – or rather, their dog.

Lewis imagined the golden retriever nosing excitedly through the grass several hours earlier, chasing the invisible scent trail that had led it to this morbid discovery. Maybe the dog had let out a fearful whine. Maybe it had wagged its tail with pride as its owner approached. But whatever it had done, Lewis was certain it hadn't responded with the full human horror its finding deserved.

The man was lying face-down in the grass, not far from a wrought-iron bench perfectly positioned to watch the sun setting over the town below. He wore a light black jacket. Lewis thought of the crumpled form of a fallen raven, wings still spread as if in flight. One arm was stretched out in front of him, as though he had tried to crawl across the clearing. The other was bent beneath his body, where he had tried to stem the bleeding. It had not rained for weeks and the parched earth drank in the blood greedily. Rather than bright red it had turned the yellow-green grass around the body dark brown in colour, like patches of shadow.

The sound of a car door slamming shut made them both turn around. Lewis watched in surprise as Chris ducked underneath the crime scene tape. Chris, who had been closer to Mark than many others. Who had – Lewis had suspected – wanted him as his partner, rather than Lewis. Who had looked up to the detective almost like an older brother. He was walking purposefully and at full pace in the direction of the body. Even at this distance, his face was dark with a strange mixture of determination and fear.

Lewis felt nausea in the pit of his stomach.

'No, not him,' said Adlington under his breath. 'He doesn't need to see this.'

'Chris,' Lewis called.

Chris ignored him. If anything, his strides lengthened. Lewis broke into a jog. He managed to intercept him at the last possible moment, half-running into the young detective, forcing out his arm as a kind of barrier, which Chris stumbled into, slowing as his eyes registered the person lying at their feet.

'The *fuck*—' he said.

'Go back, Chris. Leave it with us.'

Chris pushed away from him. He breathed heavily and raised his hands behind his head. Then he turned and headed off on his own, away from all of them.

Adlington lurched up to Lewis, clutching his side, nursing a stitch. He stared after Chris with exasperation.

'I'm sorry, but we don't have time for this,' he groaned. He patted Lewis on the chest. 'I'll talk to him. You call the super.'

Lewis circled the sycamore tree, holding his phone to his ear.

'We've got officers searching the area and knocking on doors around the park. Pathologist thinks he was killed a few hours ago.'

He heard Superintendent Warren draw in a breath. 'Christ.'

Shortly before the call came in, the superintendent had prowled through the incident room, complaining that Mark was grievously late to work and not replying to messages. It had never occurred to Lewis that the detective could be in danger – not until the body was reported and the first officers had arrived on scene.

He had never worked closely with Mark. The detective had joined the force two years ago from London, having previously served in the Met. It was Lewis's understanding he had moved to Wakestead in search of a quiet life. That he had been stabbed to death here and not in the capital seemed a cruel irony.

'So Mark was working today?'

'Yes.'

'When was he last seen at the station?'

'At around seven o'clock last night, according to CCTV.'

'He wasn't asked to attend any scenes this morning?'

'No. Nothing. And he didn't call anything in, either.'

Lewis frowned. Automatically, he had assumed Mark had been killed in the line of duty. Did this mean someone had actually targeted the detective?

'What case was he working on?'

'Aggravated burglary,' said Warren. 'No one was under suspicion yet. But you should get officers to reinterview the witnesses in that case. See if anyone had reason to obstruct the investigation.'

Lewis scanned the rolling hillside. 'Was Mark based locally?'

'No, he lived in a village nearby. Bexmere.'

'So what was he doing out here then?'

'I have no idea. Jennings, you're all right to inform next of kin once you wrap up? His wife, Olivia.'

Lewis swallowed. This was the absolute worst part of the job.

'Of course.'

'All right. Speak to you later.'

As soon as he hung up, Chris came running up to him.

'Lewis,' he said, 'they're searching Mark's car in the car park. There's an address saved in his GPS. It's a house just up the road from here.'

4

CHRIS THUMPED LOUDLY ON THE door of the house.

'Police. Open up.'

There was no response. Chris checked his phone.

'Lewis, registered owner details. It's June Golding. No criminal record. No connection to any live cases.'

Lewis squinted. Why had Mark been visiting this woman's house?

Chris's eyes darted around the closed door. 'Do we need to make a forced entry?'

'I'm not sure that's justified. Can you get the control room duty inspector on the phone now, see if they'll clear it?'

At that moment the door edged open to reveal a mixed race woman in her late twenties. She was wearing a blue hoodie and she looked like she might have just woken up. Her dark skin was almost grey with tiredness.

'Ms Golding?'

She shook her head. 'Amma Reynolds.' Her voice sounded hoarse.

Reynolds. Lewis knew that name. He was almost certain this was the sister of Isaac – the 17 year old who'd drowned tragically, more than a decade ago.

'Do you live here with Ms Golding?'

Amma nodded, still looking slightly dazed.

'We just have a couple of questions for you, Ms Reynolds. The body of a deceased male has been found at Crays Hill.'

Amma's reaction surprised him. Her lower lip trembled and her eyes seemed to cloud over for a moment.

'Can we come in?'

She nodded vaguely and shuffled out of the way to let them enter the hallway. It was like walking past a ghost. Lewis was on high alert by now. Surely this woman didn't have anything to do with Mark's death. But that reaction – was she on something?

Chris was perhaps thinking along the same lines because he started climbing up the stairs to the first floor.

'Anyone else here with you today, Ms Reynolds?'

There was a commotion at the front door. A rush of footsteps. Swinging round, Lewis watched in shock as Amma bolted out of the house.

'Shit. Chris!' he shouted. The staircase behind him exploded with noise as Chris came charging back down. But Lewis didn't wait for him. He burst out of the house just in time to see Amma run to the end of the street and disappear down a dark, narrow cycle path.

Lewis launched himself forward. Sunlight bounced off the roofs of the parked cars. Darting between them, he pulled his two-way radio out from inside his jacket. 'Suspect has run out of the house,' he yelled into it. 'Pursuing on foot.' He propelled himself forward, ignoring the burning in his legs, eyes fixed on the path the woman had escaped down. His heart was pounding but deep down he felt only a cold, calm sense of dread. Very rarely did people run. There was usually one reason why they did.

He dodged past the barrier at the opening of the walkway, which plunged down, enclosed on either side by long wooden fences half-coated in moss and shielded overhead by trees' entangled branches. The leaves glowed yellow in the sun's rays. Down this bright tunnel Lewis flew, gathering speed. Amma was close to the bottom of the pathway already. Momentum helped him close the gap between them, but not in time to catch her before she darted out of the cycle path and onto the road at the bottom.

Lewis emerged, panting, onto another street lined with houses. Amma was nowhere to be seen. He looked around desperately, trying to work out where she could have gone. Then he spotted the field gate nestled between two of the houses. Running over, he saw her over the other side now racing up the hill, along the thin parting that separated one stretch of golden barley from another. He heaved himself over the rattling fence, landing clumsily on the other side. He scrambled to right himself and took off again.

The sun was strong here and Lewis could feel his entire body heating up as he slogged up the dirt track. The incline became steeper. Amma was starting to slow down. Lewis blinked away a bead of sweat that had slid down from his forehead, blurring the vision in his right eye, and gave himself that final, excruciating push he needed to close the distance between them.

He was going to have to grab her. He was terrified of how she might react. He watched one of his hands reach for the back of her hoodie, the other for her shoulder, and felt a rush of relief as she, sensing him close behind, slowed to a halt. She lurched forward, gasping for breath. Lewis stopped too and grabbed her by both arms, careful not to grip too tightly in case he hurt her.

'You do not have to say anything,' he panted, 'but anything you do say—'

Amma dropped to the ground.

He was worried she had collapsed from exhaustion. She sat slumped with all her weight on one leg, her fingers splayed on the ground. A gentle wind swept across the barley, bending the feathered fronds in one coordinated movement, like a wave across the surface of the sea.

'Are you okay?'

The woman stared into the field, catching her breath, squinting in the sunlight. Sweat gleamed on her forehead. She lay totally still except for the white trainer at the end of her outstretched leg. It was trembling violently, like a rabbit's foot.

5

Sunday, One Day Later

THE REYNOLDS FAMILY LIVED ON the outskirts of Wakestead, in a detached house on the corner of a busy road.

Erin Crane had decided to walk there, not anticipating the deluge that would begin just ten minutes into her journey. For days the town had sweltered in the oppressive summer heat and now finally, this morning, the skies had burst open. Rain drummed across the shoulders of her light jacket as she followed the pavement up to the house.

She squinted at the large white building, its outline blurred by the rain. The parents must have moved here after it happened, so they wouldn't be haunted by the memories of their young family. But the property they had retreated to was strangely exposed. Positioned so as to face the oncoming cars as they crawled up the road and turned out of town, it seemed to only highlight the family's isolation.

A drenched cat streaked across Erin's path, shot up to the house and sprung inside through an open window at the front. Relieved to escape the downpour, Erin ducked under the shelter of the porch. But before knocking, she took two deep breaths. *Don't get their hopes up*, she thought to herself. Already she doubted she could do anything to help them.

Stephen Reynolds opened the door and beckoned her inside. 'Erin, hello. Please come in, dry off.'

Erin peeled off her dripping jacket and hung it up on the coat rail, noticing Vicky – his wife – stood at the end of the corridor.

'Cup of tea?'

'That would be great.'

She followed the couple into the house, through to an open-plan kitchen, where the cat was curled up angrily in the corner, its damp hairs stood on end.

The years had taken their toll on Stephen. In the family photos Erin had seen on the news, he had been a sturdy man looming over his teenage children. Now he was a very slight figure who shuffled across the kitchen floor in the direction of the sofa.

'I'll sit down if that's all right,' he said. 'Heart problems.'

Vicky returned with Erin's tea and sat down beside them, chewing her lip. Erin could see she was anxious not to miss a moment of this conversation.

'How long have you lived in Wakestead?'

'Thirty-three years now,' said Vicky. 'You left recently, didn't you? Good to be back, I hope?'

'Sure,' said Erin. No need to tell her she'd been dreading her return, however brief.

'We left London not long after our son was born. Stephen grew up in the area, so we wanted to move closer to his parents.'

Erin noticed a hint of resentment in her voice. How could they have known that moving here would set their lives on such a tragic course? But this was how the bereaved tortured themselves. Every decision leading up to that tragic day was dissected, re-lived, re-evaluated. *What if I had never moved house? What if I had told him not to go? What if I hadn't missed that final phone call?*

'We bought this house seven years ago,' Stephen said. 'Our friends ask us why we don't just leave the area. But it felt wrong. It felt like we would be abandoning Isaac.'

'So you already knew about the detective when we called?' asked Vicky.

'The news has been hard to avoid,' Erin replied.

It was true. The discovery of a detective's body lying in broad daylight in a country park had dominated the news cycle since yesterday. So when Vicky had called her first thing this morning, out of the blue, to explain her daughter was caught up in the case, Erin's first reaction had been one of fear. Could she really help this family? During a live investigation?

'But you didn't know Mark Stormont personally?' Stephen asked.

She shook her head. 'He joined the police after I left. So I know about as much as you do. You said on the phone you're not aware of any connection between him and your daughter?'

Vicky shook her head. 'No. But then again, she's not saying anything. Not to the police, not to us, not to anyone. We don't understand. Maybe she's in shock.'

Erin's heart sank. Arrested for murder and not speaking to the police. This really wasn't looking good.

Vicky continued: 'But I think she could be convinced to talk to you, Erin.'

'Why me?'

'She doesn't trust the police and frankly neither do we. You, you're on the outside. You could help her. Convince her to tell us what happened.'

Erin swallowed. She was internally debating how best to let them down when Stephen narrowed his eyes at her.

'You think you can't do anything to help us, is that it?' he said.

The directness of the question took her by surprise.

Reluctantly, she said, 'Your daughter needs a lawyer. Not an investigator.'

'We're getting her a lawyer,' Vicky said immediately. 'They won't do what we're asking you to do. We're asking you to find out who really did this.'

That's assuming your daughter is innocent, thought Erin.

'The police will have a better chance of finding out who did this than I will,' she said. 'The investigations where I can bring the most value are cold cases. Then I can take another look at what the police have found. But investigating during a live case…' She shook her head. 'I don't have the same resources as the police. I'll be one step behind them all the time.'

'Will they find out who did this?' said Vicky. 'Do you really believe that? After what we've been through? After what *you* went through?'

Erin nearly winced as the image of her former partner flashed through her mind. It was a good point. After seeing firsthand how easily police could abuse their power – or choose to look the other way – her faith in the institution had been permanently shaken.

'The police have already questioned us,' Vicky continued, 'and it's obvious they've made up their minds already. They think it's her.'

Stephen said, 'The way I see it, there are two scenarios here. My daughter is innocent. Which means someone else is responsible and the police are about to ruin her life pursuing her. Or Amma did kill that man.'

'Don't say that,' Vicky snapped. 'Of course she didn't.'

'I don't believe it for a second, but let's just imagine that it's true. If it is, she would have had her reasons. And if it makes them look bad, the police are not going to find that reason. Do you see what I'm trying to say?'

Erin took in a deep breath, nodding. 'What if it was self-defence?'

'Exactly. If he hurt her, then the police don't exactly have a great reputation for finding that out, do they?'

Erin swallowed. Conversations with her former colleagues suggested that things were different now. Supposedly the vetting of new officers had been tightened up. If that was true, then she struggled to see how a bad apple could have slipped through the net. But that wasn't a narrative she thought would land well with this family.

Vicky must have noticed the apprehension on her face because she said, 'I know how we must sound to you. You must think we're paranoid. But you have to understand, the police let us down so seriously when Isaac died. And now they think my daughter is responsible for the murder of one of their own. I just don't trust them to investigate this case properly. That's why we've come to you. You're not a part of the force. You can find the answers they can't. The answers we need.'

Erin clenched her fist in her lap. Could she really help these people? Or would she just be leading them into yet another crushing disappointment, when they had already been so profoundly let down?

'I'll need to think about it,' she said.

6

SILENCE FELL OVER THE OFFICERS as they waited in the meeting room for the super to start speaking. It was Sunday morning, the first time they had gathered together since Mark Stormont's body was found the day before. Warren, the superintendent, addressed the team while leaning back on a table with his hands clasped together in his lap.

'Some of you worked with Mark only briefly; others knew him very well,' he said, 'but I think I speak for all of us when I say that he was an extremely dedicated, kind, brave detective. This has been a huge loss not just to us as a team but also to the community.'

Some of the officers nodded in agreement. Lewis had never heard the super speak in such sentimental terms before. Looking around the team, he felt – perhaps for the first time since Erin had left – the invisible bonds of camaraderie between them.

'There'll be opportunities in the future for us to pay tribute to Mark and say our goodbyes,' Warren continued, 'but for now I want those of you involved in the case to focus all your efforts on bringing the person responsible to justice.'

His blue gaze swept across the room. 'As you know, we've already arrested Amma Reynolds on suspicion of murder. But until we have the forensics back, we can't be certain the killer isn't still out there. Nor can we be sure whether this attack was unplanned or if the killer had murderous intent. Finally, we can't rule out the possibility that the killer was working with others. For these reasons, I am instructing you all to take extra precaution. Uniformed or not, no officer should be out without a baton and irritant spray. Those who can should wear body armour. I want you to look after yourselves.'

Slowly, the room emptied of officers. Before getting up, Lewis glanced over his shoulder, finding Chris stood with his back against the wall. He saw his own confusion reflected in his partner's eyes. *Really?* his expression seemed to ask. Lewis pulled a face and gave a small shrug to signal his uncertainty.

We can't rule out the possibility that the killer was working with others.

Did Warren really think there was a group out there who had set out to kill police officers? That the rest of them were in danger?

He was getting ready to leave when Warren said, 'You two, stay here. Let's talk.'

Lewis and Chris approached the desk where Warren was stood. Physically, he cut a more imposing figure than his predecessor Peters, the former DCS. He was so tall that the furniture in the room seemed comically small by comparison. Lewis had the feeling he was a schoolchild about to be admonished by a headmaster.

Inside, he was squirming. They'd gotten absolutely nothing out of Amma so far and the super's frustration was palpable.

'Time's running out, you two,' he said. 'We've only got her for about fourteen more hours and we wasted plenty of time yesterday getting nowhere. So let's throw everything at it today. See what you can get from the post-mortem. Find out what we've got from CCTV, phones, social media. Find a connection.

'Officers interviewed June Golding yesterday, Amma's housemate. She said she last saw Amma the night before the murder, at a club called Prism. Amma got a taxi back early, alone, while June went to her boyfriend's. So there's no one to vouch for her whereabouts the following morning. June also claims she's never seen Mark Stormont before.'

Lewis nodded, processing this information. Still no alibi then.

Warren's gaze moved between each of them. 'This campaign group that her family set up. I don't think we can ignore it. As far as I can see, there's a clear motive here. The brother.'

Lewis bit his lip. He'd thought he was hiding his emotions well, but clearly not – because Warren lifted an eyebrow at him.

'You don't agree, Jennings?'

'Mark had nothing to do with that case. Why would she kill him over it?'

Warren shrugged. 'Perhaps it wasn't about Mark at all. Perhaps Amma just wanted a police officer dead.'

Chris asked, 'When you said there could be killers still out there… did you mean her other family members? The justice group they've set up?'

Warren raised his hands. 'It's a possibility. Whatever the case, I'm not taking any chances that will put the team in danger. Another thing—' his eyes shifted between them '—I think you were too soft on her yesterday. And I don't think it was working. Every detective's got their own style, and, Lewis – I hope you don't mind me saying this – but provoking a reaction isn't yours, wouldn't you say?'

Before he could respond, Warren turned to Chris and said, 'So Chris, if Lewis deals with putting the facts to her, I need you to be the one piling the pressure on, sound good?'

Chris nodded.

'I don't know if I agree with that,' said Lewis.

Warren watched him, waiting for an explanation.

Lewis felt a shot of anxiety, but he pushed it down. 'We know from Amma's background that she has a deep-seated mistrust of the police. That's probably why she isn't saying anything, right? Because she thinks this whole process is rigged against her.'

'Or because she's guilty as hell,' muttered Chris.

Ignoring him, Lewis said, 'The more aggressive we are, the more she's going to close up.'

Warren gave him an almost sympathetic, quite patronising look and said, 'I know she's young, Jennings. I know that makes this unpleasant. But we don't have time to play nice with her. We need answers now.'

7

Late Sunday morning, Lewis and Chris pulled on their plastic overshoes and stepped into the morgue. Cecilie, the pathologist, was waiting for them by one of the steel tables where Mark's body lay outstretched.

Lewis felt his knees go weak as he registered the detective's face. He'd had all morning to prepare for this and still it was as though his mind hadn't accepted the reality of his colleague's death.

They'd already heard from the forensic pathologist that he'd probably been dead for two hours before he was found, before rigor mortis had set in. That meant he'd likely been killed at about seven o'clock on Saturday morning.

'The victim has two stab wounds and a number of slash marks across the palms of the hands and over the chest. The slash marks make it less likely that the wounds were self-inflicted. They imply that the victim attempted to fight back.'

She pointed to a jagged hole on Mark's upper right chest. 'This was the first stab wound made…' Then indicating another, 'This second wound was fatal. The depth of penetration and the slight bruise around the entrance would suggest the attacker managed to push the entire blade in.'

'Anything you can say about the kind of knife they used?' asked Lewis.

'The stab wounds are between half an inch and one and a half inches thick. The size of the entrance wounds is consistent with an ordinary kitchen knife.'

'Can you tell if it was a woman who did it?' said Chris.

Cecilie considered Chris with her eyes half closed in exasperation. 'Stab wounds are not distinctly male or female,' she said.

'There's got to be something that points one way or the other.'

'I can tell you if the attacker was likely to be stronger or weaker, but that does not mean we can say with confidence that they were a man or a woman.'

'So which is it? Strong or weak?'

'The first stab wound was fairly shallow. Some of the others have minimal bruising. We cannot say conclusively, but these two factors imply the attacker was not particularly strong. I also suspect they were shorter than Mark, given he sustained no wounds to the face.

'However,' she said, 'to go back to your point about the victim's physical prowess, if the attacker was indeed weaker than him, smaller than him, then it is surprising that he allowed himself to be overpowered. On his body there are no other clothing fibres, no hairs, no human cells under his fingernails or anywhere else on his body. I cannot speak for evidence you found at the crime scene, but it looks to me as though he was... restraining himself.'

Sheets of rain tumbled down over them as they dashed back to the car. It was the first downpour after a long summer, and instantly the air was filled with the smell of the vegetation from the stretch of green beside the morgue. Once inside the car, Lewis swept his wet hair off his forehead and bent to put the keys in the ignition. It took him a moment to notice Chris had slumped against the inside of the passenger door. His partner was watching the rain with a hopeless expression.

Lewis sat up straight.

'Are you okay?' he said.

Chris's questioning eyes searched the tarmac outside.

'Why didn't he fight back?'

Lewis felt a wave of guilt.

'I'm sorry. Maybe you shouldn't have seen that.'

Chris rubbed his eyes. 'No,' he said firmly. 'No, I wanted to come.' He sniffed. 'Why though? You know, he was a strong guy, bigger than them too. Why didn't he just—' he curled his hand into a fist and thumped the door of the car '—fucking *do* something?'

Lewis said, 'Maybe because it was someone he knew. Because he didn't want to hurt them.'

Chris nodded. 'Because it was a woman.'

Lewis's guilt edged into frustration. 'Not necessarily.'

'Kitchen knife's the sort of weapon a girl might use, isn't it?' said Chris.

Lewis felt a strong urge to smash his own face into the steering wheel. 'Anyone can grab a knife from their kitchen. No, I think, if he didn't fight back, then that means he knew them.'

Chris bit his lip.

Lewis continued, 'That attack. It was aggressive, but it wasn't a frenzy. If they really hate the victim, you'll see dozens of stab wounds. But this… you can imagine the attacker realising what they're doing and stopping.'

'Yeah,' said Chris. 'Yeah, maybe you're right.' He continued to gaze out of the window, lost in his own thoughts.

Once they were on the road, Chris spoke up again.

'What Warren said—'

'I wouldn't worry too much about what Warren said,' Lewis interjected. 'He just wants us to be careful.'

'What if this is part of a plan, though? Killing off coppers?'

'We don't have any evidence yet that there was more than one person involved. If anything, the evidence is suggesting that this was personal.'

'I've just been having this feeling,' said Chris, directing his thoughts to the ceiling of the car now, 'that something like this was always going to happen.'

Lewis frowned.

'You know, like it was inevitable,' said Chris.

'What do you mean?'

'I don't know what it was like before. But I joined just after they caught him, right.'

Lewis felt his mouth dry out slightly. His hands squeezed the steering wheel.

'And so I was there early enough to feel this… this *shift* in how everyone saw us. You know, one moment my family's so proud of me, my mum and dad so happy I've chosen this career. And the next moment all anyone wants to ask me is whether I think any of my colleagues are pieces of shit, when we're going to sort it all out… I just think, maybe someone was always going to snap. Maybe it was always going to boil over. And it's just bad luck it was Mark.'

Lewis knew exactly what he meant. He'd felt it too – the subtle change in people's perception of his job, even from those he hardly knew. It had been difficult to ignore. There was shame where there hadn't been shame before. A feeling of impurity, like you were contaminated.

Maybe, from someone's perspective, they were. And maybe someone had decided enough was enough.

It was highly unlikely that any officer would be killed in the line of duty. Nevertheless, if you were serious about joining the force, it was a possibility you had to come to terms with. Lewis always believed he had. But now, he realised he had only accepted the possibility if it meant dying as a hero. The information they had so far suggested Mark could have been killed as part of an unprovoked attack. Targeted and slaughtered. Like prey.

As Lewis drove them back to the station through the downpour, he took a call from Rob, one of the scene of crime officers. Lewis knew immediately from the disappointment in his voice as it filled the car that his search of Amma's property wasn't going well.

'I'm afraid I don't have much news for you right now,' Rob said, 'except to say we haven't found any blood in the house.'

'None at all?'

'No drops in the carpet, no bloodied fingerprints. We'll see what comes up in the analysis. There might be smaller traces of it somewhere. But given the amount of blood at the crime scene, it's surprising not to find anything at the suspect's property. Unless she did an extremely good job cleaning up after herself. Anyway, we'll see what comes up in the analysis but, you know, it'll take time.'

Lewis chewed the inside of his mouth. Time, which they didn't have.

'Got you. Thanks for the update, Rob.'

He let out a deep breath. The results of the post-mortem had left him feeling conflicted. If Amma was innocent, then why wasn't she talking to them?

*

It was cramped and dark inside the tech team's office. As ever, they weren't short on snacks; the sugary smell wafting from an open packet of biscuits left invitingly on the desk made Lewis's stomach ache. He wouldn't have much time to eat today – he made a mental note to grab something from the vending machine before they next spoke to Amma.

Ignoring his hunger pangs, he watched the video clip play over one of the officer's shoulders. The last known footage of Mark alive, it captured his car driving up the road that would eventually lead him to Crays Hill.

One of the officers, Josh, said: 'No cameras around the park or in the residential areas near Amma's house. And this road could have taken him either way.'

'So we don't know whether he met Amma at her house,' said Lewis, 'or whether he met someone else first. What did his wife say?'

'She said he left at the usual time that morning – 6 o'clock. Nothing out of the ordinary. Although he did seem stressed, she said. But she didn't know what about.'

'He didn't say where he was going?'

'No. Apparently he usually went to the gym first thing, so that's what she assumed. But the SOCOs said his gym bag was still at the house when they checked.'

Lewis squinted at the image on the screen. Mark's face had been reduced to a blur behind the windshield. What had he been thinking? What had been going through his head in those final hours?

'As for Amma, we've found CCTV footage confirming she went to the club Prism the night before. But we can also see that she took a taxi back later that night. So no alibi at the time of the murder, as far as we can see.'

'And where are we at with establishing a connection between Mark and the suspect?'

Josh swivelled back and forth in his chair, shaking his head. 'We haven't got the passcode to Amma's phone or laptop so it's going to take a while to get her messages. However, Mark's wife knew his email password and his phone passcode so we've had a look through and found no messages between them or anything like that. He didn't receive any texts or calls from unknown callers in the days before his death. There is an encrypted folder on his laptop, though.'

'Really?'

Josh shrugged. 'I mean it could just be a load of nudes of Mrs Stormont, let's be honest.'

Lewis swallowed. Maybe the officer was right. Or was Mark hiding something else?

'How long will it take you to get in?'

'Some time, unfortunately, because we'll have to outsource the decryption. We're not getting in within the next twenty-four hours, that's for sure.'

'Can we make that a priority?'

This was their last chance. Charge her, or she would be let out. And they would have no one.

'There is one possible connection between them, though,' said Josh. 'Stormont was investigating an aggravated burglary. It bore no relation to Amma, that we can see, and he never investigated her brother's murder. But they may have crossed paths at the very start of this year.'

Josh turned his laptop around. On the screen was a CCTV still depicting a grey-and-black sea of figures packed together in what looked like a town square. A figure on the fringes of the crowd was circled in red.

'This is Stormont,' he said, 'policing a march in central London where Amma was also present.'

'A march?' said Lewis.

'It was to raise awareness about unsolved cases where the victim was black, Asian or Middle Eastern.'

'Why were officers sent to this?'

'It was just a precaution. In case anything kicked off.'

Lewis took a closer look at the photo. The scene was unsettling. Mark Stormont looked like a prowler, circling this community of angry friends and relatives.

'Do we know what happened at this march?'

'We've created a timeline of events from the CCTV footage available and various social media posts. Amma arrived early and helped hand out flyers to passers-by. She spoke at midday to the crowd. They marched to Scotland Yard. Stormont joined the whole way. But there was no trouble. As far as we can see, they didn't interact. But this is the only time when we know for sure they were in the same area at the same time.

'And that's not all. We know from a video posted on X that Amma previously had a confrontation with a police officer at one of these marches.'

He opened another tab and hit play. A jerky video, clearly filmed on someone's phone, started playing. It showed Amma in winter clothing, with a knitted hat jammed over ears, standing on the side of the road while other marchgoers filed past her. She was shouting at a uniformed police officer. The audio quality was poor but one phrase jumped out: 'You're not welcome here.' Although the officer stayed completely still, he looked seconds away from launching himself at the young woman.

'Do we know who that is?'

'An officer called Mike Nelson.'

'Can we speak to him?'

'Sure, we've got his number.'

Lewis chewed his lip, scanning the frozen image of Amma pointing a gloved finger at the officer's face. Had she and Mark had an altercation like this? Had she finally snapped and decided it was time for revenge?

He stepped out into the corridor to give Nelson a call.

'Everyone has a right to protest,' Nelson said, after Lewis had explained why he was getting in touch. 'But during this one there were a high number of people on the streets. We were there to ensure minimal disruption to everyone else who was just going about their day.' He paused. 'Except that wasn't how everyone on the march saw it. Obviously it was a protest against the police. So, from their point of view, it was offensive we were even there. Pretty soon they were hurling abuse at us. Yeah, it was very hostile.' His voice was filled with contempt.

'All of them?'

'Well, you know, a couple of them, the younger ones, were more fired up.'

'Do you remember an argument with Amma Reynolds?' Lewis asked. 'One of the women at the march.'

'Yeah. Yeah, right piece of work, excuse my language.'

'Go on.'

'So I know there's a video she sent round after. And I can't remember if it was clear from the footage, but she's the one who started on me. Screaming in my face, "you're not welcome here"… that kind of stuff.'

'Did she get physical with you?'

'I honestly thought she was going to. But I'm twice the size of her; what's she going to do? She pissed off eventually.'

Lewis checked his watch as he headed back into the main office. They were running out of time. Before midnight, they would have to release Amma or charge her for Mark's murder. There was just one more person he wanted to speak to before that final interview.

He found DCI Gregory speaking to Adlington at one of the desks where the most senior detectives usually sat. He was a tall man in his 50s with a rectangular head and a long chin, who always wore old-fashioned-looking suits that were too long for him. He had been in charge of the investigation into Isaac Reynolds' death all those years ago. Lewis wanted to find out more about the case – and whether it could have a connection to Mark Stormont's death.

'Jennings,' said Gregory, 'how are you getting on?'

'Not that well. A lot of circumstantial evidence and not much else. I wanted to ask you, as you've had the most contact with the Reynolds out of everyone here – is there anything we need to know about them?'

The heavy sigh Gregory let out was filled with resentment. 'Let me think. They come to the station every year on the anniversary of Isaac's death. It's usually the mother and daughter. They used to come round much more regularly in that first year. It's always the same thing. *Why can't you see it's murder? Why aren't you doing anything?*'

As much as Lewis empathised with grieving relatives, he understood Gregory's disdain. Nothing was quite so demoralising as having to endure a lashing from a family who believed you'd screwed up an investigation.

'Are they aggressive?' asked Lewis.

'I've never felt threatened, no. But you know how it is dealing with people in that state. They raise their voices, they point. Amma, the daughter, swears. So, yes, they're aggressive.'

Lewis chewed the inside of his mouth. 'What's your gut instinct on this? As someone who knows them?'

Gregory shrugged. 'I don't know, Jennings. They hate us. It's not impossible they would have decided to take revenge. I suppose the question is – if it was revenge they wanted – then why would they kill Mark, and not me?'

*

Amma looked predictably terrible after spending a night in the custody suite. The officer on duty had told Lewis she had left every meal untouched.

Chris said, 'It's a really tight operation you and your family have going here, Amma. You've managed to attract a huge amount of media attention over the years. And you certainly haven't shied away from the spotlight.'

Amma's chest was rising and falling as she breathed quickly in and out.

'I know you probably think there's no harm in not talking. But there is. When you don't speak, your social media presence speaks for you.' He opened the folder in front of him. 'Fifth of March. A magazine interview earlier this year. "The police have failed my family in every way. Why should they be trusted?" Last year, twenty-third of August. "The police have a lot to answer for." What did you mean by those statements? Because, from our perspective, they seem quite threatening. They make us concerned that Mark Stormont was targeted because he was a police officer. If we've got that wrong, then all you have to do is explain to us where you were on Saturday.'

Lewis stared at Amma, willing her to speak.

But the woman, who continued to gaze into the far corner of the room, seemed only to have retreated further into herself. He was close to giving up trying to understand Amma.

*

Lewis and Chris sat together in the silence of the main office, waiting for Megan from the Crown Prosecution Service to call. Lewis suppressed a yawn. It was almost the end of a long working day and custody time was running out. There were only a few more hours to go before they would have to release Amma. They had already gone to the CPS asking them to approve a charge for murder. Once the call came in, they would find out whether or not Amma was walking out of here a free woman.

Lewis rubbed his eyes. He was so exhausted he no longer knew what he wanted the CPS to say. He just wanted this to end.

Chris, by comparison, looked wide awake. The young detective was visibly tense as he sat waiting for the phone to ring with his fingertips pressed together in a tent, eyes wild with fearful anticipation.

Then the desk phone started ringing. Chris snatched up the receiver.

Lewis leant forward in his seat as Chris cleared his throat, turned away from him, and answered.

'Megan. Hi.'

Lewis could just about hear Megan's muffled response.

'Okay. Right. I understand you. No, thank you, Megan. Speak soon.'

Chris put down the phone and turned around to face him. Then he kicked the drawers underneath his desk.

8

THE EVENING OF HER VISIT to the Reynolds' house, Erin opened her laptop and gulped down some coffee. Looking out of her window – the train tracks ran straight past her Airbnb, a flat in Wakestead – she wondered what on earth connected Amma Reynolds and Mark Stormont.

Already she had become intimately familiar with Mark's face. Newspapers had emblazoned him across the front page on yesterday's papers, and it was easy to see why. He was a picture-perfect victim. Clear-blue eyes, a lopsided smile, a strong jaw. An attractive man with a reassuring presence that somehow radiated through the screen.

Tributes to the detective had poured out online. He had clearly been a popular figure, well-liked by friends and colleagues, with members of the Met having already posted online about how they would never forget the man with a 'heart of gold'. Searching through social media, Erin came across a video of his elderly parents and his wife Olivia – a beautiful woman with a mane of dark hair – huddled together at a police press conference, tearfully calling for witnesses to come forward.

With only one arrest made so far no paper had risked coming up with theories about the murder.

But people on social media were not so restrained.

Same town where Sophie Madson died. Coincidence?

Clearly a revenge killing.

I agree. Trust in the police is so broken it was inevitable something like this would happen.

Erin bit the inside of her mouth. Already a narrative was forming. And Amma fit into it perfectly.

She had already looked at Amma's X profile, but she revisited it now for a longer read. Immediately one post leapt out at her. It was about Sophie Madson. But this was not the usual commemorative post that had circulated on social media in the lead up to the third anniversary of Sophie's death. This was a photo of Amma stood against a brick wall, wearing a t-shirt emblazoned with the words 'Justice for Isaac'. She was glaring straight into the camera lens, holding in her hands a poster that had clearly been designed for a protest. Immediately Erin recognised the photograph of Sophie that had dominated the media coverage during the investigation. Next to it was a photograph of Amma's sibling, a grinning, dark-skinned teenage boy, his arms around two people who had been cropped out of the photo, the restaurant lights shining off the lenses of his glasses. They had the same narrow, calculating eyes – similar bone structure around the upper part of their faces. Under Sophie's photo, it read, 'Killer found within 12 months'. Under Isaac's, it said, 'Case unsolved 13 years on'. And beneath both photos, another line: 'Spot the difference'.

She knew the case. She recognised the boy. Every police officer in Wakestead did.

Amma Reynolds is still searching for answers after her older brother, Isaac, was found dead in a river more than a decade ago.

Isaac, aged 17, was on his way home from a Bonfire Night display he had attended with a group of friends when he disappeared. Two days later his body was found washed up on the river bank. The cause of death was drowning.

The police investigation concluded that Isaac's death was not suspicious. But his family allege that Isaac was the victim of an attack and have accused the police of failing to properly investigate the death. No arrests have ever been made.

Amma and her parents have spent years campaigning for the case to be reopened.

Erin squinted at the screen in confusion. She hadn't been working in the police when this boy died, but she remembered the family's campaign and it clearly had been gaining momentum ever since. She knew first-hand how cases could drag on, unresolved, for years, without sufficient evidence, but the pressure to allocate resources to this one seemed immense. How had Isaac's case managed to stay in a complete blind spot for the force?

She scrolled through the other search results. Amma had given multiple interviews to newspapers, websites and charities' blogs. She didn't mince her words.

'This was not investigated as it should have been. The police didn't care about my brother's death because of the colour of his skin. They abandoned us.'

In another, she was quoted as having said, 'It is institutionalised. Could she really justify taking the parents' money?

Erin winced, imagining Wakestead's police force reading through the exact same article.

Those comments weren't going to help her now.

She pushed her chair away from her desk, thinking. The more she looked at the case, the more determined she felt to try and help this family. But what if Amma had killed this man in cold blood? Could she really justify taking the parents' money?

And there was another reason, deep down, why she didn't want this case. She'd left Wakestead for a reason. Moving to London had been freeing – she'd finally put everything that had happened to her in this town behind her. She wasn't exactly overjoyed at the prospect of moving back here, even for a short while.

She opened her inbox and re-read the email she'd received last week. It was from a potential client she'd spoken to on the phone.

I found our conversation very reassuring and informative. I have thought about it and I'm happy to proceed at the fee quoted. Let me know what the next steps are.

Erin sank back into her chair. This case had thoroughly depressed her. The potential client – a suspicious spouse – had found a woman's jumper in her husband's car. Except rather than confront him about it, like a normal human being, she wanted Erin to investigate and report back with what she found. It was one of a surprisingly large number of very similar requests she had received ever since she first went private just under two years ago, from people who wanted her to follow their husband or wife and see if they were cheating. So far, she had turned them all down. It made her feel sick – the thought of getting paid to follow someone into a bar and watch them cheat on their spouse while she discreetly photographed them from a darkened corner. This wasn't why she'd gotten into policing. That was light years away from the kind of case she wanted.

But two months since work had dried up, she was starting to reassess. She'd been picky so far, and she wasn't sure how much longer she could afford to be. This month was the first time in her life when she'd had to cover the bills out of savings alone.

And then here was someone needing her help. She looked again at Amma's face and sensed, looking at the darkness in her eyes, the pain she had already had to endure for much of her life – and the huge impending wave of public backlash that awaited her if ever she was charged with this murder.

She couldn't abandon this woman. She needed to find out what had happened the night Mark was killed.

She called Vicky. After she'd told her she wanted to help, as she watched the train in the distance slip between the trees, a flash of yellow in the green, and listened to Vicky's breathless gratitude, she still couldn't shake from her bones the feeling of unease.

9

Monday

Vicky and Stephen asked Erin to come round the following day. This time, Amma was waiting for her in the living room. The parents had wanted her to stay with them after she was released on bail late the night before, rather than go back to her shared house. Folded up in one corner of the sofa, her shoulders hunched, her fist curled up under her chin, her eyes glazed over, Amma barely acknowledged Erin as she entered the room – or even her own parents, who drifted over slowly, as if scared to disturb the air around her.

'Amma. I'm Erin Crane.'

Slowly, Amma's gaze dragged up from the floor. Erin had not been prepared for the calm hatred that filled the young woman's eyes.

Vicky sat on the sofa, reached out and gripped her daughter's hand. 'Erin's here to help you, Amma. Please. If you won't talk to us, or the police, talk to her.'

Amma returned her gaze to the floor and said nothing.

'Amma, why?' said her dad. 'This is your life. Let us help you.'

Erin's entire body had tensed up. Only now that Amma was right in front of her could she understand the extent of her non-compliance. The confidence of the woman Erin had seen on social media was gone. Amma was like a statue. Beaten into silence by the stress of her thirty-six hours in custody. Knowing what the police would have made of her noncooperation, for a moment Erin felt an overwhelming sense of hopelessness. She pushed it down. This family needed her.

'Amma,' she said, 'I know you've been through a lot over the last couple of days, but your solicitor and the police need to know exactly where you were on the day of Mark Stormont's murder. They need to know everything about what happened.'

Amma looked up at her with narrowed eyes. Then she turned to Stephen.

'How can you afford this?'

Her voice – which Erin had heard only in videos until now – was deep and authoritative, not what one would expect to hear from the cowed woman in front of her.

It was the first time she'd spoken since coming back, and her parents sat there in a stunned, incredulous silence.

Amma looked back at Erin. 'How much are you going to charge them?'

'I don't care what it costs,' snapped Vicky. 'I'll spend anything it takes to get you out of this.'

Hearing this, Amma hung her head.

'I want to help you, Amma,' said Erin.

The room was silent for a few moments.

When Amma next spoke, quietly this time, her words sent a chill down Erin's spine:

'You can't help me. None of you can.'

10

Once Amma had left the room and returned upstairs, Erin nursed a cup of tea, feeling shaken by the interaction. The parents leaned against the kitchen cabinets anxiously waiting as if she was a doctor about to diagnose their child.

'So Amma hasn't confirmed where she was when Mark's body was found?' she said.

'We've heard from her friends that she was out with them the night before. She was home the morning they found him. They think he was also killed then.'

'When the police came to her house, do you know if she said anything then?'

'She ran.'

Erin glanced between both parents, trying to hide her shock.

Running from the police. It couldn't get much worse.

'They have treated us so badly all this time,' said Amma's mum. 'It's understandable she ran.'

Erin wasn't sure she agreed. She thought of the confident woman she'd seen on social media. She didn't seem like the sort of person who would run from a clash with the police rather than defend herself. And surely she should have known better than to give them such an obvious reason to suspect her. Why would she have reacted like that?

'And you two have never had any interaction with Mark Stormont?'

Vicky shook her head. 'We can't be certain. We never met him, we know that. But perhaps he worked on the investigation behind the scenes? Why would he? The police never told us they were reopening the case.'

'Had Amma told you about any interactions she'd had with the police?'

'They never see us about our son, never. If Amma deals with the police, it's when they're attending a protest or a vigil.'

Stephen added: 'There have been clashes in the past. Not here, but in London.'

'Clashes?'

'Never anything violent. She's had arguments with a few. Sometimes the police presence at these protests, you know, it feels threatening.'

'Is it possible that's how she came into contact with Mark Stormont?'

'It's possible,' said Vicky.

'Before Mark's death, when had you last seen Amma?'

'Not for a long time. She used to come round every two weeks for dinner. But recently, we've barely seen her.'

'When was the last time?'

'A month ago, maybe.'

'And how was she then?'

'We had an argument.'

'What about?'

'It was very upsetting to us. She wanted to tone down her involvement in the campaign.'

Why, after years, would she want to withdraw from that? Erin wondered. Had someone threatened her? She thought again of Amma's defeatism. *You can't help me.* Why on earth had she given up on defending herself?

A firm knock on the front door interrupted the silence.

Vicky swept into the corridor to go and answer it while Stephen lifted himself cautiously to his feet. Automatically, Erin straightened up as tension crept down her spine and over her skin. Three guesses who that could be.

She listened as Vicky opened the door. The first thing the visitor said was muffled by the rumble of a van driving past the house. But the second part, Erin heard loud and clear:

'May we come in please?'

Slowly Erin stood up to her full height. She knew that voice.

Scene of crime officers donning white overalls marched into the corridor and trundled up the stairs. Then the senior investigating officer appeared in the doorway, blinking at her in surprise.

'Erin,' said Lewis awkwardly.

She nodded in response. She'd always known this day would come, when they would meet at a crime scene, or in a victim's home, or at the house of a suspect. But she was still unprepared for the strangeness of standing there in silence, regarding each other with cold professionalism, when just a few months ago Erin had been round his for a housewarming.

Lewis looked past her, scanning the nervous faces of the family. 'I'm DI Lewis Jennings, and this DI Chris Baldwin,' he said, gesturing to his younger partner, who was eyeing Stephen and Vicky with contempt. 'We have a warrant to search the property. I'm going to have to ask that the Reynolds stay put, please.' Then he looked, somewhat sheepishly, at Erin. 'And I'm going to have to ask that you leave the property, Erin.'

She gestured towards the garden. 'Can we talk for a minute?'

His partner – Chris – shot him a disparaging look. Begrudgingly, Lewis came out with her.

'Look,' he said, once the door was shut, peering over the fences of the garden, 'let's keep this short. I don't want neighbours snapping pictures that wind up in the papers.'

'Saying what, "police and private investigator help each other solve murder case"? God forbid. Did you know him?'

'Not well, but yeah. Everyone did. He joined about two years ago from the Met. Your replacement, technically.'

'What's the mood at the station?'

'Well, one of our colleagues has just been killed so everyone's quite upset.'

'You don't say. I mean, what's the attitude towards Amma?'

Lewis lowered his voice. 'Not fantastic, given she basically spent the last few years posting on social media about how every police officer needs to kill themselves.'

'A slight exaggeration.'

'She couldn't really have a worse digital footprint, Erin.'

'Does he have any prior connection with her?'

He looked at his feet. 'I can't tell you that.'

'Any history of misconduct?'

'It's something we're looking into. There's nothing in our systems, no complaints against him that we can see. That's all I'm saying. But we'll dig deeper just in case.'

'Any others who saw Mark before he died?'

Lewis rolled his head back in exasperation and let out a low groan of distress. 'I've already said more than I should, Erin. You know I can't tell you about this stuff.'

She did know that, but even so she felt a wave of frustration and dug her fingernails into her palms. 'If I find enough evidence against someone, you'll be the first to hear.'

'I'm sorry.'

She wasn't giving up that easily. 'You don't trust me? You seriously think I'm going to tell anyone what I find out?' She glanced through the window into the kitchen, which was already filling up with SOCOs, then leant in closer. 'Go for a pint with me tomorrow evening.'

Lewis buried his face in his hands. 'No, because you're trying to make me tell you things.'

'Just an innocent pint.'

Lewis stepped back. 'Fine. But I'm not sharing details of the case with you, Erin. You know I can't.'

Erin said nothing. She could tell he had more to say. And she was pretty confident she could get it out of him.

After a moment, Lewis said, 'Can I ask you one thing?'

She waited.

'Look, we need to get her talking, right?' he continued. 'And we're not getting anywhere with that.'

'Me neither. I just tried and she wasn't having it.'

'Maybe not yet. But if anyone has a chance of making her talk, it's you, Erin. So see what you can get out of her. And tell us what you find.'

11

LEWIS SLAMMED THE CAR DOOR shut, looking out through the window at the house, picturing Erin still inside, perhaps comforting the Reynolds. They'd never worked on opposite sides of the same case like this before. The prospect made him feel deeply uncomfortable.

Chris slipped into the passenger seat next to him.

'This going to be an issue?' he asked.

Determined to hide his feelings from Chris, Lewis shook his head. 'Erin will share what she uncovers.'

Chris squinted at the house with suspicion. 'Yeah, but will the Reynolds persuade her to look the other way? If she finds evidence it was Amma.'

'She's too smart for that,' said Lewis. That wasn't his concern. His real worry was: what if Erin drove a further wedge between the police and the family, who clearly had a poor enough relationship as it was?

Chris opened his phone, looking at a photograph of Amma with a group of friends. 'So, it's this guy next, right? Emmanuel. Family friend. Also part of the justice group.'

Lewis nodded. 'Exactly.'

'I was thinking.'

'About what?' said Lewis.

'What Warren said at the start. How there could be more than one person involved. There wasn't any blood at Amma's property, right? Maybe he's right. And if he is right, then…' He pointed at the photo of Amma and her friends. 'Then they're the people we need to be looking at.'

*

They drove to the house where Emmanuel lived. Based in London for most of the time, he had come down to stay with his family specifically for the night out before Mark's death. The other reason they were interested in speaking to him was because he had campaigned aggressively alongside Amma for them to reopen the investigation into the death of her brother, also his friend.

They had barely sat down before Emmanuel spoke, in a cool, authoritative tone. 'You're making a mistake. Amma has nothing to do with this.'

Lewis got out a picture of Mark and placed it on the table between them. 'Do you know of any connection between Amma and Mark Stormont?'

Emmanuel's dark eyes flitted between the photograph and Lewis. 'No. I would have expected her to mention contact with a police officer. She never did.'

'Have you had any contact with him before?'

'No.'

'You were also friends with her brother Isaac who died, is that right?'

'Yes,' said Emmanuel.

'Did Mark Stormont ever enquire about Isaac's case?'

To Lewis's surprise, Emmanuel smirked. 'We've found that police don't usually ask about that, no. That's part of the problem, see.'

'Was reaching out to police officers part of your strategy when campaigning to get the case reopened?'

'It used to be. Family and friends of Isaac would write to detectives, turn up at the police station. But that was a long time ago. We were always told the same thing. "We'll look into it when new evidence turns up."'

'But you don't do that anymore? Is there any chance you or Amma attempted to contact Mark Stormont?'

Emmanuel narrowed his eyes. 'What you're suggesting is ridiculous. We would never have targeted a police detective. We've never instigated violence. We protest peacefully.'

'Not always, apparently,' sneered Chris. 'Didn't Amma once lash out at an officer at a march?'

'I wouldn't call that *lashing out*. That officer's presence was threatening.' Emmanuel scoffed. 'Is that your evidence? Really?'

'You've been in Wakestead with your family for a few days now, is that right?'

'Yes.'

'So you were there the night before Mark Stormont was killed? How did Amma seem?'

'Upset,' Emmanuel replied, in a reductant tone. 'You could see in her face that something was bothering her.'

'Why was she upset?'

'I don't know why.'

'I thought you were good friends,' said Chris.

Emmanuel shot him a scathing look. 'She's been through a lot,' he said. 'She has difficult moments. Like anyone would, if they'd lost a family member like that. She was upset, but that had nothing to do with this man. She didn't know him.'

The intensity of Emmanuel's tone caught Lewis by surprise. He was clearly protective of Amma. Perhaps it was more than friends between these two. What exactly, he thought, might Emmanuel have done to keep her safe?

They were heading back to the car when Lewis got a call from an unknown number.

'Yes?' he said.

'It's Callum. Mark's partner. I've been thinking about the last few times I saw Mark. Before it happened.'

Lewis felt a shot of adrenaline. 'Yeah? What is it?'

'I have a theory about the connection between him and Amma.'

12

THERE WAS AN ENVELOPE WAITING for Erin on the doormat when she got back. The conversation with Lewis was still circling her mind so she very nearly walked in without noticing it. She frowned. Who was sending her post? Few people knew she was back in Wakestead. She picked it up, recognising her mother's handwriting. She must have redirected it. Because an address in the corner told her it had originally come from somewhere else. The walls of the hallway shuddered out of focus.

HM Prison Bullingdon.

Erin realised she'd stopped breathing. She forced herself to take in a deep breath through her nose. Then she rushed into the kitchen and threw the envelope in the recycling bin. It stared up at her. HM Prison Bullingdon. Reaching into the bin, she covered the letter with a nest of paper and cardboard packaging until the words were hidden. Then she slammed down the lid and went into the bedroom.

For the next half an hour, she tried, unsuccessfully, to read up on Isaac's case. She felt as though she had left a cigarette burning in the bin. At any moment the alarm would sound, the smoke would start pouring up from underneath the door in a toxic grey cloud, a waterfall in reverse.

Where had he written it? In the canteen, sat alone? Far away from the other inmates, ignoring the insults they hurled at him, nursing purple welts on his face (because they would be worse for him, the beatings, she'd always known that; him being a detective, they would rip him to shreds) – or in his cell, with no one to confide in but a few pieces of paper?

After ten minutes she went back into the kitchen. She knotted up the bin liner as tight as she could and carried the half-empty bag to the bins outside. The metallic clunk of the lid slamming shut followed her all the way back to the flat.

Erin awoke in the middle of the night with her heart racing. She stared wide-eyed at the wall, split in half by a thin rectangle of moonlight slicing out through the not-quite-closed curtains. It was totally quiet. She glanced at her alarm clock. The red numbers glowed in the darkness. 02:13.

She knew exactly what it was that had woken her up. The impulse had seized her in a rush of adrenaline, and now there was no ignoring it. Without hesitating, she got out of bed, pulled on her dressing gown, and made her way through the unlit flat, feeling her way through the darkness. The keys clinked as she picked them up from the bowl on the dinner table. Stepping outside, she shivered in the night air.

Relief washed over once she was back in her room. She shut the door behind her. That was it. The itch scratched.

By now her vision had adjusted to the darkness and she looked down at the envelope, retrieved from the recycling bin, and the address that was printed there. This was the right thing to do. She wasn't going to open the letter; only keep it, just in case.

She put the letter out of sight, in the bottom drawer of her desk, and then went back to the bedroom, where she slept for the remainder of the night, undisturbed.

13

Tuesday

AMMA'S RESENTFUL GAZE DRIFTED TO the unlit fireplace. Erin felt her nerves tighten. Maybe she should have waited longer before trying to speak to Amma again. Expecting her to open up the following day, on their second meeting, might have been ambitious. She'd asked to be left alone with Amma, hoping after their first encounter that the young woman might be more prepared to speak. But so far she had been agonisingly quiet.

'You have every right not to comment during a police interview,' she said. 'You don't have to tell them anything if you don't want them to. But you must know how that looks to the investigators. How it looks to the Crown Prosecution Service. How it will look to a jury.'

Outside, a sparrow in a tree hopped cheerfully from one branch to the other.

'You need to give yourself the best chance of defending yourself. Even if you did something wrong, Amma, we need to know.'

Amma squeezed her hands together underneath her chin.

'You see what your parents are doing to try and help you right now? You don't think they deserve some answers from you? That they deserve to see you putting up a fight?'

Erin could see that Amma was biting the inside of her mouth in anger. She wasn't doing well to build up a rapport with her. But right now she didn't care. She knew Amma was smarter than this. Seeing the woman throw her future away for no reason was unbearable.

'I'm going to ask you some questions now,' she said. 'Please consider answering. It can be as simple as yes or no.

'Did you find out that Mark Stormont had something to do with the investigation into your brother's death? Was he responsible for some of the failings that happened?'

Amma said nothing.

'Did he assault you?' she said. 'Harass you?'

Erin saw the skin underneath Amma's right eye quiver slightly, but still she said nothing.

'Or maybe it wasn't about Stormont at all?' she said. 'Maybe, after what the police did to your family, you were angry. Maybe something happened that you didn't plan. Whatever it is, Amma, we can help you.'

Amma leant forward. 'I would never, ever have done it,' she said.

*

Afterwards, Erin drove to where Mark Stormont had lived – in a small village called Bexmere, not far from Wakestead. She breathed a sigh of relief when she saw there were no reporters lurking outside the cottage. Olivia answered the door, wearing jeans and a moss-green jumper. The redness around her eyes told her she'd been crying.

'Is now still a good time?'

'Yes. The family liaison officer's just been. I've had two reporters come knocking on my door so far today,' she said. 'I've already given an interview to the BBC.' She held herself with poise. She sniffed and put a hand on her hip. 'You didn't mention who'd hired you.'

'They'd rather I didn't say, if that's all right,' she replied.

Olivia's red-rimmed eyes narrowed slightly. If she knew the truth – that Erin was being bankrolled by the suspect's family – then there might be no chance of an interview. And an interview with Mark's wife was one Erin couldn't afford to miss.

To Erin's relief, Olivia shook her head and said, 'Fine. I don't care. The more people looking at this, the better, as far as I'm concerned. Tea?'

Light poured from a skylight above them as they sat down at the kitchen island. Olivia poured her a cup from a teapot. She was beautiful, with a mane of glossy dark hair that made her already thin face look even smaller. She anxiously squeezed the rings on her long, elegant fingers as she spoke, as if checking they were still there.

She was quiet and well-spoken. Erin was grateful for the silence of the kitchen, otherwise she wouldn't have been able to hear her. Olivia told her that she had met Mark at university and they had married a few years later. Two years ago, they had moved from London to Wakestead in search of country walks and more space and with plans to start a family of their own. Looking around at the fastidiously maintained open-plan kitchen, the photographs of friends' weddings, their own, Erin built a picture in her head of a very settled couple, feathering their nest in anticipation of children.

'When did you last see Mark?'

'On Saturday morning. Not long before the police believe he was killed. I came downstairs to find him packing a bag for work.'

'How did he seem?'

'Agitated. Distracted.'

'Why do you think that was?'

'He was working on this case that had been eating him up for a long time. A burglary. The victim was badly beaten up.'

'Did he tell you the case was bothering him?'

'No, I'm just inferring that. He didn't speak about it very often.'

'Did he often keep his work to himself?'

'There was a – a wall, yes,' she said. 'He was a very considerate person, quite protective. I suppose you may have done the same yourself. I knew if he was working on something awful like a rape case because he wouldn't tell me about it.'

As she listened to Olivia, Erin began to feel strangely unsettled.

There was something familiar about the woman that she couldn't quite put her finger on.

'Sorry to interrupt,' she said, 'but have we met before?'

Olivia shook her head.

'You and Mark never came to the force while I was there? You were never involved in a case?'

'No,' said Olivia.

What could it have been? Was Erin just remembering Olivia from the press conference she'd watched on TV? Possibly. But the recognition felt deeper than that – there was something in Olivia's manner, in the cadence of her voice, that Erin was sure she had encountered before. She pushed the feeling down.

Olivia brushed her fingertips over her lower eyelashes and swallowed.

'Have you spoken to her?'

Clearly, rumour had spread.

Erin paused before nodding.

'Do you think it was her?' Olivia asked.

'I'm not sure,' Erin replied. 'Did he ever mention Amma Reynolds? Her brother's case?'

'Never.'

'Is there any connection between them that you're aware of?'

'No.'

Had Mark really had nothing to do with the investigation into Amma's brother's death? Had theirs been a chance meeting – assuming they'd even met at all?

'He – he hadn't been around much lately,' said Olivia. 'I was angry at him for working so much. We – we argued about it.' She cleared her throat gently. 'Which I… deeply regret now.'

The question Erin wanted to ask, above all, was whether there'd been any issues with their marriage. But she needed to approach that subject very carefully. Building a rapport always required patience – even more so now that she was a PI. Family members and witnesses would tolerate a certain level of aggression from the police – they, after all, were just doing their job, a public service, and if they went against the force, they were going against the law. But Erin was someone who they could easily shut the door on and decide never to see again if she pushed it too far.

'I'm sure the police have already taken Mark's laptop and phone. Do you have access to any of his accounts?'

'The password to his email is saved on my laptop,' Olivia replied. 'That's it. He didn't really have any social media. Never liked it anyway, but being a cop…'

'Would you be happy to send me your message history with Mark?'

Olivia frowned. 'Why would I need to do that?' she asked curtly.

'The police will have an easier time than me tracking Mark's whereabouts over the past few weeks,' she said. 'I'm guessing he would text you when he was out and when he was coming back? Messages like that will help me cross-reference when I interview witnesses.'

Olivia blinked. 'I see. Well, if you think it will help. Then yes, okay.' Her brow was still furrowed. 'Only a few months' worth of messages, though. Surely you don't need more than that.'

'That should be fine,' said Erin, feeling a twinge of suspicion. Was Olivia really just keeping some of her life private? Or was she hiding something?

'Well, if that's all I can help you with…'

She led her back to the front door. Again, Erin felt recognition plucking in her mind.

'We definitely haven't met before?' she said once she was on the doorstep.

Olivia shook her head.

'I must be getting confused. I'll be in touch. You look after yourself.'

But as she walked away, Erin found herself dwelling on the look in Olivia's eyes just before the front door had closed.

Was she just imagining it – or had the woman looked slightly perturbed, as if terrified that Erin had caught her out?

14

Later that evening, Erin waited with two pints at a table by the windows, far from the ears of the other drinkers. This was the right level of busy – enough hubbub that their voices wouldn't carry across the room but not so packed they could be easily overheard. After a few minutes she saw Lewis enter the pub. Cautiously, he approached her table. Watching him glance nervously around the room, Erin resisted the urge to roll her eyes.

'I did check that your boss wasn't here before ordering drinks, funnily enough,' she said.

Lewis pulled out the seat opposite. 'Don't ask me to email you anything,' he said, pointing a finger at her. 'I want no digital trace of this conversation. You're not recording this, are you?'

'Christ.'

'I mean it, Erin.' He took a sip of his pint. His ears were glowing pink with embarrassment. 'Thank you for this, by the way.'

'So you do accept bribes.'

'That's not funny,' Lewis said. 'Okay, so tell me where you're at and I'll see if I can fill you in. No promises. But I'll see if I can point you in the right direction.'

'I spoke to his wife. She told me he was working on a burglary.'

There was a subtle change in Lewis's face at the word 'burglary'. If she hadn't known him so well, she might have missed it.

'Is that not right?'

'What? Why would you say that?'

'You just made a weird face.'

'No, I didn't.'

Erin narrowed her eyes. 'But the thing for me is,' she went on, 'his wife also said that he was becoming extremely absorbed in his work. Working late. Stressing a huge amount. Especially in the last few weeks before he died. Now, if he was working on a murder case or a rape, then sure, that would add up. But a burglary? No detective's losing sleep over that.'

Lewis eyed her carefully. She knew she was on the right track.

'So that makes me think he was lying to his wife about something.'

Lewis said nothing.

'Am I right?'

Lewis picked up a coaster and started tapping its edge against the surface of the table. 'Let's say he was lying,' he said. 'What do *you* think he was lying about?'

'We have a dead police officer who told his wife he was working late,' she said, 'and a murder suspect who's so traumatised she won't talk to the police. I don't think he was working on those late shifts. I think he was prowling.'

Lewis let the coaster clatter back onto the table. 'See, I *knew* you would think that.'

'Am I wrong?'

'*Yes*, actually.'

'Well, tell me why then. What's your evidence?'

'I'm only telling you this so you don't go barking up the wrong tree, okay. He was working on a burglary. But I'm starting to think maybe it wasn't the only case he was working on. That he was also working on the Isaac Reynolds case.'

'I thought that case was still closed.'

'It was. Is. Officially. But maybe he was researching it behind the scenes, in his spare time. That's what his partner thinks, anyway.'

'Why does he think that?'

'Apparently he was interested in the case as soon as he got here. You can see why. Cold case unsolved for years. I guess it must have seemed like an obvious example of small-town prejudice to him. But you know Warren doesn't want to reopen the case unless there's evidence of third-party involvement.'

'Do you have any new evidence? Did Mark find anything?'

'We don't know yet. The tech team's combing through his work computer and his laptop right now.'

'And what does Callum know?'

'Frustratingly little. They never spoke about it. He thinks Stormont was working away on this stuff basically in secret. But there was one thing he said. Two days before Mark's body was found, Callum dragged him out for a drink. Trying to force him out of his shell. Apparently Mark was dead quiet, totally absorbed in his own thoughts. Stressed too. And, on the way out, he asked Callum if he thought Isaac's death was really an accident.'

Erin narrowed her eyes.

Lewis leant in. 'Is it possible that Mark found out who killed him? And they did this, not Amma?'

Erin ran her thumb up and down the cold pint glass, thinking. 'Do you know anyone who could tell me more about the case? Someone who was there at the time, maybe?'

Lewis winced. 'I mean, there is someone who would know,' he said. 'But you're not going to like it.'

*

Before making the call, Erin stared at the name on her screen for a few moments, debating whether there was a way of avoiding this conversation. After all this time, she still resented ever having to ask him for help. But if Lewis couldn't give her everything she needed, then she didn't have much choice. She inhaled deeply, bracing herself for the inevitable, and hit call.

'Crane,' said Owen Walker. 'To what do I owe the pleasure?'

'How are you?'

'I'm extremely well, Crane. Picture this. I'm lying on a sun lounger beside the pool in a lovely little villa in the south of Spain.'

'I've actually just eaten, thanks. What are you doing for work these days?'

'Private security.'

Erin scrunched up her nose. 'Really?'

'Judge me all you like, Crane, but only one of us is currently basking in the Spanish sun. How does PI work pay, out of interest?'

'I don't want to go into this, Walker.'

'Thought as much. So go on, what's this about?'

'You know about the Mark Stormont murder.'

'Sadly, it's been impossible to get away from, even here.'

'The woman who's been charged. It's Amma Reynolds. You know about her brother, Isaac?'

'I wasn't on the case, if that's what you're suggesting, Crane.'

'But you remember it?'

'I do tend to remember murdered teenagers, thanks very much, Crane.' There was a long squeak on the other end of the phone line as Walker readjusted himself on his sun lounger, followed by a splash and a howl of laughter as one of his teenage sons jumped into the pool. 'It was big. Kid was missing for almost two days before they found him in the river. But they had nothing. Very little forensic evidence. No suspects ever emerged. They decided he was drunk and just fell in.'

'What about the people who were with Isaac the night of the bonfire?'

'All of them had alibis, as far as I remember. A lot of people, the family included, thought he collided with some racist bastard on the way home. Maybe. But you and I both know the odds are it was someone he knew.'

'Do you think it was investigated properly?'

'No one wanted that case, Erin. Dead black teenager, angry family and no evidence of third-party involvement. The police couldn't wait to wash their hands of it. So yes, I think mistakes were made. As I remember, one of the younger officers lost the toxicology report. Which obviously would have confirmed for certain whether the kid was as pissed as they claimed.'

Erin frowned. 'Mark Stormont. Could he have been investigating it?'

'Why would he be? Nothing to do with the Met, is it?'

'I just wondered.'

'You want my opinion on how this happened? Police had their eye on Amma. Mark attended one of her rallies as a uniformed officer. Maybe they had some kind of altercation. Amma clocked him. And started plotting her revenge for everything her family's been through.'

'You think Amma tracked down a random officer just because?'

'Don't pretend you don't have a part to play in this too, Crane.' A slightly mocking note had crept into Walker's voice.

'What are you talking about?'

'People are angry. Women are angry. This is the backlash. It was always coming for us.'

15

Wednesday

THE NEXT MORNING, ERIN BEGAN the painstaking but necessary task of trawling through every message Olivia and Mark had exchanged over the last few months. Every time Mark said he was on the way home or wouldn't be back til late, Erin noted down his whereabouts and the time in a spreadsheet. As she did this, she began to see for herself just how disconnected the couple had become. Their chat history was a litany of mundane updates, a timeline detailing when they were out of milk, when one of them was stuck in traffic, and when Mark was working late – which seemed to be almost all the time. Erin knew not from personal experience but from years of studying people's message history that conversations between long-term cohabitees were always faintly tragic. However, for a young, good-looking couple, Olivia and Mark's felt extreme. And based on these messages, Olivia was the only one who was concerned about it. *Okay. You haven't given me much warning*, she wrote in response to yet another 'working-late' text from Mark. *Next time can you tell me before I buy £30 worth of food for dinner?* Another time, Mark failed to text Olivia back for over five hours, evoking a rare expletive from Olivia: *Ffs. Will you check your phone?* Whatever had happened, Olivia had lost her husband long before he was killed.

*

Lewis walked through the office in search of Gregory, and eventually found the older detective making tea in the kitchen.

'Can I ask you something?' he said.

'Go ahead.'

'Did Mark Stormont ever talk to you about Isaac Reynolds' death?'

'Why?'

'Just a theory,' said Lewis. 'Callum, his partner, thinks he might have been working on it in his own time. Apparently he asked about it a lot. I just wondered if he'd spoken to you.'

Gregory shrugged as he stirred his tea. 'Not that I can remember.'

Maybe there wasn't much in Callum's theory then. Surely if Mark had been investigating, he'd have spoken to the lead detective on the case?

'Erin Crane has been hired by Amma's family to investigate Mark Stormont's murder.'

Gregory's eyebrow ticked upwards slightly.

Lewis continued: 'What's our position on sharing information with her?'

Gregory looked around the kitchen, checking there was no one in earshot. 'I'm surprised you have to ask me that, Jennings. We don't share information on a live case with civilians.'

His voice was firm but not unkind. Panic shot through Lewis. 'No, no, I know that. I mean, what about old cases? Like Isaac's case? I know it might not be by-the-book, but what could be the harm in sharing old case files with her? See what she makes of it?'

'And if she leaks those files to the press? If she shares them with a friend who posts them over the internet, what then?' Gregory scoffed. 'We don't farm out police work to sleuths.'

'I really don't think she would do something like that. She's not a random investigator who we don't know. She's ex-police. She knows how to be discreet.'

'Even if we were to share files with her, what would be the point? That case was closed.'

'I know,' said Lewis. 'But it looks like it could be connected to Mark's death. And it's never been reopened, even though the family's been complaining since the start.'

But Gregory was already shaking his head. 'That case was solved, Jennings. I know it wasn't the outcome the family wanted. But it was the outcome the evidence pointed to. We've got enough on our plate without opening this can of worms.'

Lewis swallowed. 'Which is why I thought, maybe Erin could help—'

'Erin Crane is a liability. She is no longer a part of this police force and that's because of her mistakes. I think it's best that you don't discuss cases with her, Jennings. I'm not sure Warren would be best pleased about this.'

Lewis felt his face flush with embarrassment.

'Yeah, I won't. Thanks for your time.'

Gregory carried his tea back to his desk, leaving Lewis alone in the kitchen with his mind whirring. He hadn't expected Gregory to embrace the idea of working with Erin. But still, the strength of the older detective's reaction had caught him off-guard.

As he was walking across the office, his phone started vibrating in his pocket. It was the scene of crime officer Rob.

'Hi, Rob. Please tell me you've got some results for us.'

'I do indeed. This might come as a bit of a shock.'

16

DEW GLISTENED ON THE GRASS as Erin walked up to Crays Hill where Mark had been found. Four days had passed since his death. The barrier tape had been taken down and the reporters had long abandoned the scene to go and knock on the doors of family and friends, hoping to provoke a newsworthy comment. The only sign that this quiet clearing had ever been a crime scene were the bouquets of flowers circling the base of one of the trees in a halo of white and yellow, like the remnants of a pagan ritual.

Erin was immediately struck by the tranquillity of the place. A bird was singing in the woods nearby. The trees' leaves glowed green, basking in the sunlight.

She glanced back over her shoulder, towards the entrance to the viewpoint.

Amma's house, she knew, was just at the bottom of the hill. Along with the friend she shared it with.

The door opened slightly to reveal a pretty woman with brown curls piled up on her head, a pink-and-white headband and an impressive array of studs on one ear.

'They said you'd be coming over,' said June, Amma's closest friend.

'Is now a good time to talk?'

'Yeah, come in.'

She followed June into the kitchen. Clearly they had just finished breakfast. Beside the kitchen sink, a small-framed man with curly black hair and pierced ears pulled off his rubber gloves, a stack of freshly washed pots and pans in the drying rack.

'I'm Neil, June's boyfriend,' he said. 'Do you want a drink?'

'No, thank you.'

'How do you want to do this?' asked June.

'I'll just ask you a few questions about Amma.'

'That's fine.'

They sat down at the small dining table.

'You've been friends with her for a long time now, is that right?'

'Since we were kids. She's like my sister.'

'This must be hard.'

June gave two sharp nods.

'If the questions I ask make it sound like I'm suspecting her, then please forgive me,' said Erin. 'I'm just trying to get as clear a picture of what happened as I can.'

'I understand.'

'When did you last see her before the arrest?'

'The night before, on Friday. We went out in Oxford. I went back to Neil's and she went back here.'

'What time did she leave?'

'It must have been about one o'clock? We called her a taxi.'

'And how did she seem?'

'Not great. She'd drunk quite a lot.'

Erin frowned. 'You live together, and she was drunk, but you didn't go back with her?'

Guilt filled June's face.

'It's my fault,' said her boyfriend. 'I wanted us to stay at mine that night. I told June she'd be alright.'

'So when did you two leave?'

'Not long after Amma,' June replied. 'At around one thirty.'

Erin was finding June oddly nervous, considering she was Amma's best friend.

She asked: 'And how was she, generally? In the days before the arrest, was anything bothering her, had she mentioned anything unusual?'

June opened her mouth to speak, but before she could say a word, Neil cut in.

'You need to tell her.'

June stared at her partner in shock. 'Neil,' she hissed.

'She's going to find out soon enough.' He turned decisively to Erin. 'Look, there's something you need to know about Amma.'

'Piss off, Neil.'

'I know you love her, but I'm not having you hurt yourself trying to cover for her. If you won't say it, I will.'

June rubbed the space between her eyes. 'Can you go?' she said to Neil.

'Huh?'

'Can you go upstairs and leave us, please?'

Neil clenched his jaw. June's eyes, now piercing, followed her boyfriend as he stalked out of the room, closing the door behind him.

Once they were alone, June took in a deep, steadying breath through her nose. 'Sorry,' she said. 'We're all very… tense right now.'

'It's all right.'

'No, it's not. It doesn't help if we fight.'

Erin waited patiently as June rocked slowly back and forth in her chair, studying the floor, lost in contemplation. She could see June was turning something over in her head.

Finally, Amma's friend said, 'He's right though. There's something you need to know.'

'What?'

June glanced up at her. 'I didn't tell the police. I just… I don't know, I was so worried about her getting caught up in this, and it was obvious she wasn't telling the detectives. So I thought, maybe if I didn't, I was protecting her.'

'What didn't you tell the police?'

'Am I betraying her if I say?'

'Would it help her?'

June rubbed a thumb over her lips nervously. 'I don't know. I think it could. But I don't know.'

'We need all the information we can get,' said Erin.

'I don't know if I can say it,' she said.

Erin was on the edge of pleading with her when June added: 'But I can show you.'

She picked her phone up from the kitchen counter, opened something on the screen, and held it out to her.

Tentatively, Erin took the phone. It showed June and Amma's WhatsApp conversation. Scrolling up through the chat and scanning each sisterly message, she wondered what exactly she was supposed to be looking for. Then finally she reached a photo that Amma had sent June two weeks before the murder. A chill spread over her bare arms and hands.

She glanced up at June, desperate for confirmation that what she was seeing was real. June held her gaze. There was a flash of fear in her eyes now.

This changed everything.

17

Erin's heart raced as she walked against the wind up the road to Amma's family's house. It was a bright but overcast day – almost the end of August. Sunlight probed through thin cloud cover, washing the street of terraced houses in a silver glow. Approaching the house, Erin felt tight-chested but exhilarated, with total clarity of mind, like she was about to plunge herself into a freezing lake.

Once inside, she asked Stephen and Vicky if they wouldn't mind giving her some privacy this time while she spoke to Amma. They willingly retreated into the garden. Erin entered the living room – where Amma was curled up on the sofa, her figure hidden beneath an oversized hoodie – and quietly closed the door behind her.

Amma studied Erin with reproach.

'I know why you aren't talking,' said Erin.

Amma's face was totally still. But Erin noticed a spark of light enter her eyes for the first time since they'd first met. Was it hope? Or fear? She couldn't tell.

'You didn't hate Mark because of what he was.'

Amma stared at her. Erin noticed the young woman's collar bones slowly starting to rise and fall as her breathing picked up.

'You were together.'

Amma looked at the wall behind Erin, her full lips pursing with discomfort, her eyes darting around, tracing the corners of an invisible shape, as she worked out how to respond.

'Tell me what happened between you and him, Amma. I can help you.'

Amma reacted by turning her face away, towards the almost-closed curtains. A band of silver light escaping through the gap highlighted the beautiful shape of her cheekbones and throat, which moved as she swallowed back her emotions. Erin couldn't have moved if she tried. Her body was frozen in place.

She said, 'I didn't run because I killed him. I ran because I knew what was about to happen. I just knew. He was gone and they thought it was me.'

The sofa gently squeaked as, very slowly, Amma swivelled her body around to sit upright, placing her feet on the floor, gripping the edge of the sofa as if to stop herself from falling forward.

'My parents hired you to prove it wasn't me,' she said. 'I've got another job for you.'

She looked at Erin, who was shocked by the sudden fire that had come into the other woman's face. This was Amma. The person she'd seen online, who had campaigned for justice for her brother, who had called the police fascists and meant it – the person she had been looking for all this time, waiting to emerge.

'Find out if it was real. I need to know how much of what he told me was a lie.'

PART II

Then…

18

Two Months Earlier

'Tell me three things about him.'

The laughter of teenagers filled the lazy Sunday summer air. The chain-link fence beside them rattled as a football was hurled into it. Amma watched June duck under a trailing rose bush reaching out from someone's garden before stopping to hold the branch out of her way.

'He's really fit. And I want to have his babies.'

'That's two.'

'I can't think of a third one.'

'Come on, Amma. I need specifics.'

She'd met him the night before at The Hollies, the family home of Neil, June's boyfriend. Most of their mutual friends had moved to London after school, with Neil, Amma and June the last remaining in Wakestead. By far the biggest of any of their families' houses, the Hollies had hosted many parties during their school years and so friends were happy to make the trip back here for occasions like Neil's annual summer party.

*

Amma had been sat outside on the patio.

She was with Neil and a number of his London friends, including Claire, who so far Amma wasn't warming to.

Earlier, when Amma had rung the doorbell, Claire had left her waiting for a few unnecessarily long moments before answering, not realising Amma could see from the shadow cast on the glass in the door that Claire was checking her lipstick and hair in the mirror in the hallway.

Now Claire was halfway through an unprompted rant about how, while she understood the desire to live close to their parents and save up for a place, there was really no beating life in the city. 'I mean, there's so much to do. I'd get so bored living out there.' She looked at Amma with her large eyes. 'Although, for you it must be important to be close to your family?'

Amma gritted her teeth.

'Yeah, of course,' she said.

Neil, clearly keen to move the conversation on, said, 'Wasn't Rory supposed to be making mojitos?'

Rory appeared in that moment as though magically summoned, carrying a tray of toxic-looking drinks that were promptly swept up by the group.

Amma ignored them. She'd never handled alcohol well, and she'd had a few drinks already.

Claire appeared not to have noticed the tension she'd introduced into the conversation. In blissful ignorance, she continued, 'I mean, I'm actually so impressed you can be in this house after—'

There was an edgy silence. Neil's eyes looked like they were going to pop out of his head.

'Why's that?' said Amma, even though they all knew. Her nails dug into her palm as she clenched her fist.

Claire's face had flushed pink. 'Sorry,' she said, sensing Amma's anger. Her voice shook slightly. 'It's just – your brother – I know this is where he had a couple of drinks before – you know, I would understand if you didn't want to be here after that. Sorry.'

Nobody said anything. Neil coughed awkwardly at the paving stones and disappeared into his drink.

Amma leant forward to pick up the last remaining drink and forced down a large gulp. It was very strong, enough to make her want to gag. Everyone seized the opportunity to talk about something else. Neil shot her a deeply apologetic look over the rim of his glass.

After that, she found it hard to rejoin the conversation. She was determined to try and enjoy herself but she couldn't ignore the new tightness in her chest, her irritability towards Claire, who started combing her hair with her fingers, looking visibly shaken by the confrontation.

What right did Claire have to bring it up like that? Perhaps she'd thought she was being kind. But Amma felt ambushed by the comment, like she had brought a ghostly presence into the party, one Amma had come here precisely to avoid. She knocked back the rest of her drink.

The next thing she knew she was staring up at the ceiling, entranced. Its light seemed to be growing and dimming every few seconds in time with the lazy reggae beat that pulsed through the closed bathroom door. Sometimes when she was drunk, Amma found it soothing to focus on a repetitive sound or motion, because it forced her to stay in the moment. But this time it wasn't working. Nothing seemed to be working.

Not again, she thought. Not here. Not now. The problem was that Claire was right. She did find it difficult to come to the Hollies. The house had always reminded her of what happened that night. Usually if she pushed the thought to the very back of her mind, she could cope. But Claire had broken down her walls in a single instant.

The other partygoers seemed to bend and warp around her, their long shadows stretching up the walls of the black and orange corridor. Their unexpected bursts of laughter felt persecutory as she wandered through rooms in search of the others. Where was Neil? She'd lost him. She couldn't see June either. She didn't recognise anyone here.

Intoxication is thought to have contributed to the cause of death.

A memory hit her out of nowhere. Of a police detective pushing a photograph towards her, showing a coffee table littered with empty beer cans and a half-drunk vodka bottle.

Amma shook her head to try and get rid of the image.

'No,' she remembered saying, 'he's not like that. You don't understand.'

She'd had enough. It was time to go home. She squeezed through the tunnel of bodies crowded along the corridor and burst out into the cool night air. Where was she? Walking along the street in the pitch-black, listening to the lonely sound of her heels clattering along the pavement, she got out her phone. She had to concentrate very hard to type her address into Google Maps. The wiggling blue line charting her 40-minute walk home looked incomprehensible.

It was as she was staring down at her phone screen, crossing the road unthinkingly, that she was suddenly engulfed in a beam of white light. Everything happened very slowly after that. Amma looked to her left and saw the bonnet of a car loom out of the darkness. The car seemed to be inching forwards. But it wasn't. That was just her perception changing. Her mind trying to buy her time as it worked out what to do. She started to run. But her front foot had barely left the ground before she realised she wasn't going to make it.

Something slammed into her back, pushing her out of the path of the car, which surged past, its car horn blaring so loudly that Amma's ears rang with pain. She stared down at the black gravel glittering in the street lights, gasping for breath. Someone's arms were fastened tightly around her middle.

'What are you doing?'

The arms around her waist loosened. She turned around. Bearded, maybe 40, in a woollen jacket. He was breathing heavily. He looked horrified by her near-suicidal display, her complete loss of self-awareness.

'Are you okay?' he asked, softer this time.

Amma was still panting hard. Relief flooded her body, numbing her extremities, as she realised how close she'd come to getting hit. 'Oh my god, that was stupid.'

'You should sit down.'

'I'm fine.'

'Come over here.'

He led her over to the curb, and Amma lowered herself down on shaky knees. She noticed she was breathing deeply. The shock had flooded her system with adrenaline and now she felt stone-cold sober and wide-awake, the night air cool on her face as she stared across the street at the orange streetlights lining the road.

'What were you doing?' he asked.

'Wasn't thinking.'

'Do you need a lift home?'

'I'm fine,' said Amma.

'Are you sure?'

Then she looked at him, still staring at her with deep concern. He was, she realised, extremely good-looking.

'Actually, that might be helpful. Is that okay?'

'Of course.'

She followed him to his car, feeling strangely content. No other cars passed them as they drove in silence down the streets bathed in amber light. The windows in the front of the car were open very slightly and she let her head roll back, enjoying the sensation of the night air passing over her face and her bare shoulders. After a long moment, she glanced sideways at the man. She liked the look of concentration on his face as he drove. Disappointment swept through her when she realised they were approaching her street.

*

'Oh my god,' June said, once Amma had finished telling her about the night before.

'I know. It was so dumb.'

'I'm just glad you're okay. So did anything happen with this guy?'

'No, I was too far gone. He dropped me off and said goodbye.'

'Do you think you'll text him?'

'Didn't get his number.'

June opened the gate, pushed past and held it open for Amma.

'Why do you reckon he was driving around so late? Do you think he works nights?'

'Who knows? Nothing I can do now, is there?'

She'd been enjoying walking outside with June, soaking in the sun, feeling the remnants of her hangover gradually dissipate. But now the heaviness in her heart – which had been there when she'd first woken up this morning, groggy and in pain – was back. She'd been on only a few dates lately, all of them terrible in their own unique way. Last night was the first time in a while she'd felt attracted to someone on sight. And she'd screwed it up.

June was a natural romantic, and she wasn't letting this go. 'He literally *saved you*,' she said. 'You could have died. It's fate, you know. I bet he'll drop round later.'

'Forget it, he's gone,' said Amma. 'Besides, I don't think I made a great impression. He's lucky I didn't throw up in his car.'

19

Amma went to dinner at her parents' that evening. Vicky, her mum, had a couple of friends over, including Emmanuel and his parents. Emmanuel had been Isaac's friend before hers. After his death he'd become one of the integral members of their campaign group, manning their social media accounts.

While their parents chatted, Emmanuel and Amma sat on the sofa discussing their next attempt to raise awareness of the campaign. He scrolled through X on his phone. 'The Sophie Madson angle is quite good for us. Trust in the police must be at its lowest in years, right? If they let someone like that operate undetected within their own ranks, what else have they let slip?'

She nodded. 'I think we should really step up our messaging ahead of the anniversary of her death. In a couple of months' time it will be three years. I'll speak to some of the journalists we've talked to in the past. Ideally we'd get a national.'

Emmanuel pulled a face. 'Ideally, yeah. But we need to have something new to say.'

Amma nodded. It was the same old issue. They'd been banging the drum about Isaac's death for more than a decade now. There was never anything new to say. But that was the only way to make anyone stop and pay attention.

She was distracted by Vicky's abrupt, shrieking laughter. Amma's mum showed love by taking the piss, which Amma would be fine with if she was actually funny. Amma could overhear Vicky entertaining her friends by recycling the same old anecdotes of when

Amma was a teenager – *remember all those fights she got into; she's so moody you wouldn't believe it.* Amma groaned and let her body sink into the sofa, trying to ignore the sounds of the gaggle of women laughing at her expense at the other end of the living room.

Another thing about her mum – she couldn't resist bossing her around like a child. 'Amma, stop flirting,' she called. 'Get the tablecloth from upstairs.' Amma traipsed up the stairs.

She searched the cupboard on the landing and found nothing so went into her parents' bedroom. She pulled out drawer after drawer and couldn't find it. Huffing now with aggravation, she stomped over to the wardrobe and, opening it, saw that the bottom looked like it could be lifted up, so she did that.

Her mind took a few moments to register what she was looking at. A colour-burst of flowers. A small and carefully tended structure like a child's dollhouse. In the middle of the structure was a candle, misshapen by the wax that had dribbled down while it was lit. Finally Amma's eyes adjusted. Behind the candle was a photo of her brother. Taken the year he died. The structure was a tiny shrine, decorated with dried flowers and a rosary, the cross casting a shadow over his face. This was somewhere a person came to pray.

Amma had barely processed this before she slammed the lid down. The sound snapped through her chest.

Her mother had been religious since she was a child, but she hadn't attended church in years, not that Amma knew.

It was a shock to come downstairs and find Vicky humming loudly and happily over a steaming pot while the radio played loudly into the room. 'What took you so long?'

Amma laid the table in silence.

'What's up?'

'Nothing.'

'Sulking because I told the girls how uncool you used to be, that's what.' She sniggered to herself and snacked on a few cashew nuts that were on the countertop.

Amma swallowed. It was not surprising, she told herself. It was not surprising at all. But listening to her mum hum away in apparent bliss, she thought how terrifying it was – how well a loved one could hide their pain.

When Amma was a child, every Saturday morning, at 5 o' clock, she would wake up to the sounds of her brother getting ready for football training. Through the wall she would hear him clattering around in the bathroom, followed by the urgent footsteps of her mother rushing down the corridor to tell him that they were going to be late if he didn't get dressed within the next five minutes. At the sound of the car pulling out of the driveway, Amma would roll over onto her side, pulling the duvet up to her chin, and flex her toes contentedly under the body-warm covers. Her last thought before she fell back to sleep was always the same: thank God I'm not the talented one.

Isaac was eleven when he announced over dinner that he wanted to become an actuary. He had just had his first career talk at school. 'What's that?' Amma remembered asking through mouthfuls of bolognese. Isaac slurped up his spaghetti loudly and said, 'I don't know, but it pays loads.'

And that was it: his future career decided. Isaac chose to study Maths and Economics at A-level and was going to apply for a mathematical degree at university, then for internships at accountancy firms. No existential crisis. No mourning over the loss of other subjects he'd enjoyed, like history. Just pure dedication to the simple goal of making money so he could give his not-yet-existent family the good life. Amma envied his ability to so easily transport himself into a future – which seemed to her so daunting and uncertain – and disregard his wants and needs of today. Amma would have to tell her kids, 'Sorry your cousins go on big holidays; your mum just had a much lower boredom threshold when we were kids.'

Isaac's maturity had made his disappearance even more difficult to fathom in those first few days. It hadn't felt real. Her smart, capable brother – missing. She felt certain he must have left of his own will. Maybe he'd met a girl and stayed with her and was too embarrassed to tell anyone or perhaps he'd decided he needed to exercise his independence and got on the first Eurostar to Paris. Neither of these were things he would do but suddenly they seemed to be the only plausible explanation. In their nervous desperation to provide comfort, her friends gave weight to the theories: 'He's at the age,' said June, with a wisdom beyond her years. 'My sister snuck off loads at seventeen.' So on the two days he was missing, when she came home from school, out of breath, Amma expected to find him on the staircase waiting for them, apologetic, perhaps, but mostly hungry, wondering where dinner was – and, above all, annoyed at her for letting Mum get so worked up.

They were having breakfast the day they found out. Her dad had already left to hand out flyers to morning commuters at the train station. Amma sat in her school uniform, her cold feet curled up under her thighs, forcing herself to eat a bowl of Crunchy Nut that was softening into a cold, unpalatable mush. Her mum stared blankly at the cereal box without reading the text. Her skin over the last few days had lost all its lustre due to lack of sleep.

When it rang, the doorbell seemed incredibly loud, the sound rebounding throughout the house. Her mum got up to answer it and Amma heard her slippers shuffling across the floor. There was a moment before she decided to follow her when Amma stared at the cooker, suddenly and inexplicably convinced that they should not find out who was at the door. She felt something she never had before – a falling sensation in her chest, like a premonition.

Amma edged towards the doorway of the kitchen until she could see, past the staircase, her mum holding the door open to two police officers. Their eyes were squinting as if it was sunny when it wasn't and there was no colour in their cheeks. They looked uncomfortable. Uncomfortable because of the pity they felt for her mum. Whenever Amma thought of it now, it made her feel angry.

She saw the police officer's lips move. Amma would never forget the faltering step back her mum took; how she swayed and almost fell and raised a hand to her chest, as if she was standing in the sea and her whole body had been wrenched back by the slow but forceful push of a heavy wave.

After Isaac died, her mum went to her room and didn't come out for two weeks.

Strangely those weeks were not the worst. With the sudden disappearance of Isaac and her mum came the sporadic arrivals of aunts, uncles and cousins, coming into the house to cook and clean and just watch TV with her, that made that stretch of time feel unreal, an alien intervention that would end as soon as it had begun. It took about a month for the numbing effects of the shock to ebb away, replaced by the realisation her brother was never coming back.

Eventually her mum re-emerged. Vicky came from a big family. She had her own mum to look after, cousins to see, their children to watch over when they couldn't. Amma learnt at any early age that having responsibility for someone or something was the best way to stop yourself from losing your mind. It was about self-preservation as much as altruism.

Then Isaac's deification started.

As time passed, family and friends began to scrub out her brother's imperfections and embellish every success he'd had in his seventeen years of life. *Did you know Isaac was top of the class for mathematics? Or that, aged ten, he climbed up his friend's house to help a pigeon out of the rain gutter? Do you remember when his other friend broke his leg clambering over a brick wall and Isaac half-carried him to A&E?* Acts of kindness were evidence of Isaac's saintlike nature. Teenage recklessness reimagined as bravery. Physical prowess seen as some deep, superhuman quality. One by one, friends and relatives adorned his collective memory with their own shiny trinket, their own tribute, until it was difficult to find the real Isaac hiding beneath the version they had created from their devotion.

Deep down, Amma knew the truth. Isaac came top of the class in mathematics, once, and never shut up about it. She also knew that in the process of climbing up his friend's house, he had broken the roof gutter in which the pigeon was trapped, dislodging in from the wall and eliciting a torrent of rage from the friend's father. And the broken leg? That was his fault – it was his idea, after all, to climb over that brick wall with no way to get down the other side except by plunging oneself down and hoping you landed well.

But Amma found that these truths were slowly pushed down to the bottom of her memory. Reminiscing with friends and family over the gilded version of Isaac they had created brought her a profound sense of comfort.

Sometimes, lying awake at night, she tried to picture what it was like talking to him. And after perhaps half an hour she would cover her face with her hands, because, no matter how hard she tried, she couldn't quite remember.

20

AMMA FELT HER HAIR TREMBLE around her face as a channel of air funnelled in her direction, signalling that a train was coming. It was Monday, early evening. She'd been working in London for several years now, commuting in and out of Wakestead. She worked for a charity for vulnerable kids – a job that brought her a huge amount of satisfaction – but until the pay improved, there would be no moving to the city for her. How much of her life had she spent on this line? Days? Weeks? Not months surely. How many times had she stared at the blackened tracks and read this week's poster and gritted her teeth waiting for a delayed train to arrive? Usually she just got on with it. But something had jolted her out of her everyday routine.

Normally she took the bus home after the train arrived in Wakestead. But today she didn't. Today she walked through town, the sun beating down on her shoulders, and headed in the direction of the bridge. As she approached the very spot where the man had pulled her out of the path of the oncoming vehicle on Saturday night, the ghost of her near-crash passed through her. The road looked so peaceful in the light of day. But immediately she remembered the huge yellow beams, the force of another body pushing her across the road, the man's eyes – bright blue – staring at her. She couldn't get that gaze out of her head. No stranger had ever looked at her with such concern. The hairs along her arms stood on end as she imagined the stare and crossed the bridge.

Why had he been out here so late? Amma found herself watching every car that passed and peering into corner shop windows, searching for his face. Suddenly she looked at what she was doing and wanted to give herself a slap on the cheek. This was insane. Any decent human being would have done what he'd done. A man had been nice to her, and now she was scouring the streets for him like a maniac. Why had she let him get in her head so much?

She rolled her shoulders, shaking off the memory, and continued walking home.

It was a hot summer's evening, the hedges outside the house almost humming with sunlight. Amma pushed open the door and headed upstairs to her room. To her surprise she found both June and Neil looking sheepish in the corridor.

'What's up with you?'

She glanced between them. June seemed bright-eyed and edgy.

'Nothing.' June pushed up her sleeves and put her hands on her hips. 'How was work?'

'Good. Sort off,' said Amma, walking past them and dropping her satchel in her bedroom. 'I was distracted.'

'By this mystery man?' said Neil, rubbing his hands together.

'Yeah, to be honest. But unfortunately I think I've scared him away forever.'

Neil rolled his eyes. 'Christ, Amma. You know we rely on you for titillation, right? Five years is a long time to be in a relationship.'

June elbowed him in the side.

Once they'd scuttled off upstairs, Amma grabbed a towel and headed into the bathroom. She was reaching over the tub to turn on the faucet when something made her stop. Two pairs of handprints were perfectly preserved in the condensation on the mirror – the larger on the outside, the smaller pair in the centre. Recalling June's half-dried hair and flushed complexion, Amma snorted through her nose. *Oh,* you *need titillation.* Dickheads.

A strangely solemn feeling came over her as she showered. Amma had moved in a few years ago after June had first gotten onto the property ladder. But their time together was coming to an end. Soon June would want to live with her boyfriend, and Amma would have to find somewhere else to live. Usually she was very content with being single. But more recently the sense that her friend's life was changing so dramatically had left her with a feeling of incompleteness.

She had just finished changing into tracksuit bottoms and a hoodie, wrapping up her hair in a towel, when the doorbell rang. 'I'll get it,' she called, heading downstairs, and opening the door. Stood on her doorstep, looking as surprised as she felt, was the Hot Man From the Other Night.

Amma suppressed the urge to rub her hands together in maniacal delight. Instead she placed one hand on the door and the other on the doorframe, spreading herself between the two, pushing out her hip. 'Oh, hey, it's you,' she said, feigning surprise. 'You helped me home?'

'Glad there wasn't any lasting brain damage.'

He had a lopsided smile that Amma found attractive. He was even better-looking than she remembered.

Then she realised what he was carrying. Her jumper. She had completely forgotten she'd brought it with her that night.

'You left this in the car.'

'Oh my god. Thank you.'

He stepped forward to place it carefully into Amma's outstretched hand, then immediately retreated back onto the patio.

'I didn't catch your name before?' she said.

'Mark.'

'I'm Amma.'

His eyes flitted from her mouth to her eyes.

This was in the bag. 'Hey, I'm so, *so* sorry about that night.'

'It's fine.'

'No, it's not.' She gestured into the house. 'Do you want to come in for a glass of water?'

He glanced into the corridor behind her, then looked at her apologetically. 'No, thanks. I'd better get going.'

He didn't want to leave. She could see it in his eyes. She heard herself say, 'Sure, no worries.'

Ask him for his number? She couldn't think of an excuse. Was she harassing him if she tried again?

'Thank you, though,' he said.

Oh god. This was awful. One last try.

'What's your number? I really think I should get you a drink sometime to say thanks.'

Mark did an odd thing. He turned his head – his collarbones really were extraordinary – and glanced over the hedge, as if scanning the road beside the house.

'Why not,' he said.

She got her phone out and typed in the number he read aloud. In between digits they briefly made eye contact and Amma felt a hot flush over her neck and shoulders.

She sent him a message. 'And that's me.'

'Nice.'

They said goodbye. He gave her one last look and then turned and headed down the garden path. Amma stared after him.

She heard footsteps behind her. June emerged on the stairs wearing shorts and a pink vest.

'Told you he'd come back,' she said smugly.

21

INITIALLY, AMMA WAS DETERMINED NOT to be the one to text first. But at work the next day, as the hours crawled by without a message, she found herself relenting.

If he doesn't text by two o'clock, then I'll text, she decided.

Two o'clock came and went. Amma, eating lunch in the courtyard outside the office, typed out a message – *hey, thanks again for returning my possessions :) when are you around for that drink?* – and hit send.

Almost immediately she regretted it. Sending the message and waiting for his response only amplified her anxiety. Unable to concentrate on her work, she continually unlocked her phone, sneaking glances at the screen for a message that never came. After each obsessive check she would re-evaluate the message she'd sent. *A drink*. How original. Maybe she should have suggested something with a bit more imagination. Pretended she had a cultural side.

Okay. End of the day. If he hasn't texted back by then, he's not interested.

She couldn't remember the last time a man had gotten her this worked up. It was stressful and exhilarating at the same time, that something as banal as a text message could put her on high alert.

Her heart sank when she got back that evening and realised June wasn't in. She rang her and they spoke over the phone while Amma reheated a chilli con carne.

'If he doesn't get back to you, he's insane and not worth your time,' June said decisively, which calmed her down for a bit.

But the deadline she'd set for Mark wouldn't leave her mind. As the time approached 10 o'clock, she pulled on her pyjamas and slid into bed. She checked her phone one final time.

No messages.

Ah, she thought. Too eager. Fucked it.

She put her phone on charge, curled up in bed and tried to forget about it until eventually sleep came.

A slither of morning light woke her up. She'd forgotten to close the curtains fully last night, and a beam slanted across her face, directly into her eyes. Almost immediately she noticed how different she felt compared to yesterday. The traces of anxiety in every corner of her body were gone. She felt calm and well-rested. She was going to stop caring about Mark now. She'd decided.

She rolled onto her side and checked her phone. A message was there waiting for her.

Sorry for the late reply. Are you free Saturday?

Her new resolution not to care was quickly cast to the wayside.

*

As Amma walked over the bridge into town on Saturday, she felt beautiful. She was wearing a skirt and sandals. Her hair, loose, tumbled in thick curls around her head. She'd been to the gym an hour earlier, and she could still feel the rush of endorphins as she took in the strip of yellow splitting a darkening sky, silhouetting the steeple of the church and gleaming off the bonnets of the cars parked along the street.

They were meeting for an afternoon drink in a pub Amma and her friends usually skipped because it was too expensive. Amma felt a rush of panic and excitement when she spotted him waiting at a table. They exchanged the hug that typified first dates – quick and awkward, with both of them angling carefully so as not to press their chests together or bump noses. In their swift exchange, Amma drank in the smell of the cologne he'd sprayed under his jaw.

'What do you want?' she asked.

'Obviously I'm not actually going to let you buy me a drink.'

Very quickly Mark started to tick an alarming number of boxes. When he went to get their drinks, he moved his body with a calm authority that made Amma's skin shiver. He asked questions, lots of them, one after the other, about her family, her friends, her job, and when she replied he listened attentively, following up with questions that were thoughtful and considered. But despite this Amma struggled to fully relax. She'd been on so many shit dates lately she'd lost faith in her own judgement. Was this guy an absolute catch? Or was he just the first man who'd been nice to her in a long time?

He was leaning forward to ask her something else – a question about a holiday she was describing – when Amma interrupted him.

'Wait, wait, I feel like this is just turning into an interview now,' she said, gesturing between them with her hands. 'Let me ask you something.'

'I'm cripplingly shy,' he said, giving her another lopsided smile.

'No, you're not getting away with that. Sooo, what do you do?' She took a sip of her ice-cold rose, studying his face.

'I'm in the army.'

Shit. Amma tried to hide her disappointment.

'Oh, so do you move around quite a lot?'

He nodded.

The slow responses over text. The caution. That explained it.

'How long are you here for at the moment?'

'It's hard to say. I'm waiting to hear about a deployment.'

Amma nodded, trying to hide her disappointment. Typical. You finally find a good one and they might disappear at any moment.

'So you live near here?'

'Not in Wakestead, no. I'm staying with some friends at the moment, closer to Oxford.'

'Oh sorry, I didn't realise you weren't local. I hope this wasn't far for you to travel.'

'No, it's fine.'

'So why were you here that night then?'

'I have some friends here as well. It was a bit of a late one.'

No mention of a girlfriend so far, Amma had noticed. He looked out of the window as a beam of sunlight came slanting into the pub. Amma registered the genuine appreciation on his face as he soaked in the warmth.

'Do you want to go for a walk?'

'Yeah, why not?'

They walked through town to Crays Hill. The June heat rose until it swallowed her whole. In yellow patches of grass scattered throughout the park, friends and couples lay sprawled in various states of blissful lethargy, legs spread, sandals removed, their heads either lolling on the chest of a sleeping lover or tilted up to bask in the rays of her sunlight. Next to her, she heard Mark draw in a deep breath. Then he got down and lay on his back, eyes closed. Behind him was an old stone monument speckled with yellow lichen.

He squinted at her with one eye closed. With one hand he beckoned to the space next to him. 'Come on.'

Amma joined him. The dry grass prickled her bare arms. It took her a few moments to relax her body. She closed her heavy eyelids. When she did she saw nothing but dark red.

They lay side by side, comatose. After a while she opened one eye to sneak a peek. Mark's eyes were closed as though he was sleeping but his lips were half-smiling. His shirt's top buttons were open, exposing the beautiful drama of his collarbones. A pleasant heat thrummed between her legs. An ant followed a sloping blade of grass down into an unseen insect world. Birdsong came and went, floating above their heads, the only sound disturbing her quiet euphoria.

As she looked at him, Mark's eyes slowly opened. He smiled with knowing pleasure that was almost post-coital. Amma felt another flush of embarrassment. She sat up quickly, smoothing her skirt over her thighs. She never usually got this self-conscious around men. The flush in her cheeks deepened as she realised Mark was watching her hands. He pushed himself up onto his elbows. Amma got the impression he was waiting for a signal from her.

They weren't far from hers. She could invite him back right now. But she knew if she did that, there was an 80 per cent chance she'd have sex with him. And it was too soon.

'I'd better go. I'm seeing some friends later,' she said.

Which was true. She'd known there would be a clash and said yes anyway, pre-empting this moment, where she would need a reason to escape before she did something stupid.

They got up.

'It would be nice to meet up again,' said Mark.

'Yeah.'

He stuck out his hand.

'Urgh, I hate that,' said Amma.

She went in for a hug which Mark returned, a little cautiously. Amma felt a tug of dissapointment in her chest. They'd broken some kind of barrier there, in the grass. And now it was up again. Mark had turned back into the guarded person who'd knocked on her front door earlier that week.

They parted ways, walking in opposite directions down the hill.

22

BIRDSONG WOKE HER UP THE next day. Amma stretched out her limbs underneath the fresh covers, soaking in the knowledge that this was Sunday, the gentlest day of the week. Bit by bit, yesterday's date with Mark slipped into her mind.

When she'd returned home, she'd stood alone in the kitchen for a few minutes, dazed and delighted, feeling as though an electric current had woken up inside her. She could still sense it now, humming quietly beneath her skin. She closed her eyes, letting her hand drift down into her pyjama shorts. She remembered the heat of the sun's rays beating down. The presence of Mark beside her. Tiny arrows of pleasure shot up her body. Then a glow spread across her whole head. Her free hand scrunched up the covers as she floated away and up through the ceiling.

*

The bucket bumped against Amma's thigh as she hauled the mop upstairs.

'This feels excessive,' said June, following behind.

It was Saturday night and in a few hours' time Amma would be going on her second date with Mark. The furniture in her room spilled out in the corridor. Manoeuvring around her stranded belongings, Amma put down the bucket and started aggressively swabbing the floor. June was watching her from the doorway with alarm.

'He must be a big deal. You never clean.'

'You don't understand. He's an adult.'

'So are we?'

'Can you just be mature if we come back here? I don't want to find you and Neil lounging on the sofa eating Pringles out of the box. I don't know, maybe watch the news or something.'

'Watch the news? What are you talking about?' June watched her push the mop underneath the bed. 'How old did you say he was again?'

'I didn't. He's thirty-three,' she mumbled as she swabbed the floor.

'Is this why you're freaking out? You think you'll seem immature to him? Because you definitely won't.' She got out her phone. 'What social media does he have? So I can look him up.'

'He told me he doesn't.'

'Really?' June made a face. Then her expression softened. 'Maybe that's a good thing, you know. Grounded. Not vain.'

'Hopefully,' said Amma. 'Annoying for me, though. Makes it harder to work him out.'

June leaned against the doorframe. 'Soo…'

'What?'

'So you think he's coming back here?'

'I don't know. Maybe. Maybe back here.' Amma momentarily stopped mopping, staring at the empty room. 'Oh my god what if we have sex? I think I'll die.'

'I've just remembered I definitely won't be in.'

*

They stepped out onto the doorstep of the pub. The sky was a deep dark blue. Mark stared up at the roofs of the buildings along the street.

'So do you want to come back to mine?' she asked.

He looked at her. His eyes moved slowly between each of hers. 'Sure.'

They chatted all the way home but Amma was hardly aware of anything they said. Her heart was doing back-flips in her chest. She was never usually this nervous inviting a man back. Her legs were shaky and she had to keep her eyes trained on the garden path as she led him up to the house because she was worried about tripping on the paving stones.

She hadn't put any wine in the fridge. Once inside, she rummaged around in the drinks cabinet.

'Is rum and Coke okay?'

'Sure. Thanks.'

He looked very tall in the cramped kitchen. Their age gap was showing.

'So we could have these on the sofa,' she said, handing him his drink, 'or in my room if you like.' The final six words tumbled out of her.

Mark paused. His expression was hard to read. 'Your room sounds good.'

Amma swallowed. 'My room. Great. One second. Just going to the toilet.'

She dived into the bathroom, had a two-second breakdown, frantically reapplied deodorant, then re-emerged and threw Mark an easy smile. Leading him upstairs, she swayed her hips from side to side, hyper-aware of the sound of his gentle footsteps behind her. By the time they reached her room her skin felt very hot. Mark stepped inside – once again seeming too big for the room – and looked around with curiosity.

'It's nice.'

She shrugged. 'It's small. It does the job. Mates' rates.'

She listened to him inhale deeply through his nose as he pressed closer, his chest against her arm. She could feel his heart beating hard.

She had wanted this all week and now they were here she felt unsure. It had been a long time since she'd liked someone this much. Maybe she should hold back. Avoid crossing this threshold so soon. Sensing her hesitation, Mark moved his head back and touched her elbow.

'If this is too early, that's okay.'

The slightly chaste gesture panicked her. 'It's not too early,' she said.

She kissed him. Amma had had so many bad kisses lately – too much teeth, too much spit, too much tongue – that she'd almost forgotten what it felt like to have another mouth melt into hers. They moved onto the bed. Gently he slid one hand around her waist and lowered her down until she was pressed into the sheets. Then they started kissing more deeply.

He got on his knees in front of the bed. He kissed her bare thighs without opening his mouth. 'Move this way,' he said, placing his hand to the left of her. The gentle instruction made her spine pinch in with pleasure. Her leg trembled as she edged along the bed. Mark pushed his hands up her skirt and pulled down her pants. Then Amma felt his mouth press against her and open.

Her head rolled back. The shadow of the lampshade stretched across the ceiling. After a few moments she looked down and his eyes met hers. His pupils were dilated. Her cheeks flushed with heat.

He got up and pulled off his t-shirt, then started unbuckling his belt. As he pulled down his trousers, his eyes never once left hers. She moved up the bed to give him space, spreading her legs wider, her heart racing as he clambered across the mattress. When he entered her, she let out an involuntary cry. Mark, almost alarmed, responded by moving gently. She dug her nails into his shoulders. 'Go faster,' she said. He did as she said, kissing her. A fire spread across all of Amma's skin and up her spine.

Afterwards, for a few moments neither of them said anything. Then Mark kissed her shoulder, his beard hairs tickling her skin. 'You're unbelievable,' he said.

They lay there talking for an hour, still glowing with the rush of endorphins. Eventually Amma disentangled herself to go to the toilet. She darted out of her room in her t-shirt, confident she wouldn't bump into June on the way. She couldn't think of the last time she'd been this excited just to be at home. Somehow even her bathroom seemed brand new. She appreciated the smooth tiles beneath her bare feet, the sound of water streaming out of the tap, the feeling of its coolness over her hands.

When she returned, Mark was sat at the edge of her bed, shirtless, his beautiful back to her. He was holding something in one hand. Erin realised he was staring at the framed photograph of Isaac she usually kept on her desk. He looked back at her, his expression pure and quizzical.

'That's my brother,' she said. She slipped back under the covers. 'He was killed.'

Mark looked back at the photograph. 'I'm so sorry.'

She wanted him to get back under the covers with her. But his attention was still fixed on the photo.

'Killed how?' he asked.

'He drowned. The police said it was an accident. But it didn't look like an accident.'

He looked back over his shoulder. 'Really?'

She nodded. To her relief he got up and came to lay beside her.

'Who would have done something like that?'

'Some of his friends think he was targeted. That it was a racist attack. Unprovoked.'

She'd never spoken about her brother to a man this early on while dating. She was surprised at how natural it felt. Mark's tone was calm and sympathetic, without probing too much.

'But you don't think that?'

She studied the ceiling. 'I don't know. Maybe. I would almost rather believe that. But…'

'What?'

'I think it's more likely the person who did it probably knew him.' She paused, correcting herself. 'Which means I probably knew them too.'

23

After work the following Tuesday, she bought a lemonade from the corner shop and drank it in the garden while reading. The air started to cool as evening approached. It came as a huge relief after the stifling heat of the day. Amma flexed her toes on the garden seat, enjoying the faint breeze over her bare legs. It was three days after she'd slept with Mark and her body was still fizzing with excitement and satisfaction. She looked up at the silver birch in next door's garden, half-dangling into theirs, its leaves whispering as the wind passed through them.

Just as she was starting to think about dinner, the doorbell rang. Amma groaned. Slowly and reluctantly, she extrapolated herself from her reclined position before heading inside to answer the door. When she opened it, her heart stopped. Mark stood on the doorstep, dressed in a black bomber jacket.

'Sorry to just turn up. Can I come in?'

'Sure.'

Amma stepped back to allow him into the house. This wasn't good. His expression was grim. Shit shit shit, she thought as she led him into the kitchen.

She wanted to ask if it was because of the nature of his job – because he too was scared he might get deployed at any moment – but she didn't want to put words in his mouth. If he had a problem with her specifically, she needed to hear what it was.

The cries of a bird – perhaps disorientated by the light from the rooms downstairs, perhaps warning of danger – floated in through the kitchen.

'Last time… That was stupid of me,' he said.

Amma flinched.

'I don't mean I didn't… I had an amazing time with you, I just—'

'You don't have to—' She dismissed him with a wave of her hand.

'No, I did. I had an amazing time. I'm just not in the position to…' He cleared his throat. 'I'm not in the position to give you what you deserve.'

'Why did you walk away the first time?' she said.

'I was scared.'

Amma chewed the inside of her mouth.

'Do you have a girlfriend?'

'No,' said Mark decisively.

She nodded. 'Okay.' She was getting frustrated now. If he did have a problem with her, she'd rather he just said. 'If you're not sure about me, that's fine, you know.'

Mark reacted to that immediately. His chest inflated as he drew in a slightly panicked breath.

'No, it's not, it's—' He turned around, gripping the chair behind him. 'I think you're incredible.'

She watched Mark stare at the floor. Agonising over every word.

Suddenly, she started to feel a tiny glimmer of confidence grow in her chest.

Hang on, she thought.

He didn't have to do this. He didn't have to come here and tell her to her face. They'd only just met. He could have texted her. Anyone would – wouldn't they? – rather than put themself through the ordeal of letting someone down in person?

Mark looked at her. 'I came here to say that this can't happen again,' he said firmly.

'Okay,' she said.

'It just can't.'

'Okay.'

She felt a small, playful smile creep onto her face.

Mark bit his lip and looked away. He rubbed his mouth with his hand in frustration. At almost the same time, his body turned in her direction and drew closer, as if magnetised towards her. Amma tilted her head and he bowed hers to her shoulder. With his face buried in her t-shirt, she heard him inhale deeply through his nose. His mouth found hers and they started kissing.

Afterwards, when they were naked under the covers, she said cheerfully, 'Don't feel bad. I can tell you did try really hard,' at which point Mark covered his face with his hands.

24

Amma was never more aware of how small her room was than when she and Mark were having sex. The five-metre-by-four-metre space seemed to shrink. The double bed became a single and, through the walls, her housemate and neighbours were an almost constant presence. Mark would be holding her face to his while he slid inside her and upstairs there would be a creak across the floorboards, followed by a scuttling of footsteps downstairs, as June or Neil nervously passed her room on the staircase. They would be in the middle of sex and have to stop to laugh because next door a man had started loudly celebrating a goal. While she didn't exactly enjoy these interruptions – the sound of a whirring dishwasher, the laughing of June on the phone to her mum – somehow they heightened her sense of intimacy, reminding her of the depth of her own feelings. She could be in a crowd with Mark and still feel like they were alone.

This is what she was thinking when they were lying in bed together afterwards, drugged by the rush of hormones to the head. And then as they were heading downstairs, Amma in her dressing gown, Mark fully clothed, about to leave, another thought occurred to her. Something that had been bothering her all week.

'You said you live with friends, right?'

Mark was putting on his jacket. He ran his hands up and down the collar, adjusting it. Amma had noticed that when he was thinking his eyes dropped down to the left. 'Just temporarily.'

'Maybe we could stay at yours next time? It would be nice to meet them.'

'It's quite rowdy. Not very private.'

She almost scoffed. 'And this is?' She was grateful that at that moment June, cooking with Neil in the kitchen, let out a shriek of laughter over the clanging of pans.

Mark looked mortified. 'I'm sorry. Living with men is something else.'

'Don't worry about it. In your own time.'

Mark zipped up his jacket. It was always Mark who left first. Always Mark who had chores to do, people to see, work to prepare in advance of Monday. His ability to extricate himself from their world and prioritise other things terrified her. Amma felt like she would push back all her plans just to spend ten more minutes with him.

He kissed her, pulling her in and squeezing her around the middle, and then he was gone, leaving her alone.

Gradually, she became more comfortable working on the campaign in Mark's company, if he happened to be around at the weekend. One day, while they were drinking coffee in the kitchen, Mark watched her screen as she wrote up an opinion piece for the *Examiner.*

'Do you not worry about yourself in all this?'

Friends had asked her the same question in the past so his concern hardly registered, and she gave the answer she always gave them: 'Isaac would have done the same for me.'

Mark's face was strangely still. 'He might not have faced the same risk as you.'

She lowered her phone, giving him her full attention.

'What, because I'm a woman?'

Mark said nothing, which meant yes.

'You must have seen at some point what they say online.'

She had. Years ago. And then she had decided she would never read the comments on social media.

The unsettled look in Mark's eyes told her he must have come across some bad ones.

'It's not real. All that shit.'

'I think ninety per cent of the time it's not real. But some of them mean it.'

'I'm not going to let a minority stop me. What kind of person would I be if I did?'

It surprised her that Mark could be so un-enlightened about this.

'This isn't the only way you can get the police to reinvestigate. I'm not saying you shouldn't campaign. I just don't know if you and your family need to put yourself in the firing line like this.'

Amma fundamentally disagreed with him. After all, they were what connected people to Isaac. They represented the real-world consequences of his murder. When people saw their grief, they saw him as a living person and not just another faded photo in a newspaper. Amma had only seen evidence that the best strategy for putting pressure on the police was one that involved her and her family leading the publicity.

If it was anyone else she'd have come out with this in a heartbeat. But looking at Mark's blue eyes she couldn't bring herself to say it. He had seen a post online from someone who said they wanted to find and kill her, and he was, understandably, uncomfortable with that.

'I appreciate your concern,' she said – she always became more formal when she was trying to stay calm. 'But trust me, we aren't seeing results with the police. This is what I want to do.'

'It's just—' he rolled his shoulders, searching for the words '—are you going to get those results if you keep saying the police were racist for not investigating properly?'

Amma had that familiar sinking feeling she'd had previously on dates, where an otherwise promising date said something that was a massive red flag.

'Are you serious?'

'Why was it racist?'

'If a white teenager – similar to Isaac in every way apart from his skin – went missing that day, they'd have reacted faster. And then when they found him, they'd have immediately asked why an intelligent, hard-working teenager with offers from Bristol and Warwick who barely drank was dead in a river.'

Mark's jaw clenched slightly as he decided not to say something. Amma felt anger rising in her chest.

'The police do take complaints like this seriously. More and more. So does the police watchdog.'

'I'm not saying these people were intentionally racist. I'm saying the air they breathe is racist.'

'What you're talking about is being unknowingly racist.'

'So?'

'So if you can't find any evidence about someone's intentions, I don't see how it would ever be fair to charge them. They might well be racist. But if you can't prove it, I don't see what's the point in chasing them.'

'What do you mean, you don't see the point?'

'That is the most incendiary claim. That is the thing they'll hate you for. The noise you've created around that. Wouldn't the police be more likely to reinvestigate if you dropped that claim? If all you want is for them to help you, then why do you have to go there?'

'Because—' Amma found herself scoffing '—because it's true.'

There was no singular version of that first week searching for Isaac. Grief made her obsessively circle back over the memories, checking under the rugs, peering behind the curtains, searching and searching for clues she might have missed. She never found anything. Except those things her parents had tried to hide from her, which she had been ignorant to as a child.

When the police had first came swaggering into the house with their black stab-proof vests and walkie-talkies, straight-backed and purposeful, Amma found their presence both intimidating and comforting at the same time. She was then fully confident of their ability and drive to help them find her brother.

Only much later did Amma's mum tell her how the officers had behaved that day. As Amma waited upstairs in her room, the officers had stood there, shoulders slack, hands in their pockets, watching with vacant eyes as her parents had retold the story of Isaac's disappearance. Her mum told her she couldn't believe the lack of energy in their demeanour. They had asked if Isaac had ever done this sort of thing before. She had said no. They had asked if Isaac was involved in a gang. She had said no. One of them had said, 'You'd be surprised how often this happens. He's probably burning off steam.' Her mum said she had frantically gathered up photo frames round the house, because she was scared they wouldn't recognise him from his old school photo on the window sill alone, and when she'd showed these photos to the officers one of them had said, 'Look at him, strapping lad, he can look after himself.' Amma remembered her mum was horrified that the officers had seen a man in the photo and not what she saw – a young teenage boy. Clenching the steering wheel as she recounted the meeting to Amma, she had hissed through her teeth, 'You can't say that, that's my baby.'

Amma thought that when they searched for Isaac as a family, putting up posters on streetlamp poles, visiting the homes of every friend he had ever had – whose parents greeted them with a look of pity in their face that made Amma feel paralysed with fear – that they were doing this as a supplement to the police investigation, so their odds of finding him were even higher. In fact, the police hadn't even started looking yet. For those two days when Isaac was classed as low-risk, not another living soul had looked.

There was one detective she remembered more than any other. DCI Gregory should have been completely forgettable. He was a greying middle-aged man who'd still worn an eighties suit that was too squarish in the shoulders and too long in the middle, elongating him into a rectangle, a slab of stone. But he'd carried himself in the slow, purposeful manner of someone who knew everyone was watching them and that made him memorable. The officer who had been waiting with Amma had sat up and watched him read the case file as though it was a piece of homework he was going to mark. Once he was done reading it, he'd looked at Amma. He had a very strong browbone that kept his face in a permanent frown. Under his pale-blue gaze Amma had felt small, stupid, worthless. *My brother fell into that river*, she'd thought to herself. *I'm wrong and they're right and I'm wasting their time.* She would forever feel sick with herself that one unkind look from an old man had made her think those thoughts.

It was him she'd seen at the station several times since, whenever she went in person to pile on the pressure and ask them to look into the case. Whereas the other officers were ignorant or uninterested, Gregory seemed to want to belittle her. 'We have something in common, Amma. I lost someone I cared very deeply for recently. Cancer. She was in her mid-forties, so not as young as Isaac, but still young. Too young to be taken away like that.' He shook his head. 'I remember I was so angry. But you learn to deal with it. What I'm trying to say, Amma, is I understand the irreplaceability of that relationship especially with someone you grew up with. I know the pointlessness of his death must be hard to accept.'

What the police never seemed to understand was that if Isaac's death was murder – then that meant the killer was still out there. It was an idea that had always terrified Amma, much as she hated to admit it. There was a time not long ago when she had been so immersed in her brother's case that she became intensely paranoid. She obsessively checked the number plate of a car that had started parking down her street until one day she saw a young family pile inside, because they had just moved in. She took better care of herself now. Things were different.

Suddenly Amma had become someone who watched the clock at work, who ran down escalators to get to a restaurant booking. She kept expecting to turn up and find Mark had done a no-show. She was in disbelief that she could rely on this feeling. The happiness seemed to be a well she could repeatedly draw from without it ever running dry. Seeing him transformed her mood so completely that when they were together she felt annoyed at herself for letting things bother her earlier in the week.

After her brother's death, life had become incomplete. There was always more she could be doing to put pressure on the police and compel them to reinvestigate. Periods of rest were hard to justify. She dedicated hours of her free time to the campaign, and if she could not find the time, she berated herself and pledged to do more the next day. Sometimes it seemed her life couldn't truly begin until they had found a killer. The possibility loomed so large in her imagination that it sometimes cast a shadow over her whole future.

Now she had found something that left her wholly satisfied with the present moment. For the first time in her life, she was free.

Day by day, without even noticing, she stopped messaging Emmanuel. She stopped organising vigils and marches and press interviews. Slowly, she stopped thinking about her brother.

25

Amma crouched on the balls of her feet to inspect the lasagne bubbling away through the orange-black grime on the inside of the glass. She felt giddy even though she had no plans tonight, full of energy at the prospect of a weekend away with Mark. He'd booked two nights for them in the Lake District, the first time in a long time that she'd been away with a boyfriend. Excitedly, she picked up her mobile and gave him a call. How nice that they were close enough now to do something like this – and that she could just contact him out of the blue.

'Hey, so tomorrow. What time do you want to meet at the station?'

'I don't know. I'll text you.'

He sounded stressed. Amma loosened her grip on the handle of the oven door.

'Are you okay?'

'Look, I'll talk to you later. Now's a bad time.'

The line cut out.

Amma lowered her phone and stared at the screensaver, which showed her and June laughing, and thought she might cry.

A few seconds later a WhatsApp message appeared on her screen.

I'm sorry, I should have said. I'm at work and I can't take personal calls when I'm working. Best to text.

*

'That is fucking weird.'

Amma sawed through the crust of the lasagne – which had burnt while she went in search of June to have a small cry – and deposited a wedge onto June's plate.

June didn't react. She was still glaring into space, one elbow on the table, hand open and twisted to express her disbelief.

'Never call, just text? What if you get locked out of your flat? What if your car breaks down?'

Amma slumped down opposite June, picking despondently at her own slice of over-crisped lasagne. 'He works really hard.'

'I hate that. So do you. He needs to give a proper explanation if he expects you not to be hurt by that. Setting boundaries is normal but that's not a boundary. That's a huge emotional wall that sends the signal you can't rely on him.'

Amma tucked her arms and legs in a little. She usually loved June's willingness to launch into an attack on any man who fell even a little short of her very high standards for her friends. But Amma had never heard her do it with Mark, and she didn't like it.

June continued: 'You should tell him. Say something like: I respect your boundaries but if this is going to be a serious relationship, I need to feel I can rely on you for emotional support and you doing this makes me feel like I can't—'

'It is a serious relationship.'

June hesitated.

'I know but it's early right? You guys need to have these conversations.'

She almost wished she hadn't said anything. Hadn't tarnished his until-now-spotless reputation with her friend.

'What's the worst thing that can happen if you say something?'

'He might think "you needy bitch" and leave?'

'He's not going to do that. Honestly. Say something. Have you met his friends yet?'

Reluctantly, she said, 'No, to be honest.'

'Just ask, if you want to. I'm sure he'll introduce you to some.'

'Yeah.'

Amma cut into her lasagne and forced down a couple of bites. This conversation was making her feel uncomfortable. With this trip to the Lake District, she'd felt for the first time like her and Mark were finally an established couple. Now June was making her realise she still hardly knew Mark at all.

*

Long, mist-blue grass. The sound of trickling water. Amma and Mark wound their way along the curving pathway through the forest of pine trees that swept down the mountain. A stream ran beside them, over algae-slicked rocks, low-hanging branches dragging inside the clear spring water. Her calves burned pleasantly from hours of walking.

She looked up at the sky. It seemed impossibly open and clear, impossibly blue.

She tried not to think about the argument she'd had with her dad the day before.

*

Her throat felt dry and scratchy. Her temples burned. Theirs was an argumentative family. But what she was about to say to her dad, she had never said before.

'I can't make it to the vigil for Isaac's birthday. There's a clash.'

Her dad blinked twice. Then his eyes narrowed. 'A clash with what?'

'I'm going away then.'

It felt too early to mention Mark. Her parents would ask when he was coming round for dinner. She wasn't ready for that kind of pressure.

His moustache twitched. 'On holiday?'

He made no attempt to hide the judgement in his voice.

Amma felt her discomfort turn into anger. 'Every single year since he died, when have I ever missed a vigil? Or a march? Or the chance to hand out fliers?'

'Exactly.' The chair creaked as her dad sat up straight, arms cradling his stomach as if he had an ulcer, moving around in his seat. 'Why – why now?'

'This is going to happen more and more. In the future I might need to pick up my kid from a sleepover. I might have a work trip.'

'This isn't either of those things. You aren't obliged to go on holiday. A holiday is a choice.'

It didn't feel like a choice. She wanted it so much she couldn't imagine doing anything else.

'I decided this. I want to live my own life.'

'We're doing this because he didn't get to live his.'

Amma felt like he had slapped her. What she said next she would always regret.

'It's been thirteen years. We aren't going to find out who did it, Dad.'

A hundred different thoughts passed over her dad's face. Amma saw him decide not to put any of them into words. He got up and left the kitchen, leaving behind him a devastating silence.

*

Now, her lungs burned as they approached the top of the hill. Amma kept her eyes focused on the trail beneath her feet, the tiny pink flowers dotted in the short, coarse grass. With some effort, and accepting Mark's outstretched hand, she clambered up onto the large pockmarked rock that jutted out of the hillside, where he was already standing. They celebrated their ascent like children. Whooping into the sky. The wind was more intense here. Gripping Mark's middle and looking back at the seemingly impossible route they had taken over the landscape, Amma felt her body sway in the wind, as if she might blow away at any second. They were so high up it was a struggle to make out buildings nestled in the rolling hillside. She felt they were all-seeing and powerless all at once, like small gods.

*

There was no light pollution here. The sky was a deep black, a vast peaceful nothingness. Amma rested her head in Mark's lap and stared into the crackling fire. She held Mark's hand against her chest, as if his arm was a blanket she had pulled over herself. His other hand stroked her hair in a slow rhythm.

Even now, she could feel a knot of discomfort in her stomach. All day she'd been waiting for the perfect moment to speak to him. She was only just realising that that moment wasn't going to come. No matter when she spoke, she would always feel she had disturbed some sacred peace.

'I don't want to hide things from you,' she said.

She felt Mark's stroking hand slow to a stop.

She curled her fingers more tightly around his. Nervously she glanced up at him.

'I just think you should know everything about me if you're going to make an informed decision.'

There was a flicker of concern in his eyes.

'I feel like—' she sat up straight '—I feel like you've met me at a time when I'm doing pretty well. But I wasn't always. After Isaac died, I had issues. With my mental health.'

'That's completely understandable.'

'I didn't know how to talk to people about what happened,' she said. 'And they didn't know how to talk to me. I got into fights at school. I drank too much, smoked too much. The campaign, it gave me a sense of purpose. It helped me come to terms with what had happened, I think. But it also took its toll. What you said about how I deal with trolls online. You're right, it is hard. I guess I've gotten a thick skin over time. But at first I became extremely anxious, paranoid. I imagined people were following me.

'I just feel so ashamed about everything that went through my head at that time. I was so – so powerless, so pathetic. So suspicious of everything. I don't know, I just feel I want you to know that that happened. 'I'm a much stronger person but I just want you to know about that time in my life.'

Mark placed his hand over her forehead. It felt warm. 'It doesn't change anything,' he said.

She'd hoped by sharing something so personal he'd feel compelled to do the same. But in the long moment that followed, Mark said nothing.

*

The turquoise hills rolled past them as Amma drove them out of the Lake District and back down south. Back to normality.

Her mind kept circling over last night's argument. What had started out as a beautiful moment by the fire – her first time really opening up to Mark – had quickly turned into something ugly. She wanted to apologise again for losing her temper. But she'd already said sorry so many times this morning.

He'd told her over and over again that it was fine. Except it wasn't fine. She had to be more careful than this.

26

AMMA HAD STARTED TO NOTICE something was up with June. She was slouching around the house, barely reacting when Amma came in from work except to murmur a 'hey' from where she was huddled up on the sofa.

Slowly, silently, they had adjusted their routines so as to share a space while avoiding the other completely.

Amma kept intending to ask if she was okay but she was in and out so much these days, it was a conversation she kept pushing back. Then one evening in August it was forced on her.

She was stuffing her bed sheets into the washing machine when she heard the mournful shuffle of June's flared jeans. She was in her comically oversized slippers and holding a mug that said 'don't talk to me before my morning coffee'.

'Are you free for a drink on Friday?'

She sounded almost tentative, as if they didn't know each other that well. Amma's heart squeezed.

'Really sorry. Me and Mark are going to dinner.'

The look on June's face told her she'd expected as much.

'You are seeing a lot of each other.'

There was a judgemental tone to her voice that Amma tried to ignore as she shut the door to the washing machine and turned it on.

June added: 'I barely see you any more. Neil said the same.'

Amma felt June's hurt cut through her. It was true. It had occurred to her yesterday as she was rushing off to work and saw June's gym trainers by the door. They used to go to the gym together on Saturday mornings, then reward themselves with a glorious mountain of eggs on toast at the local café. Now that Amma reserved her weekends for Mark, entire weeks had gone by without her seeing June.

'I'm sorry, I know. We could go for a drink on Tuesday?'

'You're saving a Tuesday evening for me? Wow, I feel special. When do you next have a Friday or Saturday free?'

'I can check. I usually keep those free for Mark.'

'All of them?'

'He sometimes can't let me know if he's available til the last minute.' Amma felt her cheeks flush with heat as soon as she said it.

June blinked at her, very slowly, in total disbelief. 'I'm sorry, what?'

'It's the job. He sometimes has to work weekends.'

June stepped back. 'So you can't ring him in case he's at work. And also you need to keep all of your Fridays and weekends free in case he decides he wants to hang out? Are you serious?'

Amma suddenly felt very curled up in front of the washing machine. She straightened up but kept her eyes to the floor. She didn't want to engage with this, didn't want to validate June's reaction.

'Did you say anything about that, by the way? The phone calls.'

'No.'

June said nothing for a second. Amma could tell she was trying to choose her words carefully.

'This isn't like you,' she said.

Yeah, well, I've never felt this way before, have I? Amma wanted to say, but she stayed silent.

'Look, it's your relationship. But don't limit your own happiness just to make space for him, Amma.'

'I'm not.'

June shook her head. 'I just don't like to think of you sitting around on a Friday night waiting for someone to text you.'

Amma bit the inside of her mouth. She was never ever going to say this to June, but this was what she thought. June and Neil spent their weekends binge-watching their favourite TV shows and ordering takeaways. Domestic responsibilities dictated everything in their relationship, and these slovenly days were their only relief. They didn't have what Amma and Mark had. Amma had never felt so attracted to someone in her life. She couldn't imagine watching even half an hour's TV with him without wanting to have sex instead. The feeling was so strong it drove everything she did, even if it looked crazy to an outsider. If June felt this way too she'd also feel perfectly fine hanging around waiting for the phone to ping, clearing out her evenings, obsessively washing bed linen.

But she was never ever going to say that to her, so they each mumbled a half-felt apology to each other, promised they'd go for a drink soon, and then went to their respective rooms. It only hit Amma how awful that had been when she heard the sad sound of June's door closing.

When they'd argued in the past, it had usually been a blazing row over something that ultimately didn't matter, like leaving the other waiting at a bus stop for too long. Now they were arguing about something that really did matter, and the atmosphere that followed was bitter, ashen.

She thought about what June had said on the train home from work the next day. The carriage was so hot she had had to peel off her jacket and heap it in her lap as she sat in her seat. The man opposite her was drinking greedily from a water bottle as if it would be his last drink for days.

Don't limit your own happiness just to make space for him. Amma chewed over the expression as she swayed with the train's sad rocking movements and stared at her own resentful eyes in the reflection of the window. What a ridiculous thing to say. Amma was blissfully happy. Happier than she'd ever been. June was probably limiting *her* happiness by allowing Neil to slouch over and force her to watch a football game for two hours while June painted her toenails and tried her hardest to seem interested. It seemed to Amma that everyone made concessions for the people they loved, and frankly she would rather make the concession of waiting around and obsessively checking her phone than be inauthentic, as June sometimes seemed to her when she was around Neil.

The train jerked to an awkward halt and the doors hissed open. A woman in an immaculate jumpsuit boarded and sat herself down. The jumpsuit was pearl-white, flawless against the mottled design of the carriage seats. *I need to dress better*, Amma thought to herself. But unfortunately she couldn't afford the number of dry cleaning bills it would require. She had started doing this ever since going out with Mark – staring at white women on the train who looked more Mark's age and wondering what she should do to more resemble them. She didn't know why. It wasn't as if Mark had ever implied that was what he wanted. *Pathetic, you need to stop this*, she scolded herself internally.

There was something about train journeys, the noise, the sweaty bodies packed in together, the stress replicated on the faces of everyone around her, that pushed Amma into a deeper state of irritability. She knew that was why the argument with June was bothering her so much now. Almost as soon as one of the passengers gave in and opened a window, letting in a wave of fresh air, Amma felt her head clearing. She started to feel disappointed in herself for the thoughts she'd had about June not ten minutes earlier. She saw June's intervention for what it was. A good friend, voicing her concerns. June hadn't said these things to upset her. She didn't even have a vendetta against Mark. She had said these things because she cared about her. The realisation filled Amma with alarm as she watched the woman in the jumpsuit gaze out the window, sunning herself in a rectangle of orange light that streamed in. When had she become someone her friends worried about?

And so the anger towards June ebbed away. Instead she felt angry with Mark.

Why couldn't she call him? Why did he only arrange plans with her at the last minute? Why hadn't she met anyone in his life? They'd been dating for almost two months and Mark was still a half-drawn figure in her head. There was an implication in June's words that she found unbearable to contemplate but that deep down she knew was true. He was asking too much of her, and not pulling his own weight in return. A year ago, she'd have never put up with this from a man. She suddenly felt furious with herself for becoming so submissive. June was right. She deserved more.

She was going to confront him.

27

IT WAS ANOTHER WARM SATURDAY evening. Amma and Mark had taken a couple of beers out to Crays Hill to watch the sun go down. With their backs against the monument, they looked down at the trees at the base of the hill which were awash with amber light. It was an idyllic view. But Amma's stomach was churning. *Now*, she thought. *Say it now*.

'I wanted to say…'

Mark looked at her innocently. Amma felt her insides squirm.

'I really feel – you know, I really haven't felt – I don't think I've ever felt this way.'

The wrong thing to say? He'd been in relationships before; he probably couldn't say it back and be truthful. Air rushed into her chest when Mark reached over to squeeze her hand and said, 'You've changed everything for me.'

Neither of them had addressed their feelings as directly as this before. Amma wanted to stretch this moment out for as long as she could. But she needed to get this out now, or she might never say it.

She said what she'd been rehearsing in her head all week: 'I just want more of you. So I really want to meet your family. Your friends. I like everything about you so I just want to see all of it.'

Mark's hand loosened slightly. There was a nervous movement in his eyes.

Please no, she thought.

'It would mean a lot to me if I could come round yours,' she said.

Mark looked at the rim of his beer bottle.

'That's not going to be possible unfortunately.'

Amma stared at the ground. All at once, a wave of frustration and after that fear crashed over her. She had the sensation of water wrapping around her ankles and pulling her out to sea, the darkness rushing around her.

'You're not serious about this, are you?' she said.

Mark rubbed a hand over his face. 'I am. I am.'

'I'm getting screwed over, aren't I?'

'Amma…'

She'd been trying to steady her breathing and speak with confidence. But Mark's response tipped her over the edge. She asked, her voice cracking, 'Why are you doing this? Please just say.'

Mark shook his head. 'I'm so sorry.'

She was crying now. 'Is it something you're ashamed of? Because I don't care. I want to know. Is it me? Are you ashamed of me?'

'No. Absolutely not.'

'Then why?'

He turned his head away. At the sight of his exposed neck, Amma felt a surge of love so strong it filled her with panic.

'This is not… okay,' he said.

She swallowed before speaking.

'You mean us?'

'Yes.'

Amma took two slow breaths in and out. She could smell the salt of her own tears on her face. Okay, she thought. This is it. This is how it ends.

'What do you mean?'

'This is not okay,' he repeated. 'Not yet. I can make it okay. But I'm scared.'

'I don't understand.'

'I think I love you more than you love me. I know you'll hate me for saying this, but I've been through enough to know what I want. And I know it's you. How would you know?' He looked at her. 'You're young. Meeting new people all the time. What if this is just fleeting for you?'

'It's not.'

'Yeah but how would you know? You haven't been here before. I have. And sometimes this is as good as it gets. You're gorgeous. I don't think you see yourself the way I see you and realise that from my perspective you could fuck off with literally anyone at any moment.

'One day, I want to drive to your house and have no baggage, nothing with me. To know it will just be me and you from that moment on. But to make that happen… to make this work, I need to change things. I'll lose everything. That's a fact. And I'm scared that when I do, you won't be there.'

Amma waited for a few moments. She took a deep breath.

'That is the stupidest thing I've ever heard,' she said.

Mark's eyes widened.

'You're holding back because you've decided I'm too young to know what I want? Because I can't guarantee what's going to happen in ten years' time? Literally fuck you. Yeah, you're right. I do meet new people all the time. And you know what? I literally don't care. For the first time in my life. None of them come close. And no, there isn't anything I can do to prove it. You do need to take my word for it. So, yeah, fuck you.'

For a few moments Mark stared at her. Then he leant forwards.

'Come here.'

He pulled her into a deep hug. Amma buried her nose in his shoulder, letting the smell of him surround her.

'No more secrets. I'll do it.'

After a few moments they parted. Amma sniffed. The tears and Mark's confession – however limited – had left her feeling raw but cleansed, as if all the emotion of the last few weeks had been washed away.

But still her mind was racing.

Baggage. What did he mean by 'baggage'? *I'll do it.* Do what?

'I'm going to go quiet for a week,' he told her.

Amma wiped her eyes. 'Don't do that. No more not calling. No more power plays.'

'Just a week. I promise. And then I'll be back. And then no more secrets. And it will just be us.'

He squeezed her hand in her lap. 'A week.'

Suddenly Amma had the feeling she was being watched. She turned around sharply, just in time to catch a movement of pale brown in the dark foliage, behind the closed gate. She blinked. There was nothing there.

'Everything okay?' asked Mark.

'Never mind,' she said.

She squeezed his hand, returning her attention to the sunset, and took a sip of beer.

For a second there, she thought she'd seen a figure watching them.

28

THE OFFICE WAS STIFLINGLY HOT. Amma and her colleagues worked on the edge of the desk, away from the window, to avoid the rectangle of blazing sunshine it cast over the table surface. One of them, Maisie, had a fan going on the floor. Every ten seconds it would circle round, sending a sudden blast of cool air over Amma's legs. But it provided only a temporary relief.

Saturday. She just had to wait until Saturday.

Amma had never known how excruciatingly slow the passage of seven days could be. Anxiously tracking the passage of time, everything seemed to take longer than ever before. Every train journey between Wakestead and London seemed twice the duration these days. In the office with Maisie and Sarah, the time trudged along, as they sat in silence at their computers, sluggish in the heat. Even seeing her friends felt like a chore she'd created for herself; something to pass the time, and when she was there she wasn't really there, just hovering anti-social and unpleasant to be around at the corner of the pub table.

She had begun to worry there had been some kind of accident since she last saw him. In moments alone she pictured a crossroads, bike wheel rearing up, spinning. Mark's precious brains splattered across gravel, glistening in the summer heat like pink jewels.

She hadn't told anyone yet. She couldn't bear to tell June because she knew exactly what she'd say. That this was ridiculous, that she was being led on, that she shouldn't put up with this from a man any more. Better to wait. Because then whatever this was would all be over. And their relationship would emerge shiny and new, unmarred by this terrible week.

She saw how ridiculous it was that until this week she'd never asked herself what could be the reason for all the secrecy. Now it was all she could think about. She had narrowed it down to a number of theories.

The first. Unbearable. Mark was in a relationship and had been all along. In her heart Amma knew this couldn't be it so she pushed this theory out of her mind.

The second. Mark didn't think he could handle a relationship alongside his job. This seemed the most likely. The job after all had been his excuse this whole time, whenever he had been unavailable for a date, whenever he had had to leave early in the evening.

The third. Mark had lied to her about his job. And somehow starting a relationship with her had crossed a line at work. This was the most absurd theory, by far. For a few days Amma had refused to give it too much consideration because of how ridiculous it was. But now, having pored over her last conversation with Mark for days and days, reviewing every word, every micro-expression, she was convinced this was the only theory that made sense. *I have to change things. I'll lose everything.* There was no getting around it. He had sounded scared.

*

Friday morning. Just a day left to wait. Grey light outside. Amma rolled over in bed and instantly checked her phone. No text. She rolled back onto her side.

It took every ounce of strength in her body not to call in sick and stay there, sinking deeper into the mattress.

Later that day, Neil texted asking her to come round after work. It was still light outside as she walked through the field leading to The Hollies, trying to control her imagination. But even then she had visions of Mark emerging from Neil's living room, the house she was in the night it began for them When Neil opened the door she glanced hopefully over his shoulder into the corridor.

When he led her into the living room, where June was cuddled up on the sofa, her eyes searched the room as though Mark was about to step out from behind a curtain. June untucked her legs and smiled at Amma. They'd been watching TV together. The sight of their happy domesticity made Amma feel like an alien.

'We were thinking we might go out tonight,' said June.

Amma stared at her. She couldn't think of anything she felt like doing less.

Mark had said she would hear back from him within a week. That meant she could still hear from him today. What if he turned up this evening, announced, and she wasn't there?

Two days ago, she had given in and called June to tell her what Mark had said to her. Not even her friend's warm, soothing words had calmed her down. Instead they only made her feel more alone with the feeling that Mark hadn't come back and perhaps that was because something was horribly wrong.

Neil shook out his curly hair awkwardly. 'You should come with us. Emmanuel's coming, plus a couple of others. It'll be fun. Take your mind off things.'

She looked between them, processing the strangeness of the situation. Neil's simpering expression. June's hand gesturing towards the cushioned seat next to her. They were both moving very carefully, like Amma was a wild animal they needed to catch that might bolt at any second. This felt like an intervention.

'I really don't feel like it,' said Amma.

'Please come,' said June. 'For me. I just want you to have a nice time.'

'What if something's happened to him?' said Amma.

She didn't have time for this. She needed to find him. The days were slipping away. Memories flashed through her mind of Sellotaping posters to lampposts as they flapped in the wind, of traipsing along damp streets while other kids from school hung around outside McDonalds, of wading through damp grass, desperate yet terrified to find something, anything. *The longer you leave it, the more evidence disappears—*

'Look, if he texts you, he texts you and you'll meet up. If he doesn't, well, you should enjoy yourself anyway. I hate seeing you like this.' June had raised her voice. 'Just come for an hour, if you want. I promise it will make you feel better.'

Amma was absolutely certain that it wouldn't. But the desperation in June's voice stirred something inside her. She couldn't leave her friend feeling like this. She couldn't turn her down.

'Okay,' she said. 'I'll come out for a bit.'

The music was so loud it took her ears a moment to adjust to the shouting voices in the smoking area. Amma, Neil and Claire squeezed through the crowd of clubgoers until they found their own spot to get some air.

'How are you feeling?' asked June.

'Better,' said Amma. It was true. The company of her friends, plus several drinks, had softened her emotions. For the first time in days, she wasn't worrying about Mark.

Neil and June looked at each other. Then Neil opened his mouth, lacing his fingers together in front of him, and said, 'Mark isn't a good guy, Amma.'

Amma swayed on the spot. 'Yes, he is.'

The pitying look on both of their faces filled her with a deep and visceral rage.

'Why are you looking at me like that?' she snapped. 'Something might have happened to him and you're looking at me like he's – like he's dangerous or something.'

'None of our friends have ever heard of this guy. He met you in the middle of the street at two o'clock in the morning, outside a party full of people in their twenties. And now—'

'And now? Say it, Neil.'

'He's using you. Who the fuck is this guy?'

'I don't need this, Neil. I don't fucking need this.'

She turned around, ignoring June calling out her name, and disappeared back into the heat of the club.

*

A beam of light forced Amma awake. She untethered herself from a deep sleep and crawled with some effort towards consciousness. Once she came to, she realised she was lying in her bedroom. The light shining directly on her face was pouring through the curtains, still open a gap after she had failed to fully close them last night.

Her throat felt raw and scratchy. Her eyes were puffy from dehydration. When had she got back? She didn't remember. She couldn't remember anything. How much had she had to drink?

She searched the room for clues. Last night's dress lay in a crumpled heap on the floor. For a moment she panicked because her phone wasn't in its usual place, charging on her bedside table. But then she got up and found it inside the bag she'd taken with her.

Immediately her thoughts jumped to Mark. Saturday. Surely today.

She opened her phone, which told her it was eleven o'clock. Nothing from him. Just a few unread messages from June. *Please text me when you get home xx*, read the last one. Amma hadn't responded.

She was hit by a wave of helplessness. What had happened last night? Why couldn't she remember anything?

Then there was a knock on the door. Followed by a loud voice.

'Police. Open up.'

PART III

29

THEY SAT IN TOTAL SILENCE after Amma was finished. There was no sound apart from faint birdsong outside. A robin hopped from branch to branch of a large shrub extending across the window, like a hand shielding them from view.

Telling her story had changed Amma almost beyond recognition. She seemed at once brought to life and at the same time completely exhausted. Tears gleamed on her cheeks but her eyes were now lit with determination and fire.

'And that's the last time you saw him?'

Amma nodded.

'And you don't remember anything else about that night?'

Amma shook her head, still not looking at her. 'I don't know. I remember that argument with Neil and June. And then, I don't know, I had way too much to drink. I can't remember anything else. I sort of remember June helping me into the taxi, and then I woke up. The next thing I knew, the police were knocking on my door.' She pressed her temples with her fingers. 'Why can't I remember? I don't know why I can't remember.'

'Why didn't you tell me all this at the start?' said Erin. 'Why didn't you tell the police?'

'Because when I found out Mark had been in the police, I was in shock. I couldn't believe what they were telling me. I thought it was all part of some trap. I just… I gave up, to be honest. Besides, they've already made up their minds, haven't they? They've decided it was me.'

'What do you mean?'

She shot Erin a furious look. 'How would telling them I had a relationship with the victim make me any less of a suspect? It's worse, right? You're an investigator. You figure it out.' She stared, wide-eyed, at the carpet, despair creeping back into her face. 'Besides, I don't – I don't have anything to give them. I don't have any evidence about who could have done this. I don't have an alibi. I don't remember what happened that night. And all the evidence points to me.'

Erin said: 'I believe you, but it doesn't matter. If you didn't do it, the evidence will show that, Amma.'

'What if there isn't any?'

'There will be. Did Mark ever talk to you about difficult relationships he was having? Or suggest he felt threatened in any way?'

Amma's eyebrows furrowed in distress. 'No. No, never. I never—' she sniffed, her voice vibrating with emotion '—I didn't know he had a wife. I swear, Erin.'

'I believe you.'

'I didn't know any of it. The police. Why wouldn't he say?'

'I think maybe because he knew what your opinion of them was,' Erin said. 'And that you might turn him down.'

'What he said to me… *I have things I need to do*… was he going to leave her?'

Erin shook her head. 'I don't know. Perhaps.'

Amma sniffed again, her eyes searching the walls. 'That's the only thing I can think of. What if he did? What if he did and she—'

Erin thought of Olivia's poise, her nervous hands, her fearful eyes. 'It's possible.'

'But I don't know,' Amma continued. 'I don't know this woman, I can't just say that—'

Talking about Olivia had made Amma twist and turn with anxiety, running her hands up and down her arms and squeezing.

Eventually, in a quiet voice, she said, 'Do you think you can love two people at the same time?'

Erin swallowed. She couldn't in good conscience withhold from this woman the one piece of knowledge she had that might bring her some solace.

'It sounded like their relationship was suffering. Like it had been for a while.'

Amma's eyelids flickered. 'Maybe I was just a breath of fresh air, you know. An escape.' She half-laughed bitterly and placed her face in her hands. '*I don't have a girlfriend.* Jesus Christ. Why did he lie? Why?'

'The police must already know about the relationship by now, but they need to hear your account. So I'm going to share this with them, okay? And then I think you need to tell them yourself.'

'The evidence didn't matter with my brother, did it?'

'Lewis Jennings is a good detective.'

'It doesn't matter. Not while Gregory is there. He was in charge of my brother's investigation. You didn't know that?'

Erin felt a chill spread over her skin.

'He was hiding something then. And he'll hide this now.'

'Why would he do that?'

'I don't know. But he hates me. He always has.'

Amma drew in a deep breath through her nose, steadying herself.

'Can I ask you something?'

Erin nodded.

'Do you think he was going to come clean? Do you think he was going to end it with her and tell me the truth? If we ever met again?'

Erin swallowed. 'I have no idea, Amma.'

'Can you try and find out for me?'

'I'll try.'

Erin understood her desperation. Amma had suffered a double death. She had lost Mark at the exact same time she had lost the very idea of who he was.

But there were some answers Erin was afraid she was never going to be able to find for her.

30

'SHE'S TALKING,' SHE SAID.

Lewis's eyes widened. Straight after hearing Amma's story, she'd texted him saying she needed to see him. Now they were standing together in a quiet corner of a busy pub with wood-panelled walls.

'So I know they were seeing each other,' she continued.

Lewis looked relieved that she had found this out for herself.

'I'm guessing you found hairs, fibres from his clothing, in her house.'

Reluctantly, Lewis nodded.

'And there must be text messages.'

'We've got hers. Mark clearly had a second phone. We haven't found it yet. Where did they meet?'

'He saved her from getting hit by a car at two in the morning after a party.'

'Two in the morning? What the hell was he doing?'

'Exactly. Amma told herself it was a coincidence but obviously her friends had their suspicions. He never told her he was a police officer. Or that he was married.'

'Christ. He didn't seem the type, you know?'

Erin shrugged. 'Takes all sorts. Any evidence he's done this with other women before?'

'Not so far. Did Amma suspect he had?'

Erin shook her head. 'She was besotted. Still is, it seems.'

'When did she realise he was lying?'

'There were signs that something was up. I'm guessing you've got a sense of this from their text messages, but apparently she confronted him about it and he said he was going to disappear for a week while he "sorted some things out". And then it would be happily ever after. So what do we think? Was he phasing her out? Or did he try and break up with Mrs Stormont?'

'Olivia hasn't said as much to us. Did Amma tell you what happened the day Mark died?'

'She says she doesn't remember getting home after that night out. She woke up to you and Chris knocking on the door.'

Lewis bit his lip. 'Do you think she would tell this to us? Now she's spoken to you?'

'She let me record her story, and she's happy for me to share it.'

'Knew you could do it,' he said warmly.

'You get why she wouldn't talk to the police though, right? She didn't trust them to begin with, and now she finds out her boyfriend's been killed and he was one of them. It looks like a conspiracy to her, you know?'

She didn't know how much she should tell Lewis but she was determined for him to see things from her perspective. She couldn't believe that Amma had anything to do with Mark's murder.

But Lewis's mind was elsewhere. He took a sip of his pint and asked, 'Have you received a letter? By any chance?'

Erin looked up, startled. How could he know? Unless—

'You still see him then?'

Lewis coloured. Anger rose within her and she took a gulp of wine, trying to push down her emotions. Emotions about Sophie Madson, and Tom, and the slow realisation that the detective, her partner, had murdered a teenage girl and nearly got away with it.

At the start, she'd tolerated Lewis's solitary prison visits. She hadn't understood them, but she'd tolerated them. What had happened to them was a shock, a trauma, and they were each entitled to process it in their own way.

But that was early on, when Tom had first been imprisoned. Now two years had passed – and he was still doing this.

'Why, Lewis? I'm surprised you can even stand to see his face.'

'He doesn't really have anyone, Erin.'

'So this is an act of charity from you, is what you're saying?'

Lewis shrugged. 'Well, kind of, yeah.'

'How nice of you. So what do you two talk about?'

'Police work. Old cases. New ones.'

'*New ones*?'

'Obviously I don't share anything important with him, do I? It's just, you know, he misses it.'

There was a flicker of embarrassment in his eyes. Erin had this horrible feeling the look meant: *and you do too*. Her chest tightened.

'Look, I think you should see him, Erin.'

'What are you talking about?'

'No, it's not what you think—'

'He's a murderer. A lying, cowardly—'

'He knows something about Isaac Reynolds.'

Erin felt her heart sink.

'Of course he does,' she said bitterly. 'How does he know about it?'

'He was there in the early days, right? Not when Isaac died, but afterwards when the family were first pushing to reopen the case.'

'So what does he know?'

'He wouldn't say.'

'How convenient.'

'He said he'll only tell you. No one else.'

Erin glanced into the pub, at the men laughing around a wooden table.

'That's him playing games, Lewis.'

'Yeah, it might be. I get that. But you should still hear what he has to say, right?'

Erin's insides squirmed. She twisted on her feet. 'I just don't believe for a second he knows something.'

'Look, I really was bricking it before I saw my ex to pick up some stuff I'd left at hers, but then—'

'Lewis, shut up.'

'I appreciate it's a bit different, but—'

'A bit different?'

'Okay, really different. I just mean, when I actually met her, it wasn't that bad, you know? I'd made it into a real thing in my head.'

Erin felt an overwhelming urge to grab her hair by the roots and pull it out.

'I'm not *scared* of him,' she said.

'I didn't say you were!' Lewis raised his hands defensively. 'It's just, you know, Isaac's case – I think you're right, I think we do need to understand what happened there. And surely, for the family, you have to explore every possible avenue. I'm not gonna lie, I feel like that's what you taught me. The family always come first.'

Erin felt like he might as well have slapped her across the face. Was he implying she was putting herself first?

She leant in, lowering her voice. 'I got more first-hand exposure to his bullshit than anyone else. It took me a long time to recognise when Tom Radley was manipulating someone. But let me tell you, I recognise it now. And this is what it looks like. He finally knows about a case we're both working on, and he's using it to get to us. God knows why. God knows what he's trying to get out of it.'

She was so angry her cheeks had flushed with heat. She couldn't be here any more. She retrieved her jacket from the table, getting ready to go.

'Tell him I'm not coming. And he needs to give you the information. If he's so interested in reliving the glory days, he can help us out. But I'm not seeing him.'

The sunset had turned the river water pink and blue. Walking back to her Airbnb, Erin zipped up her jacket against the encroaching cold. Up ahead, facing the river, was a black bench. Passing it, she dropped her eyes. Whenever she walked this way, a memory edged into her mind's eye, of her former self seated there, and him right beside her. She'd been getting better at forcing the image out. But today she could almost sense the presence of the two ghosts as she passed the bench, in the direction of the town.

She felt a strong urge to smoke. But she'd given it up after she left the police and she was loath to return to nicotine now – all because Lewis had brought up Tom and his letter. Lewis didn't understand. He thought she didn't want to see Tom because it would be too gut-wrenchingly painful to see the face of the man she'd once loved. That was completely wrong. Insulting. The reason she couldn't see Tom was because if she did, he would win.

Years of obediently limping after Tom. It had taken her two years of reflection to understand. She had been solitary – obsessively wrapped up in her work, where he had been a central figure. She hated to think of the drippy, compliant person she'd been with him. She was never going to be that person again. And that meant never again doing what he wanted.

So no, she wouldn't see him. He could rot there in that prison. In all likelihood, he knew nothing about Isaac's case. But even if he did, she didn't care. She'd get there herself. Without him. Without anyone.

31

Thursday

THE SUPERINTENDENT HAD ASKED HER to meet in his office the next day. Warren stood up to his full height and thrust out a hand for her to shake. To her surprise, DCI Gregory was sat beside him, watching her cautiously. Erin remembered what Amma had told her about the SIO on her brother's case. She wished she could speak with Warren alone.

'I'm sure I don't need to say this, Erin,' the super began, 'but I just want to reiterate how important it is for the sake of the case, that none of your findings reach the press.'

Was he serious? As if she needed to be told that. 'Of course.'

'So,' he said, 'I understand Amma has spoken to you. She's claimed she had a relationship with Mark.'

She nodded.

'You have a recording of this?'

'Yes.'

'Then I'm going to have to ask you to give us a copy of that to aid with the investigation.'

'Sure,' said Erin. But deep down guilt gnawed inside her stomach. By handing it over, she almost felt like she was betraying Amma.

She gave him the USB stick, which he promptly stuck into his computer. Watching the file upload, he said, 'Does she say in this where she was the day Mark was killed?'

'At home. She was out the night before but she says she can't remember what happened.'

'Well, that's very convenient,' sneered Gregory.

She ignored him. 'Something important. Mark told Amma a week before he died that he was going to make some changes in his life. He suggested they could then be together. It's possible he was planning to leave his wife or his job.'

Gregory narrowed his eyes at her. 'I find it strange,' he said, 'that she was comfortable to reveal all this to you, but not to our officers.'

'Do you? Amma's not been quiet about her mistrust of the police.'

'You'd think being arrested on suspicion of murder might make her open up a little though, might you?'

Erin shrugged. 'Well, we've got there now.'

Warren smiled insincerely, as if she'd forced him into an awkward position. 'We have to question every piece of information that comes our way. And I suppose what I find myself questioning is why she told *you* this story. I hope you'll see what I'm getting at?'

'I don't see what you're getting at.'

He opened and closed his hand.

'It seems lost girls come and find you, Erin,' he said. 'But perhaps you're also drawn to them? If you were going to create a sob story that Erin Crane would buy into, might this be it?'

Erin gritted her teeth.

'It is Amma's word against a dead man's, isn't it? Perhaps that was their last conversation. Or perhaps their last conversation was an argument. Perhaps she asked him to leave his wife, and he said no.'

You can't stand the fact it happened on your watch, thought Erin. *An affair with a police officer. During your clean-up operation.*

'Thank you for coming forward. I want us to work together, as much as we can, on this. I don't want you to work against us. And on that note, there was something I wanted to ask you.' His blue eyes flashed. 'How would you feel about coming back?'

Erin shook her head. 'Thank you, but that's not possible.'

'Anything's possible, Erin. Large parts of the force are in agreement that what happened to you was very unfair. Swathes of the public too. You could appeal the decision. And then we could get you back on board. Think about it.'

Crossing the car park, Erin couldn't help but look back at the familiar building and imagine Warren watching her through the dark windows.

Why was Warren – who had always given the impression that he didn't take her seriously as an investigator and that he saw her only as an irritant – offering her a job?

She couldn't deny that the offer had filled with a sense of longing. Visiting her old workplace always brought with it mixed emotions. Although she had become used to life as a PI, she still missed the camaraderie, the stability and the excitement that came with working as part of the CID.

There seemed to her to be one obvious explanation for Warren's sudden change of heart. Because if she was on his team, she would be easier to control. And if he wanted to control her, that suggested there were things in Isaac Reynolds' case that he would rather keep hidden.

She ducked into her car.

She was about to drive off when something made her stop. It was the empty seat next to her. Suddenly she was hit by the mental image of Amma in Mark's car, the first time they met on that June night.

The jumper in the car. It was such a small detail in Amma's story. Yet why did Erin feel like she'd heard it before?

Slowly, as she stared out the window at the wind-swept trees, a memory came back to her. A memory of a well-spoken, very controlled voice, so quiet it was almost like a murmur.

And suddenly she remembered.

She remembered where she had first met Olivia Stormont.

32

'WE HAVE SPOKEN BEFORE,' ERIN said.

Olivia's face paled.

Erin had driven to Bexmere immediately after meeting Warren and Gregory at the station. Now she was stood in the kitchen with Olivia, whose eyes were wide with trepidation.

She said: 'You got in touch with me a week before Mark died. But using a different name. We spoke on the phone. You wanted me to follow your husband. Because you were worried he was having an affair. And I said no because I don't do that kind of work. I couldn't remember you from your voice alone. But I remember now. Your evidence was that he was working late nights. That you'd found a jumper in the car a couple of months earlier that wasn't yours. You knew about the affair.'

'Yes,' she said breathlessly.

'Why didn't you tell me?'

'I know I should have done. But I – I knew how it would look. My husband was gone. Before I'd even had time to process what was happening between him and… her. I found a woman's jumper in the car. He told me it was a colleague's, and he returned it. I'd known for a while, though. Deep down I knew.'

Olivia was scratching unconsciously at her collarbone in a hypnotic, gentle motion as she spoke. Erin recognised the trance-like state she was in. This was how people behaved when they were sharing something they'd buried deep inside.

'I knew I was losing him. All the late nights. I wasn't born yesterday. I—' Shame creased the skin next to her eyes and over her forehead '—I had a doctors' appointment one day when he said he'd be working late. But instead of going home afterwards, I drove to the police station. I waited outside. I wanted to see if he actually did stay there til eight o'clock, like he'd said he would, or if he left.' Her lips pursed. 'When I saw him leave that building at five on the dot, I was so angry.'

Olivia's quiet voice had turned to a low, threatening whisper that gave Erin a chill.

'I drove after him and followed him all the way to – her house. I didn't see who let him in. I kept telling myself, maybe this is work-related. Maybe he's interviewing someone. But I knew from his demeanour when he went in. He was relaxed. He was visiting someone.'

Olivia swallowed. 'I just wanted to know. I wanted to know even if it killed me. I parked right opposite the house. There's a door in the living room that lets you see through into the kitchen. They were just shadows. There was light coming in through the kitchen and it silhouetted them. They came out and walked to Crays Hill. I followed them. They sat together by that monument up there. Just talking. Holding each other. They looked like teenagers.'

'When was this?'

'A week before he died.'

Erin thought back to her conversation with Amma. Their last meeting at Crays Hill. The figure Amma thought she had seen. Olivia.

'Did you confront him?'

She pressed her lips together, shaking her head.

'I was going to. I was in shock. Still trying to work out what to do, what to say.'

'Am I the first person you've told?' she said.

Olivia locked eyes with her. She gave a small nod.

'I couldn't stand it,' she said quietly.

'Why didn't you tell me? Or the police?' Erin couldn't get her head around it. 'Did you not think this might happen? That Amma might tell the truth?'

Olivia clutched her sides. 'I didn't want to breathe life into whatever they had. She already took him from me. I couldn't let her take everything else as well.'

Erin tried to imagine it from her perspective. Could the desire to hold onto the memory of her husband's love really override her need to get his murderer imprisoned? Evidence of an affair proved a connection to Amma, the main suspect. But perhaps Olivia really was so proud, so infatuated with her husband, that preserving their relationship has become to her the most important thing.

But there was, of course, another possibility. Another reason why Olivia may have chosen to say nothing. Knowledge of the affair gave her a clear motive. Olivia had seen her husband with another woman at Crays Hill. And a week later, he was dead.

Perhaps she was still lying. Perhaps she had confronted him after all.

33

LATER THAT DAY, ERIN MET June and her boyfriend again at The Hollies. She looked through the kitchen window into the overgrown garden, trying to imagine that night when Amma had left this house in a wild panic – before running into the road where Mark had saved her from certain death.

'Whatever you did worked,' said June. 'Amma wasn't talking to us before. But now she is. She's going to come back to live with me for a bit. Try and bring back some normality.'

'It's gut-wrenching seeing her, though,' said Neil. 'She's like a different person. Before all this happened, she was so bubbly and confident. You can't imagine.'

'I wanted to talk to you more about Mark,' said Erin. 'You told Amma you suspected he wasn't a good guy. Why?'

June exhaled deeply.

'I think he was a liar,' she said. 'I thought that then and now we know for sure.'

'What made you think it at the time?'

'He was hiding. He had weird rules about when she could call him. He wasn't introducing her to his friends and family. He was working mad hours. He was unavailable. I thought for a long time he was cheating. But how do you say that to your friend? When they're so happy and your evidence is so flimsy?'

'Did you ever suspect he was lying about his job?'

June looked at the ceiling.

'No, I never thought that. But now I know, I – I need to know.

The night he met her, was that planned? Was he investigating her?'

Erin took a sip of tea. June was right. There did seem to be something pre-planned about Mark's first encounter with Amma. Surely he had known who she was when he met her. Could he even have been following her – gathering information on this woman who was campaigning for her brother's case to be reopened? She thought again of Gregory and Warren. Their apparent desperation to get her to look the other way.

Erin said, 'I also wanted to ask you about that night before he was found. The last time you saw Amma before all this happened. If someone's framing Amma, then they needed to be certain she'd be home that day. And as far as I can tell, the only people who knew she was out the night before are your group.'

Neil and June stared at her wide-eyed.

'Another thing. Amma drank more than she normally would. Apparently slept in really late that Saturday. Which is very convenient for the killer, because it means Amma has no alibi for the morning Mark died. Is there any chance someone spiked her drink?'

'Shit,' said June. 'It's possible. I didn't even think of that.'

'What about your friends? Who bought rounds?'

They were silent for a moment.

'I'm not sure,' said June. 'We all bought one, to be honest.'

'You think one of her friends killed Mark?' said Neil incredulously.

Erin replied: 'We can't rule it out. As I said, you were all the last people to see Amma.'

June's eyes were narrowed. 'Barely anyone knew who he was, though. Amma hadn't told many people.'

'Someone might still have worked out they were together.'

'Why would anyone, though? Kill him?'

'A number of your friends are part of the campaign group, aren't they?' said Erin. 'If one of them found out Mark was actually a police officer, it's not impossible they'd lash out.'

'You know,' June said, 'I'm here saying I was suspicious of Mark.

So maybe that gives me a motive. But why would I then try and frame Amma? I love her. Anyone who had a problem with Mark would have also loved her so why would they do that?'

She had a point. If a member of Amma's circle was responsible, then they had to have a grudge against her. And right now it wasn't clear why they would.

Neil was squinting at the carpet. It looked like he'd just remembered something.

'Actually,' he said, 'she did flip out at someone that night.'

'What?' said June.

'After we spoke to her in the smoking area, she went off. We found her, danced together for a bit. Then we lost her again. Couldn't find her for like twenty minutes. The next time I saw her, she's absolutely losing her shit at this guy. In the middle of the club. It looks like she's started it because a couple of guys are getting in between, trying to get her to back off. I've never seen her like that before.'

'Did you see who it was?'

He shook his head. 'No idea. It was so busy. They'd disappeared before we could get a look at them.'

'And did Amma say anything about this afterwards?'

'She was so far gone, she wasn't making any sense. She was just crying. June was looking after her. Then we called a taxi for her.'

'Why didn't you mention she had a fight?' said June. 'I didn't know that was why she was upset.'

'Hey, I was pretty drunk too,' said Neil defensively. 'Amma's never been able to handle her drink, not since she was a teenager. I have to admit, when she was kicking off that night, I thought she was having an episode. Wouldn't be the first time.'

He said it offhandedly, clearly assuming that Erin knew what he was talking about.

Erin's pulse quickened. 'What do you mean, wouldn't be the first time?'

'Look, she's been through a lot. Like, I lost my mum quite young,

I know how it is. But she's not the most stable person. When she loses her temper or drinks a lot, she disappears. And ever since the campaign, you know, she's had times where she's been very paranoid. She gets a lot of attention online. She's had to deal with trolls. She started getting really paranoid thoughts. Imagining people were following her.'

34

SHE MET WITH AMMA LATER that day. They sat together on the table in her parents' garden in the cool breeze.

Amma pushed her fingers into her hair, over her scalp. 'I honestly can't remember that.'

'You don't remember having a fight with someone?'

She shook her head. 'It's all a blur. Honestly, after that argument with Neil and June, I can't remember a thing.'

'You don't remember anyone else being there?'

'I remember June, Neil, Emmanuel. I can't think of anyone apart from that.'

'Neil mentioned that you'd had some issues with mental health.'

'My mental health isn't me,' she said.

'I know that. But the police won't see it that way. Any information they get, they'll use it to build a case against you.'

'I'm much better now. I used to be very anxious. I thought people were tapping our phones. Recording us. Filming us. I kept the blinds closed permanently.'

'Why did you think that?'

'I don't know. We'd received a couple of threats online. Initially I took it very seriously. That's all it is, I swear. I'm over it. I didn't have some kind of psychotic episode that night.'

Erin tightened her fists in her lap. She wanted to believe Amma. But she found herself struggling to.

A woman with mental health problems, who sometimes had

paranoid thoughts, who didn't have an alibi for the morning of Mark's death.

However much she empathised with her, Erin struggled to completely rule out the possibility that it had been Amma who met with Mark at Crays Hill on that Saturday morning.

*

'Anyone we recognise?' asked Lewis.

He looked at the officer's screen. It showed, from above, a queue of young clubgoers in puffer jackets shuffling towards the entrance of the night club.

The force had requested the CCTV footage when Amma was first arrested, to confirm her whereabouts that night and identify who was with her in the club – Prism – and whether Mark was one of them. After Erin's tip-off, he had asked the officers to look at the footage again, scanning the queue for anyone else they recognised.

'So here's Amma coming in with her group of friends. June, Emmanuel, Neil.'

Even having seen this still before, Lewis felt unsettled as he looked at Amma. While her friends laughed among themselves, enjoying their night out, Amma stared into the distance with a troubled, far-away expression, her eyelids weighed down with drink.

'So Mark wasn't there that night, as we already know. And we can't see anyone connected to him, as far as we're aware.'

He clicked through the stills.

'However, about half an hour later, this lot show up. Recognise them?'

Lewis squinted at the screen. Three men were standing shoulder-to-shoulder in the queue. One of them had a beanie hat pulled down over his head.

'Not at all,' he replied.

'One of those men, Aaron, is an old friend of her brother. Also a member of the campaign group.'

'Did any of Amma's group mention bumping into them?'

'No.'

Lewis frowned. Had Amma lashed out at one of her brother's friends? Why would she do that?

*

Lewis walked up to the front door of the apartment block and rang the doorbell for Flat 14. It had been years since he was last in London for a case, and he'd forgotten how much he disliked the city. Everything from the fumes of the busy road to the sight of the rubbish bags spilling out of the building's overburdened bin store made him desperate to be let inside.

After a few moments, a blurred figure appeared through the mottled glass in the door. It opened to reveal the person they'd seen on the CCTV: a tall man, in his late 20s but already bald, with pointed ears.

'Aaron?'

'Yes.'

Lewis showed his warrant card. 'Mind if I come in?'

For a moment Aaron's eyes widened with alarm. 'Er, sure,' he said.

Aaron led him upstairs and through to the living room, where he turned off the TV. It was quite clearly a shared flat. There were a few photographs on the mantelpiece of the blocked-up fireplace, but otherwise the space was devoid of personality and slightly neglected, with the plaster cracking in the corners of the walls. This was a transitory space, somewhere people were just passing through.

'Anyone else in today?'

'My flatmates are out at the moment. What's this about?'

'You knew Isaac Reynolds?' he said.

Aaron nodded. Lewis could tell he worked out a lot. His t-shirt fitted tightly around his vast shoulders and wide biceps. Yet his head was very small by comparison, as though it had been photoshopped onto another's body.

'We were in the same year at school. Same group of friends.'

'You're still in contact with the family?'

'A bit, yeah. I go on their marches when I can.' He scratched his ear and looked Lewis up and down. 'Is this about…what happened?'

'Where were you on the twentieth of August?' Lewis wanted to see if he lied.

Aaron scoffed and wiped his nose on the back of his sleeve. 'Am I in trouble or something?'

When Lewis said nothing, he continued, 'Er, I was out. At Prism. It's a club.'

'Did you at any point come into contact with Amma Reynolds?'

His eyes widened. 'So she was out that night? Before… shit.'

'Did you see her or not?'

'It was Emmanuel who mentioned they were going out. So yeah, I guess I wondered if she'd be there. Didn't see her though. Never bumped into any of them. Eventually gave up trying to find them and left at about 2 a.m.'

That tallied with what they'd seen on the CCTV.

'And where did you stay?'

'I was staying with some friends just outside Oxford.'

'And the next day, what were you doing?'

'Just hung out at theirs. I can give you their names.'

Lewis wrote down their names on his phone while Aaron read them out.

'We've heard that Amma had some kind of altercation inside the club before she went home.'

Aaron shrugged. 'I wouldn't know.'

Lewis resisted the urge to sigh out loud. He was starting to get the feeling this had been a huge waste of time.

Aaron looked him up and down. 'So it is true then? You think she killed him?'

'What do you know about what happened then?'

'I know that a police officer died. And I know Amma was arrested for it right after.'

'Does that surprise you?'

Immediately Aaron shook his head. 'I can't imagine her doing it. No way. She's a good person.'

35

Friday

AMMA HUNG UP HER JACKET and was about to go upstairs when someone grabbed her. It happened so quickly that she barely had time to register the sound of footsteps sweeping across the floorboards for what it was before she felt their arms fastening around her middle from behind, pulling her towards their firm body. They must have been in the bathroom. Waiting for her to get home. For a fragment of a second she felt something almost like exasperation. You idiot, she thought. Dozens of threatening messages and tweets. This was always going to happen and you know there is only way this can end.

Then the adrenaline kicked in. The moment of existential dread passed. She screamed. She sprung out of the intruder's arms and whirled around to confront him. Once the room stopped spinning, the figure slid into view.

Blue eyes. Deep blue eyes filled with concern.

It was Mark, panicked and breathing hard. And very much alive.

He said, 'It's all right. I can explain. I can explain everything…'

Coming up through a tunnel. Grey morning light poking through the closed curtains.

Amma woke up and looked around the room, populated with dark furniture that looked strange and unfamiliar. It took a few moments for her to realise it was her own. The dream was over.

She finished her breakfast and washed up her bowl in the kitchen sink. She had gone back to stay at hers and June's place last night for a few days. The attention of her parents had been much-needed but now she wanted some time alone to gather her thoughts.

To her surprise, as she was washing up, she heard the doorbell ring. Anxiety spread across her chest. Her immediate thought was that it must be the police. But when she went to open the door, it wasn't DCI Gregory standing there. It was Mark's wife. She was beautiful and angular. A hateful part of Amma noticed the three wrinkle lines crossing her otherwise unblemished forehead. The two women looked absolutely nothing alike.

'Can I come in?' Not a question. An order. Still in shock, Amma gestured lamely inside the house. Olivia brushed past her. Amma watched the mane of brown hair tumbling down Olivia's back as the woman walked into her living room.

Olivia was as out of place as her husband had been on his first night here. Ignoring Amma, she looked the walls up and down with a fastidious air, as though she was a prospective buyer coming to view the place and was so far painfully disappointed.

Amma thought of all those older white women she'd ever watched enviously on the train. Olivia looked exactly like them all.

Seconds dragged by with neither of them speaking. Amma waited with baited breath for Olivia to say something. The woman – no, Mark's wife – seemed to be vibrating on the spot. As she studied the painting on the wall, her beautiful mouth started to turn down at the corners. She raked a trembling hand through her hair.

'So this is where he was going?' she said. She fixed her bright-blue eyes on Amma. 'Here?'

Amma swallowed.

'Did he tell you he was married?'

Amma shook her head. 'I – I didn't know.'

Olivia looked away sharply, composing herself for a second. Then she looked right at Amma again. Amma noticed now that the rims of Olivia's eyes were pink, the corners wrinkled from lack of sleep.

'Are you a vile person? Or just an idiot?'

The fear she'd felt ever since she opened the door to find Olivia standing there amplified. Amma's throat tightened with suppressed emotion.

'Because only an idiot could be with a man like that,' said Olivia, 'and not think he was taken.' She pointed at the sofa. 'Did you fuck here?' Then at the floor. 'Or here?'

Amma felt her mouth soundlessly open and close.

Olivia's arm came up and down in jerky motions. She looked like a recording of a woman on film, freezing as the internet connection timed out. 'Tell me. Fucking tell me.'

'I didn't know,' said Amma. 'I swear.'

Olivia ignored her. Perhaps she hadn't even heard her speak. The tendons in her neck were sticking out. 'None of it was yours. It was mine. *Mine.* you fucking bitch.'

Amma stood there frozen, speechless.

'Who are you? Who the fuck are you? You're not even his type.' Tears poured down her face. 'We fucked two weeks ago. In our bed. At home. Me and my husband. How does that make you feel? How much do you think he fucking loved you then?'

For a few horrible seconds, Olivia blurred to a shimmer, backlit by the window behind her, through which white light was pouring through.

'God, I could kill you. I could fucking kill you.'

She sounded shocked by the realisation. She looked like she would too. Amma felt her back freeze up. June wasn't home. They were alone. Olivia was so animated with fury that no matter how thin her limbs were Amma felt convinced they could rip her to pieces.

'I just want to know what happened. As much as you do.'

'I know what happened. I know who you are. You killed him. You dragged him down into your world and you killed him.'

*

Erin knocked on Olivia's door. There was no answer.

She knocked a second time and suddenly the door was yanked

open, revealing Olivia, hard-faced, eyes blazing, dressed in a long dress and knee-length boots.

She stormed past Erin.

Erin followed. 'Exactly what else are you hiding?'

The sound of Olivia's heels angrily striking the pavement was the only sound down the quiet empty street.

'Amma told me you threatened her. Why would you do that, Olivia?'

'I didn't threaten her,' Olivia half-shrieked over her shoulder.

Again and again she had ignored Olivia's lies. But there was no smoke without fire.

'If I didn't know any better,' she said, 'I'd say you didn't want me to find your husband's killer.'

Olivia whirled around.

'You've already found his killer,' she said. 'And you're protecting them.' She was bearing her teeth. 'You're on her side. You always were. Don't deny it.'

Erin said nothing.

'I speak for Mark's family,' she continued, 'when I say we want absolutely nothing to do with you. Don't come here again.'

36

Saturday

AMMA AWOKE EARLY THE NEXT day and lay there for ten minutes. She closed her eyes and remembered the park in the height of summer, sunbathers wiped out by the sun's formidable rays. She tried to conjure up the sensation of the dry grass beneath her fingers, the sound of insects and the feeling of Mark's body lying beside her. What had they been talking about before they'd reached that moment? What had he said to her afterwards? Why couldn't she remember? She should have written it all down, every word he ever said, every moment that her former self had squandered, letting them wash over like waves that would pass over her again and again, ceaseless.

She could tell she wasn't going to go back to sleep. Eventually she got out of bed and approached the window. Pulling open the curtain, she looked out at the early morning light, the road turned amber by the beam of a single street lamp, completely empty apart from the line of parked cars. The silence filled her with a strange calm. She felt her heart rate begin to slow.

Then something moved. The shadow beneath her car grew suddenly larger. A man emerged from beneath it. Amma stopped breathing. Automatically, she stepped back behind the curtains, watching in horror through the gap between them as the man stood completely upright and walked around the outside of her car. Ice-cold fear ran through her as he glanced back at the house. Then, with a straight back, he walked down the street, behind the tree at the end of it. As quickly as he had appeared, he had vanished from sight.

*

The engineer sucked in his lips and shook his head. He was stood in the car park with a clipboard in one hand. 'Nothing.'

'Are you sure?' asked Amma.

'Not that I can see. No trackers.'

Amma felt a surge of panic. She scanned the car obsessively, searching for any scuff or scratch that might suggest it had been tampered with.

'Did you check inside?'

The engineer shrugged. 'Look, I've checked everywhere. There's no devices. Nothing like that.'

She swallowed. She knew she looked crazy right now. But she didn't care. She'd seen no other option than to get the car checked out by a professional.

After she'd seen the man outside her house, she'd crept outside, gotten on her knees and started searching every corner and crevice of the car for a device. Finding nothing, she'd decided then and there to take it to the garage. She couldn't drive in peace without getting it checked out. Now the engineer had given his verdict, her mind raced with images of driving it around again knowing someone might be tracking her every move with a GPS device, or watching her through a hidden camera, or listening to her through a microphone.

The man must have put something on her car. She was certain of it. But what?

Amma had already paid. Too flustered to feel embarrassed, she thanked the baffled engineer and edged her body into the car. Even the steering wheel felt unfamiliar. With a jolt of fear, she imagined that as she pulled out of the garage and joined the main road, the movement might trigger some lurking explosive device and the whole vehicle might be engulfed in flames.

She couldn't live like this. She'd have to sell the car. As soon as the thought occurred to her, she realised how irrationally she was behaving. Had she definitely, definitely seen the man?

Her mind had been unclear ever since Mark had been killed. The line between reality and imagination had become increasingly blurred. Sometimes a whole hour could pass by in a fog, as if it had never happened. Other times she found herself so lost in the memory of him that she felt almost convinced she was in a dream.

Her chest tightened. Perhaps she hadn't seen a man. Perhaps she'd imagined him.

But if that was the case, then that meant she was losing her mind.

She needed someone else's perspective. As soon as she got home, she'd call Erin.

37

Amma's voice was shaky down the other end of the phone. 'I feel like I'm going insane.'

'You're not,' said Erin.

There was a crackling sound as Amma breathed out. 'There wasn't anything on the car, though. Maybe it was nothing. But I saw him. I definitely did. I wasn't imagining it.'

Erin bit her lip. Amma sounded completely convincing. But she would be an idiot if she ignored what she knew about her mental health history right now. Was this how it manifested itself? With visions of strangers loitering outside the house?

'I used to feel it all the time. I used to ignore it because it's a symptom, you know. Paranoia. A therapist once told me to try journalling. I used to keep a note of my thoughts. Including times when I felt someone was watching me. I looked at it last night. I thought – I don't know, maybe this is stupid – but I thought I could share the entries with you.'

'Of course.'

Erin wrote down the dates as Amma slowly worked through her diary, noting two separate occasions when she thought she had seen someone following her. One day in the previous November she had sensed she was being watched on her way to Emmanuel's to discuss an upcoming march. Another time she had noticed a figure in the darkness outside her house, only for them to disappear the moment she approached the window.

Once the call was over, Erin looked at the dates.

They all fell within the past year.

She checked her notes on the Mark Stormont case. A wave of cold hit her.

She rang Amma back, trying to hide the tremor in her voice.

'Can I come over? I need to see you in person.'

38

Erin waited on Amma's doorstep. She gritted her teeth so tightly it hurt, imagining what she was going to have to say.

After a few moments, she heard footsteps shuffling down the carpeted stairs in the hallway and Amma opened the door. She looked weaker and thinner by the day. Her cheekbones stuck out and her lips were cracked.

'Come in,' said Amma. 'I'll get you a tea.'

'Don't worry about it,' said Erin, stepping inside. She didn't think this would be a long visit.

There was a flicker of surprise in Amma's face. Erin could tell she knew something was up. In silence they walked into the living room. Amma turned around to face her and crossed her arms over her chest.

'What is it?' she asked.

Erin sighed, trying to find the words. 'Amma...' she began.

Amma's eyes went wide with panic. 'Is it to do with what I said earlier? Was a man planting something on my car? What else have they planted?'

Erin felt nauseous. She wondered if she'd made a mistake coming here. She wished she'd had more time to formulate her views.

'I have a theory,' she said.

'What?'

Erin took a deep breath.

'The officer you saw. He wasn't placing a tracker on your car. He was removing the one that Mark put there.'

39

FROM THE MIDDLE OF THE living room, Amma squinted at her in disbelief. Under her clothes, Erin felt heat spreading across her skin. She prayed she was right. Because she could sense from the cold fury in Amma's eyes that this was an accusation the woman would never forgive her for. There was no going back from this.

'What are you talking about?'

'Amma—'

'Do you have evidence?'

Erin said nothing.

Amma scoffed. 'Is there anything behind this?'

'Mark's partner thought he was investigating your brother's death without anyone's knowledge. Because he kept mentioning the case and working late in his own time. What if that wasn't true? What if they told him to investigate? But not – not in your interest, Amma.'

Amma swayed slightly on the spot.

'You have been a problem for the police for years,' Erin said. 'You know that. Maybe they genuinely thought you were a threat. If your brother was killed, then it's possible the police either missed something or deliberately obstructed the investigation. If that's true, then maybe they wanted to keep that buried. And their only way of doing that was to silence you. And maybe they thought they could do that by gathering information on you.'

'What are you talking about?'

'Were there ever occasions when police turned up at speeches, marches, vigils, and you didn't know how they knew about them?'

Amma frowned.

'The dates you told me about… I checked them against the timeline I have of Olivia and Mark's messages. Both days, he said he was working late. The same excuse he gave whenever he lied about meeting you. Then the night you met Mark… he wasn't just in the area. He followed you to the party. Mark was following you for months before you met.

'You said you became less and less interested in your brother's case after meeting Mark. What if that was what he wanted? What if he was manipulating you?'

Amma stared at her, her eyes burning with rage. 'You didn't know him.'

'You told me to find out if it was real,' she said. 'This is the answer. It wasn't real, Amma.'

A silent tear rolled down Amma's face.

'What happened to you,' she hissed, 'is not what happened to me.'

Erin flinched. It was the first time Amma had ever alluded to her past. Her throat grew hot with emotion but she stayed silent.

'That's what this is about,' snarled Amma. 'You can't stand seeing two people in love. After everything you went through. Even the memory of it – you have to stamp it out.'

'That's not true—'

'Get out.' Amma shook her hands at Erin. 'Get out.'

Erin left the house and walked at speed down the street, her breath coming out in sharp, shaky gasps. She touched her cheeks and noticed with surprise that she'd been crying. Her fingertips came away hot and wet with tears.

Mark couldn't have been working alone. If he really had spied on Amma, then someone had ordered him to do it. Someone senior. She thought of Gregory and Warren.

There was something she couldn't work out. And that was: why would Gregory have gone to such lengths? What was so personally devastating about the Isaac Reynolds investigation, and the way it had been carried out, that he would jeopardise his whole career by spying on the victim's sister?

In her mind, there were two possible answers. The first was Gregory had failed to investigate the case properly. He had failed in some career-destroying way – perhaps by accidentally destroying crucial evidence – and he knew that if Amma ever found this out, his career would be over.

Or, the second, Gregory was somehow personally responsible for Isaac's death.

But why? Why would Gregory have ever crossed paths with Isaac?

She needed answers. Checking her phone, she saw it was almost 5 p.m. Lewis might still be at work. She texted him: *Hey, any chance I could see you at the office?* Then she hit send.

40

ERIN STEPPED THROUGH THE AUTOMATIC doors and into the police station. She walked through the dimly lit, almost-empty office until eventually she found Lewis working quietly in one of the smaller rooms.

He looked tired. Seeing her, he blinked slowly and forced a half-hearted smile.

'You want a tea?' he said.

'Yeah, sure.'

Lewis disappeared for a few minutes and returned with two cups.

'This takes me back,' she said, taking hers. 'Hiding out in different parts of the office working on Sophie Madson's case.'

Lewis said, 'It's nice to come into work not absolutely bricking it every morning.'

'Must be,' said Erin, before adding: 'Was quite exciting, though.'

Lewis smiled. There was something bittersweet about reminiscing. The truth was things were nothing like they were before. A gulf stretched between them now.

'Funny you texted,' he said. 'There was something I was going to ask you.'

'What?'

'We're interviewing Amma again tomorrow,' he said.

Erin swallowed, though her throat felt totally dry.

'We want you to be watching,' he said. 'In the observation room.'

Erin frowned. 'What? Why?'

'It was Gregory's idea. He wants you on the same page as us.'

Erin's mind was whirring. Gregory wanted her to watch the interview. It was a change of tune since she'd last seen him and Warren – when both had seemed desperate for her to back off. What did it mean? Her only guess was that they had built a strong case against Amma, strong enough they believed Erin would give up once she'd heard it. Fear bubbled in the pit of her stomach.

'So,' she said, 'the night before the big interview.'

Lewis nodded.

'What are you thinking?'

Lewis reached up to run a hand through his hair – a nervous impulse she thought he'd abandoned a long time ago. He seemed to sense what he was doing because he snatched his hand away before it could make contact.

'I don't know. A big part of me doesn't believe she could do it. But then…' he shrugged, 'the fact they were in a relationship, and he was hiding so much, it doesn't help her case.'

'What if that wasn't all he was hiding?'

'What do you mean?'

'Has Gregory been acting strangely?'

Lewis's eyes rolled to the ceiling. 'Christ. Are you really going to do this here?'

She leant in, keeping her voice low. 'So you think a new detective flew in the face of his superiors' orders and decided to investigate an unsolved cold case all by himself?'

'Possibly.'

'And he just so happened to fall madly in love with a woman who'd been causing the force grief for years?'

'What are you getting at here?'

'That if the police planned all this, it wouldn't be the first time.'

Lewis stared at her open-mouthed. His cheeks and ears had flushed pink with anger.

Erin continued: 'There is a precedent for the police instructing officers to infiltrate people's lives, sometimes through artificial relationships.'

Lewis covered his face with his hands in frustration. 'Oh my *god*,' he groaned.

'Amma posed a threat to the police. She was campaigning for them to reopen a case that – for whatever reason – the police didn't want to reopen. What if Mark was ordered to spy on her? What if he took it too far? Or, what if he was told to form a relationship with her to distract from the case? Convince her to drop it? If that's true, then at least one person high up made him do this. You and I both know who that is.'

Lewis brought his hands down and gripped the edge of the desk. 'You know, I never wanted to say this to you.'

'Go on.'

His eyes had lit up with rage.

'You can't get over it. He fucked us over and you're the only one who can't move on. You're projecting yourself onto this case and you're imagining he, or someone like him, is behind it all over again, because you can't stand that you got it wrong the first time!'

Before Erin could think of a response, he pushed his chair out and leapt to his feet.

'You're paranoid, Erin! All you see now is the absolute worst in people. Their worst possible intentions.'

'That's our *job*, Lewis!'

'And if you seriously think this is all part of some conspiracy, then what the fuck must you think of me? That I'm complicit? Or that I'm so shit at my job that I'm ignoring the signs staring me in the face?'

Erin had never seen Lewis so angry. His words hung heavy in the air around them during the silence that followed. She felt like someone had punched her in the chest.

When he next spoke, his voice was quieter and laced with a faint tremor.

'I've always defended you. When people talk. When they say you've lost it. I don't know if I can do it any more.' He glared into the distance.

'When they say I've lost it? Wow. Thanks for that.'

Lewis didn't look at her. His eyes scanned the half-closed blinds. 'I think it's best if you go.'

She chewed her lips. There was one more thing she'd come here to say. And she wasn't leaving before she said it.

'There's something I want you to see before tomorrow. I've emailed it to you.'

Wearily, Lewis said, 'What is it?'

'It's a spreadsheet of every diary entry where Amma noted feeling paranoid. Feeling like someone was following her. And alongside it are messages exchanged between Mark and Olivia, which show that Mark wasn't home on those days.'

She started zipping up her jacket.

'Unlike me, you can actually check CCTV systems. So maybe you can do more with it than I can.'

'Erin,' said Lewis. 'Diary entries? Seriously? This is completely insane.'

'Just think about it,' she said.

She stormed out.

Once she was inside the safety of her car, she allowed herself to draw in a deep breath. She ran a trembling hand through her hair, catching sight of her own eyes in the rear-view mirror. They were watery and clear and her cheeks were blazing with emotion. She clenched her teeth, suppressing the urge to cry.

She forced herself to take out her phone and text Amma: *Interview in the morning. Be ready.*

This was the end for her and Lewis. She could feel it in her bones.

But she had got what she needed.

She slipped a hand into her pocket and pulled out the USB stick.

The moment Lewis had left the room to get their teas, she had swiftly and quietly parked herself in front of his computer, where she had gone in search of the file she needed and hit 'copy'. Now in the palm of her hand she held the entirety of Isaac's case file.

41

Sunday

AMMA WOKE UP EARLY, BEFORE the sun was up. She had intended to get as much sleep as possible so she could be well-rested for the day's events. But a sense of fear and urgency had nestled deep inside her bones. It trembled underneath her skin like an electric current, preventing her from rolling over and going back to sleep. She needed to be ready. Today was the day.

She crept downstairs to the kitchen, made herself a cup of tea and looked out into the garden. In the darkness she could just make out the shape of a well-kept fox nosing through the grass on its narrow legs. Would she be here tomorrow morning? She didn't know. It was possible she wouldn't be back here for years. The thought – hard to fathom – made a deep pit open up in the bottom of her stomach.

The numbers on the oven clock glowed red: 05:43. She thought about what Erin had told her yesterday. It was too horrible to comprehend. So she'd given up on the idea Erin could help her. She felt more alone than she had ever felt in her life.

The sound of the kitchen door opening made her jump. She turned around to find June standing there in a fluffy grey dressing gown. Her skin was dull with tiredness.

'Can't sleep either?' she said.

Amma nodded.

At the sight of her, June's face crumpled as she held back tears. Amma opened her arms and held her.

'It'll be all right,' she said, though she wasn't sure she believed it.

They came at just after nine o'clock. She watched as a police car appeared behind the shrub outside the living room window, its nose just poking out of the foliage.

They were back.

*

For the first time in two years, Erin entered the observation room. None of the officers were here yet. Stepping up to the one-sided mirror and seeing Amma sat in the interview room, looking tired but defiant, with her lawyer beside her, Erin's heart tugged with emotion. The young woman shouldn't have been sitting in that room. Erin blamed herself. She hadn't moved quickly enough. Hadn't found evidence pointing to the real killer. She bit the inside of her mouth, pushing the thoughts down. This was exactly what Gregory wanted – to demoralise her.

She heard the door opening and turned around to see Lewis and his partner pushing into the room.

'Shouldn't you two be in there?' she asked.

Lewis's eyes were still dark with last night's argument. He shook his head.

Erin frowned. If they weren't interviewing her, then there was only one person who could be. Gregory.

*

Amma pressed her knuckles into her forehead and breathed deeply, gathering her thoughts, blocking out the white walls of the interview room. The solicitor her parents had hired – Thea – edged her chair closer. 'It's important to remember, Amma, that if they've discovered any forensic evidence connecting you to Mark, that doesn't necessarily link you to the scene of the crime. Your relationship would have made it more likely that hairs and clothing fibres might still be on his person even a week after you last saw him.'

Amma nodded to show she understood. She had imagined coming back here many times since she was let out. She had emotionally prepared herself for what was about to happen. At any moment now the detective Lewis Jennings and his partner Chris would be coming through that door. They would present her with all the information they had gathered about her relationship with Mark – everything she had kept secret from them. This time, she needed to use her voice. She needed to have her reasons. She couldn't just give up, turn inwards, hide away like she had done before.

After a few moments, she heard the gentle sound of the door opening and closing, followed by footsteps clicking across the linoleum floor. One pair of footsteps. Had Lewis come alone this time?

At the sound of the detective pulling out a chair and sitting down, Amma looked up, lowering her hands.

Then she felt her heart drop through her body.

Grey-haired, square-shouldered, and just as she remembered him, Gregory was watching her from the other side of the table.

'I'm DCI Gregory. But we don't need introducing, do we, Amma?'

This man had reduced her to tears as a child. She was still scared of him.

'So, we have an answer. You were in a relationship with DI Stormont. You must have realised we would work this out, right, Amma? You strike me as an intelligent woman. You must have known we would find the text messages, the skin cells, the clothing fibres.'

She imagined Mark's dust coating the furniture in her house. Hairs on pillowcases. Tiny threads of clothing hidden in the carpet. A final layer of tangible parts of him, soon gone forever.

'Yes or no, Amma?'

Gregory's bark brought her back into the room.

'Did you realise we would find out?'

'Yes.'

'You did. Okay, so then, what reason did you have for wasting police time and stopping us getting to the truth about your boyfriend's murder?'

'I – I—'

'Didn't you care? How quickly we found his killer?'

'No – I mean, yes, of course—'

'Did you love him?'

'Yes.'

'Do you think he loved you?'

A pause. 'Yes.'

'You hesitated. Perhaps you weren't sure, Amma? Tell me what happened during your last conversation.'

'He said he had things hc needed to do. And then we could properly be together. I didn't know what he meant.'

'But you must have your suspicions now?'

'I think he was going to leave her.'

'You know what I think, Amma? I think you got impatient. He'd told you not to contact him for a week. It was only natural that you began to worry.

'I think you started following the trail. I think you found out about Olivia.'

'No, no, I didn't.'

'I think you found out he had a wife and you realised he had lied to you.'

'That's not what happened.'

'So when he asked to see you, you were ready. You turned up with a knife that day. You killed him on that hill.'

Amma was shaking her head non-stop. She could feel herself turning inwards. She hated how he made her feel – small and speechless like a child.

Gregory sighed heavily. 'I'm getting very fed up of this game of yours, I have to say.'

He pushed something across the table.

'You know this person?'

It was a photograph of June.

'Yes. June.'

'Your friend and housemate?'

'Yes.' Amma felt her heart rate increase.

'Let's imagine that you really don't have anything to do with this, Amma. In that case, I need to start looking elsewhere. June knew about your relationship with Mark. Like you, she chose not to tell the police. I have to ask why. Perhaps she was simply protecting you. Or perhaps she had something to do with this.'

Amma felt like her organs had disappeared all at once. She shook her head. 'No.'

'June had her suspicions about Mark. I doubt she approved of your relationship. Perhaps she snapped. Found out he had a wife and killed him for betraying her friend.'

'She wouldn't do that.'

'Or perhaps your friend Emmanuel had something to do with it? He can't have been happy if he found out you had a boyfriend. Particularly not as he'd spent so long himself hoping you two might eventually end up together.'

'How do you—'

There were only a handful of people who knew about Emmanuel's feelings for her. Had one of her friends told him? Why would they have done that? Had they not realised it would make Emmanuel a possible suspect?'

'Perhaps he lashed out. Perhaps he was jealous. Perhaps it was him who killed Mark. And perhaps you're protecting him now.'

She dragged her fingers across her scalp.

'You're wrong,' said Amma.

Thea, her solicitor, stepped in then. 'Is it my client you suspect, or her friends, detective? Or are you simply trying to provoke a reaction?'

Gregory ignored her.

'If I'm wrong, then tell me what happened, Amma.'

'I don't know.'

'Ah yes. You don't remember. You don't remember the day before someone you loved was murdered. Are these memory issues a common problem? Have you ever suffered from paranoia, Amma?'

He squinted at her. Was Amma just imagining it, or was there a knowing glint in his eyes?

'What?'

'Have you ever thought someone was following you? Imagined someone was standing outside your window only to turn around and discover they weren't really there?'

Crackling fire. A warm hand stroking her hair. Clear blue eyes.

'You – you can't know that—'

'Is that a yes, Amma?'

All through her body her muscles clenched with horror. She imagined Gregory's face glowing orange in the firelight.

'No, I—'

'There's something we've found among Mark's possessions. Something I want you to listen to.'

Amma could barely breathe. Gregory opened his laptop and turned it around to show her what was on the screen.

It was an audio file.

He pressed play.

42

A RUSTLING SOUND EMANATED FROM THE laptop, filling the interview room and feeding through the speakers into the darkness of the observation room.

After a few moments, Erin realised what it was. The sound of a fire crackling.

She felt her shoulders seize up as she watched Amma react with horror, eyes widening, lifting her head to stare at Gregory.

'What the fuck is this?'

'It's a recording that we found on Mark's laptop. In an encrypted folder,' he said calmly.

The popping sounds as the firewood split, releasing steam into the fire, were followed by a softer but louder noise – the murmur of fabric on fabric, as someone near the recording device shuffled where they were sitting.

A voice said, 'Has anything ever happened to you that changed you? Something so big it made you feel like a different person by the end of it?'

It took Erin a few moments to recognise Amma's voice. This version of her sounded like a different woman; so relaxed she seemed almost sedated.

Amma's solicitor sat totally still. Erin recognised the fearful expression on her face. That was how lawyers looked when evidence emerged that their client hadn't told them about.

In the room, Amma said, 'Turn it off. I know what happened. I don't need to hear it.'

But Gregory made no move to stop the recording.

Another voice on the audio file replied: 'How d'you mean?'

Erin knew instinctively who this was.

Amma's chest started to rise and fall rapidly as she stared at the laptop, entranced by this apparition of Mark that had been conjured into the room.

She hadn't told Erin about this.

With cold accusation, she said to Gregory: 'You recorded this. You did.'

Gregory shook his head solemnly. Then he raised a finger to his lips, signalling silence.

The Amma on the recording said, 'Do you feel like you've always been the same as you are now?'

'More or less,' Mark replied.

'Really? So you just haven't changed at any point in your life?'

'Not that I can think of. Not on a fundamental level, no.'

Mark was holding back. And Amma could clearly tell.

'I just feel like I know so little about what your life was like before I met you.'

Even listening to this conversation with no sight of the two people speaking, Erin could sense the tension growing between them.

'I feel I don't know much about you now, to be honest,' Amma continued.

There were a few moments of silence filled only with the spitting and sizzling of the fire. It sounded like the scratching sound of audio on an old film, as if this conversation had been recorded decades ago.

'Well, I'm sorry about that,' said Mark.

Gregory held his clutched hands up to his mouth. He looked like he was almost in prayer, but his eyes remained fixed on Amma, watching every micro-expression.

'Really? That's what you're going to say to that?'

There was a loud rustling on the recording. Amma sitting up.

'I don't know what you want me to say,' Mark replied.

'Maybe something that fills in all the gaps you've created for me? Do you know how weird it is to have absolutely no idea what your boyfriend is doing as soon as they walk out the door? I feel like you stop existing. Like you disappear.'

The tone in Amma's voice had changed in an instant. She was talking quickly and confidently, her voice high-pitched with anger.

'Why aren't you on social media? Why can't I call you whenever I want? Why have I never, ever come round to yours?'

'I already told you—'

'Oh yeah, sorry, it's not private enough. Yeah, great excuse. So it's me always having to clean up for you before you come round, never the other way round. Let me ask you something. Can I come round to yours next week?'

'What?' Mark sounded surprised by the mundanity of the question asked with such viciousness.

'Can I come round to yours next week?'

'I'm not sure.'

'Are you serious?'

'You can, you can. Of course you can.'

'I'm freaking out now. I'm really freaking out.'

In the interview room, Amma was curled up, her hands over her ears, unable to bear the reliving of this hated memory – the memory of berating someone she would never speak to again.

'Are you seeing other people?'

'No.'

'Do you live with someone? Is that what's going on?'

'No.'

His voice was low, tentative, unconvincing.

Listening to Mark lie, Erin felt her chest tighten painfully as she imagined Amma's despair.

'Why can't you just tell me the fucking truth? Why are you lying to me?'

'I'm not.'

'Yes, you are!'

Amma was shouting now and as she shouted the sound of shattering glass exploded through the speakers. It was so unexpected it made Erin flinch.

Immediately afterwards, there was a sharp intake of breath.

Amma's past self said, 'Oh my god, I'm sorry. I'm so sorry.'

'It's fine,' Mark replied quietly.

'It's not. Oh my god, I'm so sorry, I didn't mean to – here—'

Amma was still curled up in her seat. Her shoulders shook as she cried.

That was when Erin realised what she was listening to. This was Mark's betrayal.

Gregory pressed stop.

43

GREGORY BROUGHT HIS THICK FINGERS together on the table.

'Let me explain my understanding of what just happened there, and you can correct me if I'm wrong, Amma.

'You opened up to Mark about your mental health problems. You asked him about his past, hoping he would reciprocate and open up to you. When he didn't, you started interrogating him about his secrecy. You suggested he might be seeing someone else. And in your rage at the idea, you threw an almost-empty bottle of wine at him.'

He reached into the folder and pulled out a large photograph, which he placed in the middle of the table.

Amma's stomach lurched. She looked away.

'And Mark sustained an injury to his hand.'

'Don't, I don't want to see that.'

'Look at it, Amma.'

She forced herself to look at the photograph. It showed an open hand. She recognised that perfect white scar slicing over skin, disturbing the unique creases of a familiar palm. But that familiar palm was grey, drained of all the colour of life. The hand was lying on a metallic table.

She lunged forward, sending the photograph across the table and fluttering down to the floor.

'You are a violent person, aren't you, Amma? A paranoid, violent person.'

'No.'

Thea jumped in. 'This is outrageous.'

'Why did you throw a bottle of wine at Mark?'

'I wasn't trying to throw it at him, I swear. I swear. He – he tried to catch it—'

'Why was Mark recording you, Amma?'

'I don't know.' She sobbed the words out.

'Was it because he felt unsafe, perhaps? Because he wanted evidence?'

'He wouldn't. He wouldn't.'

'How many times have you been violent towards a partner, Amma?'

'Never – that was the only time – I wasn't violent—'

'Did you know Mark had a wife, Amma?'

'No, I didn't.'

'But you suspected it, didn't you? Do you live with someone – that's what you asked Mark.'

'I didn't know—'

'You didn't tell Erin Crane about that argument.'

'I – I – it was nothing, that was why – it was nothing – and I was ashamed—'

'Or was it because this was the first time you'd lashed out at Mark? Because three weeks after this assault, you killed him?'

'I wasn't violent – I never would have—'

'Paranoid thoughts. Difficulty controlling anger. Violent behaviours. It was you, Amma, admit it. You were on the edge for years before Mark came along. And then his betrayal finally pushed you over it.'

'No—'

'You realised it was never serious between you two. Just a summer. And you couldn't stand it. And you killed him.'

Her throat felt so hot and tight she was almost gasping for breath as she cried. She couldn't believe she was crying here, like a child, in this bleak white-walled room in front of this grey-suited man.

She broke.

'I never,' she sobbed.

She held her hands over her face, which now felt wet and hot with tears.

'I never would have done it.' Her voice sounded thick and muffled.

Gregory's hand was pressed flat on the table, fingers splayed, commanding the space between them.

Slowly, it withdrew from the table as he sat back.

'I think we'd better stop there.'

44

Erin hung back while the custody officer on duty processed Amma for detention. His name was Liam and he was in his mid-forties. He had a kind voice that meant he was usually very good at dealing with even the most volatile detainees. He managed to make one of the worst moments of someone's life sound like they were at a travel agent.

'So you're being charged with murder, Amma, do you understand that?' he said from behind the protective glass.

Amma stood at the front desk with her head bowed. 'Yes.' Her voice was raspy and defeated.

'You're going to stay in a holding cell until we can get you booked into the first available court hearing at the magistrates' court. There's a quad where you can exercise. If you need a GP you just let us know and we'll get someone to see you, all right.'

Amma swayed on the spot. She stepped away from the front desk and let her back touch the wall. Her body was shaking.

'Amma,' said Erin, 'call your parents. Tell them what's happened.'

Amma looked at her. Her eyes were cloudy with despair.

'I didn't do it, Erin,' she said.

'I know. You've been charged, you've not been convicted of anything. I'll visit you, we'll talk on the phone.'

'That's enough now, come on,' said the officer.

Erin watched as he steered the new detainee towards her cell. Amma moved like a ghost, feet seeming to hardly touch the floor.

Once they'd disappeared round the corner. Erin let her back hit the wall. She felt as though there was a huge weight in her chest, dragging her down.

'You need a glass of water, Erin?' asked Liam.

'It's all right.'

'You just take a minute.'

She couldn't manage a response. She slid down the wall, crouched down on the balls of her feet and closed her eyes. She opened them again when she heard footsteps approaching.

Gregory was stood over her.

'I know that must have been hard to watch,' he said. 'I can see you've become fond of her.'

Erin rose to her feet.

'So you can't share evidence with me,' she said, 'but you can if I have to watch you torment an innocent woman?'

'I thought it would help if you could see what we're seeing.'

'Why was Mark recording her?' she asked.

'As I told Amma,' he said, 'I suspect he had begun to feel unsafe. He's a police officer. He would have known the importance of hard evidence.'

'Were there other recordings?'

'You and I both know, Erin,' he said, 'that a vast number of cases are just between a man and a woman. Sometimes it's as simple as that. You've been a huge help. You've helped her, by encouraging her to speak. And you've helped us to get to the truth.'

Erin felt herself sway on the spot. Was this her fault?

'But I really think you should leave this to us now.'

*

Lewis stared at the half-eaten tuna sandwich in his hands as the noise of the office canteen swirled around him. Every bite had turned into a dry claggy mush in his mouth. He felt certain he couldn't have any more because his stomach was churning with guilt.

Chris, beside him, had already finished his sandwich and was happily working his way through a packet of crisps.

'Cheer up, mate,' he said. 'It's done. We did it.'

'What was that about?' he asked.

'What?'

'The way she reacted to Gregory when he came in.'

The older detective had insisted he should interview Amma, after Lewis and Chris had failed so miserably to get a comment out of her last time. But when Gregory had sat down, something strange had happened. Amma's despondency had seemed to disappear in an instant. Looking up at the newcomer, she'd drawn back from the table until her back had touched the chair. She'd looked like an animal drawing in on itself, ready to pounce. It was the most visceral reaction Lewis had seen in her so far.

Chris shrugged. 'It's her narrative, isn't it? She thinks Gregory didn't find this mystery killer. She hates him.'

'And then Gregory… the way he acted…'

'Can you blame him? All those sulky silences when she obviously did it. She had it coming to her.'

Lewis looked at the empty seats inside the room. 'That just seemed – I don't know. More intense than I would have expected.'

'That's how hard we should have been on her from the start.'

But Gregory had been harsher to her than he had expected. Far harsher. As if it was personal.

Lewis forced down the remainder of his sandwich. He noticed his hand was shaking slightly.

45

'I'M SO SORRY.'

Pale light shining through the windows of the Reynolds' living room silhouetted Vicky and Stephen. Coils of silver steam drifted up from their respective coffee cups.

Vicky reached a hand across the table, fixing her with a look that was almost stern.

'It's not your fault. You listened to us. You helped her. We're grateful for that.'

Erin was completely unprepared for this. From her perspective, Amma's parents had every right to hate her right now. She was struggling to keep up her professionalism. She felt like pulling her hair out and begging them for forgiveness.

Stephen said, 'And think what we've found out now. This means she was right. She was never paranoid. They were spying on her. He was spying on her. Recording her.'

Erin tugged her sleeves up to cover her hands. 'They've already decided his intention though. He felt unsafe. I don't know how to prove otherwise.'

'You're not planning on stopping, are you?' Vicky said. 'I'm sorry, but I'm not letting you. They said my son was so drunk he fell into a river on his way home. My son who barely drank. Now they've gone after my daughter. Saying she's a violent killer.' She shook her head. 'They can't do this to us. They can't get away with it. Whatever's going on, it's got to be linked, hasn't it? Whoever did this, they know what really happened to Isaac. They know why he died.'

'I have been thinking,' said Erin, 'that maybe I'm looking at this the wrong way up. I'm starting from the finish. When I need to be looking at that night. At what happened to Isaac.'

'We've got a box full of everything the police ever told us in the attic. Which, I have to warn you, is not very much. But you're welcome to it.'

'He was last seen with a group of people from school. Do you have any suspicions of those people?'

Vicky and Stephen shared a long look.

'The only ones we ever knew were his friends,' said Stephen. 'And I mean, I'm ruling nothing out, but I can't see any of them doing it, could you?'

Vicky pursed her lips in disagreement.

'Could you, Vicky?'

'You know how it is at that age. The bad behaviour you'll ignore in order to fit in.'

'Do you know if any of them had a problem with Isaac?' asked Erin.

'A couple of them did,' said Vicky. 'The best person for you to speak to about that is Rory. His closest friend from school. He lives in London now but we can put you in touch.'

'Do you think it could be the same person?' asked Stephen. 'Isaac's killer and Mark's?'

Erin shook her head. 'I don't know.'

Vicky clenched her fist on the table. 'Whoever it is, I want to see who did this in court,' she said. 'I want them to see the pain they've put me through. And I want them to spend years having to contemplate what they did, the same way I do every day. If they die without punishment, they get off scot-free, as far as I'm concerned.'

46

ERIN DIDN'T NOTICE SHE WAS being followed until she was halfway down the street.

Suddenly she became aware of the sound of footsteps clicking over the pavement behind her. In her mind's eyes she saw something that had happened just seconds ago but must have registered only on a subconscious level – the figure of a man in a long coat slipping out of his car at the exact same moment she left the Reynolds' front garden.

She started walking more quickly. Then he appeared in front of her, walking backwards, hands in pockets, smiling effortlessly.

'Erin,' he said. 'Free for a quick chat?'

Erin made no attempt to hide her exasperation.

'Do you not think that you should be more careful about sneaking up on people when there's a murderer potentially still at large?'

'At large isn't what I've heard. What I've heard is someone's been charged for the murder of Mark Stormont.'

A local news reporter, he had been among those following the Sophie Madson case. He had documented the fallout religiously, and Erin had since learnt his name: Alex Spencer. He bristled with energy, as though he could hardly bear to stand still. His body language alone gave the impression that he could flit effortlessly from one story to the next – provoking a reaction and then disappearing off to interfere in someone else's life.

'You're not getting anything, Alex.'

She manoeuvred past him. He fell into step with her.

'So are you working on the case then?'

Erin said nothing.

'Obviously you are, given you just walked out of Stephen and Vicky Reynolds' house. Did they hire you? Do they not trust the police to do a good job?'

'Exactly how long have you been lurking outside their house?'

'I'm not bothering them, Erin. I do have some respect, thanks very much. I'm just seeing if any interesting figures like yourself turn up.'

Alex swerved in front of her again.

'It was Amma Reynolds who was arrested for Mark Stormont's death, wasn't it? She's the one they've charged.'

Erin hated the gleeful look in his eyes.

She gritted her teeth and continued walking. Alex sped up to catch up with her.

'So, how bad is it looking?'

She kept walking in silence.

'You're not under the same restrictions as the police any more, Erin. You're free. Nothing's going to happen if you talk to me. It might even help shed more light on the case. Encourage witnesses to come forward.'

Erin turned towards the road.

'You know, we could really help each other.'

She waited for a car to pass. 'How could you help me?'

'You're self-employed now, right? You need to promote yourself. Raise your profile. I can do that.'

'No, thank you.'

'Are you sure? It can't be all that easy getting work. We'd make you look good.'

'I'm not talking to you.'

Another car rushed past. Erin stepped forward.

'What if I could tell you about her brother's murder? Stuff that didn't make it into the papers. Stuff the police won't tell you.'

She stopped. She turned around.

There it was again. That gleeful little look in his eyes – because he knew something she didn't know, something the public didn't.

'Have you reported on that case before?' she asked cautiously.

Alex unlocked his phone. 'One sec.'

Erin gritted her teeth with impatience as he tapped his phone screen.

Then he stepped forward and showed her a long list of articles, all about the case, all of them for the *Examiner* and written by him.

'A fair bit, yeah,' he said smugly.

He had come close enough that a wave of his aftershave had hit her. Erin backed away.

She was aware she was standing very straight.

'We could get a pint,' he said.

Erin felt heat crawl up her neck. 'A coffee,' she said.

'Sure thing.' There was no indication in his voice that he was disappointed.

Afterwards, as she walked to her Airbnb in the dark blue dusk, Erin felt angry by how flustered the encounter had made her. Alex thought because he was good-looking he could use that on her. He couldn't.

Once back, she made a cup of tea and took it through to her bedroom, where she turned on her desk lamp and opened her laptop. She got out the USB, pushed it inside and clicked on Isaac's case file.

Included inside were witness statements, screenshots of surveillance footage, text messages and forensic reports. Bit by bit she started combing through the case the police had built up after Isaac's death.

Some stills in the report she had seen before. The final sighting of Isaac had been widely circulated in the media after the police released them early on in the investigation, asking any witnesses to come forward. The lonely images showed the lanky teenager walking unaccompanied down the high street. He looked angry. His head was bowed and his fists were stuffed in the front of his jacket.

What was new to her were the interviews. Erin read through the transcripts of conversations the police had had with Vicky, Stephen and also Amma. Anxiety knotted in her stomach at the intensity of their desperation, which leapt off the page. But apart from these interviews, no one had been formally questioned in relation to Isaac's disappearance or death. So instead of transcripts, there were only officers' reports of conversations with witnesses.

Erin opened her notebook and started creating a timeline of events that night. Isaac and his friends – Emmanuel, Neil, Rory, Aaron and Jack – had gone to The Hollies after school to drink and play games. A number of witnesses, including Neil's dad Ian, reported that Isaac had become withdrawn and irritable partway through the night. The group was then seen arriving at the firework display – 'reasonably intoxicated', according to one eyewitness – at 8 p.m. Rory reported that Isaac left early, just an hour later – something other witnesses corroborated. Rory had followed Isaac away from the crowd and asked him if he wanted company, to which Isaac had said he wanted to go alone. This had been the last time anyone had spoken to Isaac. The time of death was estimated to have been at around 10 p.m.

Because of Isaac and Rory's unannounced departures, the rest of the group had splintered off into search parties and quickly lost each other. All of them reported traipsing home, either alone or in pairs (Aaron with Jack) at around 10 p.m. or 11 p.m.

It struck Erin reading these reports that no attempt had been made by police to verify the boys' accounts. She knew from first-hand experience just how overcrowded and chaotic those firework displays could be. It would have been very easy for one of the boys to sneak off after Isaac without anyone else noticing. How could the police have known that someone hadn't followed Isaac home – and encountered him later on his journey, after that final CCTV footage was captured?

Also included in the folder was a copy of the results from the post-mortem. Hope grew in Erin's heart. She knew the pathologist.

47

'DO YOU REMEMBER THE DETAILS?'

'Yes. I've returned to this one again and again myself,' said Cecilie. In the background of the call, Erin heard a metallic clunk which she recognised as the sound of a mortuary cabinet being slid open, either to remove a body or return it to the cool darkness. A small wave of nausea rose inside her at the thought.

'Why's that?'

The family were so certain there was murderous intent, I wanted to make sure I hadn't missed anything.' She continued: 'The cause of death was drowning. However, he had sustained a number of injuries before his death. His left shoulder was dislocated. And there was bruising around his wrist.'

'His shoulder?'

'Yes.'

'Do you know when he sustained the injury?'

'Shortly before his death, judging by the level of bruising and the swelling.'

'Can you think of any reason how that could have happened?'

'It could be that he sustained the injury lowering himself – or falling – into the water. If there was a rock there, for example. However, the bruising around his wrist makes that unlikely.'

'How so?'

'The pattern of the bruises suggested to me that something constricted around his wrist. As if he was tied to something.'

Erin felt her heart beat faster.

'That made me wonder if it was a suicide attempt. He could have tied a rock to his wrist before jumping in. But if that's true, they never found anything like that in the river. Or it may be that he sustained this injury before he even got in the water. Maybe someone tried to forcibly restrain him.'

Erin clenched her jaw. This didn't sound accidental. It sounded violent.

'And one more thing. How do you fall into a river on your way back home? On a route you must know like the back of your hand? The suggestion has been that he was drunk and he fell in. But a toxicology report found, I remember, that he was underneath the drink driving limit. I know he was young, but the level of alcohol he'd consumed wouldn't suggest to me that he would be intoxicated or disorientated.'

Erin clicked through the files inside the folder in search of any document labelled toxicology report. No, it was as she remembered. There was none there. Suddenly she recalled what Walker had said – that someone had lost it.

'Have you heard of any documents going missing in relation to this case?' she asked.

'I haven't personally, no. But it wouldn't be the first time, would it?'

48

LEWIS FINISHED TYPING OUT HIS email and hit send. Sinking back into his chair, he felt relief spread through his body. That was it – his final report on the Mark Stormont investigation, done. Now he could put the case out of his mind until the trial began.

He looked out the window, watching the tangled branches of a nearby tree swaying in the breeze. An image of Amma curled up in the custody suite flashed through his mind. No matter how hard he tried, he couldn't get that final interview out of his head. It had left him with a feeling of unease deep in his bones. He thought of what Erin had said to him. That spreadsheet she'd sent him was waiting, unread, in his inbox. Biting his lip, he glanced around at his colleagues to check that none of them were watching him, then opened her last email.

The spreadsheet noted down every message exchanged between Mark and Olivia, along with occasional entries from Amma's journal. He scoffed. This really was ridiculous. So Amma had felt on-edge a couple of times when Mark just so happened to be out of the house. So what? It was crazy to suggest there was a connection.

But still. That recording. It kept creeping into his thoughts. It was a blatant invasion of Amma's privacy. It seemed so unlike Mark to do something like that. And he found it difficult to believe Gregory's explanation that Mark was scared for his life and wanted evidence he could use to defend himself. He was a detective. A married one. Why wouldn't he have just walked away if he felt unsafe?

He opened the location data for Mark's car on his laptop and searched for the days listed in Erin's spreadsheet. One by one, he clicked through each still showing where Mark's car had been picked up by various cameras.

Eventually one still appeared that sent a chill down his spine.

'What does that look like to you?' he asked.

He'd summoned Chris into a small meeting room. Chris hunched over his laptop and squinted at the screen.

'Is that Mark's car? And is that—'

'Amma.'

Realisation filled Chris's eyes.

'What does it look like?' he repeated.

'Well, it looks like he's following her,' said Chris quietly.

'Yeah. Yeah it does, doesn't it? Following her a month before they even met.'

Chris straightened up. He put his hands in his back pockets. Lewis could see he was struggling to process this new information.

'I mean, it could be a coincidence. They just so happen to be down the same street.'

'Maybe. Or maybe not.'

'Does this change anything? You're acting like it's really significant.'

'Does it change anything?' said Lewis incredulously. 'It looks like the victim was stalking our suspect.'

'He wouldn't do that,' Chris snapped. 'You didn't know him like I did. He was not like that.'

'So how'd you explain this then?'

'Maybe he just saw her and liked the look of her and was thinking of stopping and asking her out.'

Lewis bit his fingernails. He couldn't understand how unphased Chris was by this image that had nearly given him a heart attack.

'It's just—'

'What?'

'Following her. Recording her. That doesn't ring any alarm bells for you?' He noticed his voice had grown louder and quickly lowered it. 'What if that meeting between Mark and Amma was supposed to happen? What if it was planned?'

'By who?'

Lewis said nothing.

'By the super? Or Gregory? Is that what you're saying?'

'What if he wanted Mark to keep tabs on her? On her campaign? Because if he was, then he's hiding something, isn't he?' Lewis said. 'And if he's hiding something, then he would have a motive to get Amma done for this. He would have a motive to—'

He didn't need to say it.

Chris's face darkened. 'Jesus Christ. This is Erin, isn't it?'

Lewis covered his face with his hands. 'I don't know what I'm saying. She's just got these ideas in my head. And now I can't get them out.'

Chris crossed the space between them and placed a hand on his shoulder.

'Seriously, you need to take a break from this. Whatever's happened here, it's between Mark and Amma. They had an affair and it all went wrong and he wouldn't leave his wife and she killed him. We've done all we can. It's up to the courts now. Erin's just bitter because we're here and she isn't. Don't let her theories get to you, all right?'

Lewis nodded. He felt embarrassed that his younger partner was having to calm him down.

'Yeah. You're probably right.'

'I am. Just put it to bed.'

49

ALEX PLACED THE COFFEES HE'D ordered on the table between them.

'It must be quite isolating, being a PI,' he said.

'I'm fine by myself,' said Erin.

'It's impressive, honestly. I couldn't hack it.'

Erin shrugged. Was he trying to flatter her? She wished they'd just get on with it.

'So,' she said, 'what do you remember of the way the case was investigated?'

'You must have seen it yourself, right? Confirmation bias. They decided what happened to Isaac, and then they stuck with it.

'So the story is that Isaac drowned, right?' he continued. 'Didn't see the river and fell in. It's not insane a teenager might do that, with enough alcohol in their system. But where did he fall in? He didn't need to cross the river to get home. So what was he doing over there? I know some people think it was suicide. But there was nothing about his family life or behaviour that suggested he had mental health problems.

'I went knocking on doors asking if people had heard anything, seen anything around the river,' he said. 'And there was one person who had heard something that night. A man who lived right up against the bank. He said he'd heard a boat going up the river. A motorboat, because he'd heard the engine. And laughter.'

'Laughter?'

'Yeah. He said it sounded like a party.'

'Did he report it?'

'Oh yeah. But the police did nothing with it. When we asked for a comment, they just told us they were looking into it but it didn't seem relevant. My editor said there wasn't enough in there for a story so we never ran with it.'

'Is this guy still around?'

He shook his head. 'Died of a stroke a couple of years ago. But that's where I would start, if I were you. By working out who owned a boat in the area at that time.'

'What do you think happened?'

'Some kids in that school were lying.'

Alex glanced down at their empty cups before scanning the café and arching his eyebrow at her.

'Do you want a proper drink?'

The first pint went down surprisingly easily. Alex pushed their glasses across the bar and ordered another round.

This wasn't going the way Erin had planned.

'Is it mainly cold cases people want you to solve?' he asked.

'No.'

'What else then?'

'Women want me to find out if their husbands are cheating on them.'

Alex's eyes lit up. '*Really*?'

'Yes.'

'And do you?'

'I can't think of anything worse.'

'What if someone said they'd pay you a million pounds?'

'No.'

'Yes, you would. For a million pounds.'

Their next drink arrived. Together they took sips.

'I wouldn't. Anyone paying someone to spy on their partner is a piece of work. You should just get divorced if you feel that way.'

'I don't know, that's their problem though, isn't it? At least you'd give them the truth. And expose some lying arsehole who might otherwise have given his wife an STD. Does it not surprise you that it's women approaching you with these kinds of jobs?'

'How do you mean?'

He shrugged. 'I'm generalising, but do you not think men are more jealous? And more predisposed to that kind of controlling behaviour?'

'I guess women see a kindred spirit.'

'What does that mean?'

'Never mind.'

He cocked his head to one side. 'Can I ask you something?'

'What?'

'Tom Radley,' he said, 'was that just partners?'

'Is it a gossip column you're writing now?'

'Just between us.'

'Maybe I don't want to tell you in case you publish something.'

'Maybe I don't publish stories like that about people I like.'

Erin scoffed. Neither of them said anything. The music blasting into the pub suddenly seemed incredibly loud.

'Was that awkward?' asked Alex. 'I feel like that was awkward.'

She stared into the remainder of her pint. 'I'd better head.'

'Really?'

'I have interviews in the morning.'

She pulled on her jacket and reached under the table for her bag, heat flushing her face.

'Have I overstepped the mark? If I have, I'm sorry. I didn't want to make you feel uncomfortable.'

'No. You haven't.'

She pushed through the pub door and onto the street, already regretting what she was doing.

50

Monday

IT WAS EARLY IN THE morning, nine days since Mark's murder. Lewis was driving Chris to the station when he heard the noise.

They fell silent. In the distance, people were chanting in unison. The noise grew steadily louder until they turned into the station and saw a group of protesters clustered outside the building. Some were white, some black. Most were young. Lewis recognised some of them. Members of the campaign group.

He realised what they were saying. 'Free Amma! Free Amma!'

Seeing them, the group surged forwards and within moments the car was engulfed. It shook as the protesters hit the exterior with their posters and bare palms. The chanting now had dissolved into a frenzied, uncoordinated shouting.

'Are you fucking serious?' said Chris.

Heart pounding, Lewis inched the car slowly and carefully through the group. Their faces were filled with anger. The chant began again.

'Free Amma! Free Amma!'

Then something exploded next to the other passenger window. Chris, having flinched away from the noise, lifted his head up from beneath his arms to study the window with incredulity. It was glowing red. It took Lewis a few moments to realise it was not blood splattered across the glass, but paint.

'Right,' said Chris decisively.

He scrambled to unbuckle his seat belt. Lewis's heart filled with dread as he realised what was coming next.

'Don't!' he yelled.

But it was too late. Chris had freed himself and now he was opening the door and stepping into the mob.

Lewis exited on his side, emerging into a ball of noise. Someone's warm spittle landed on his check as the protestors shouted at him. Disorientated, he turned around just in time to see Emmanuel – his eyes lit up with rage – hurling a bucket towards Chris, covering him in thick ropes of scarlet paint. A moment later Chris grabbed him and shoved him up against the car. His white shirt was splattered with lashings of red.

Then Lewis saw the officers pouring out of the station.

*

The officers took Emmanuel and a number of other protestors down to the custody suite while Lewis escorted Chris up the corridor into the main office. Beside him, the younger detective was shaking with anger.

'Maybe it was him,' he gasped. 'Maybe *he* killed Mark. He has a motive. Maybe it's him.'

With his shirt sleeves streaked bright red, he looked absurd, like an extra in a horror film.

Lewis clenched his fists. 'Why did you have to get out of the car?' he said through his teeth.

'How could you stay in the car?' Chris snapped. 'Seriously, people are literally attacking our station, and you just sit there—'

Lewis couldn't take it any more. They'd been walking side by side but now he abruptly stopped and grabbed Chris's arm, pulling the younger detective around to face him.

'Do you have any idea what you just did? How bad that looked? What it means for you? What it means for everyone else in this building? Jesus Christ. It'll be a miracle if you don't get a complaint.'

The younger detective said nothing. To Lewis's satisfaction, he saw a flicker of fear in Chris's eyes.

'Go and clean up.'

*

Erin met Emmanuel in the graveyard. She found him crouched on the balls of his feet in front of Isaac's grave. It was the first time she had visited it. A photo of the family stood against the headstone, inside a weathered metal frame, next to a vase of fresh flowers.

'Criminal damage,' he said, answering the question before she asked it. 'Like it's that expensive to get some paint off a car. My first hearing's on Thursday.'

Erin sighed with frustration. The pointlessness of it. After everything Amma had been through.

'I don't care,' said Emmanuel. 'They need to know we're not just going to let them do this.'

He showed Erin a video on his phone. But she'd already seen it this morning, plastered all over social media. The clip showed Chris emerging from his car, his jaw set with rage, into the crowd of protestors, grabbing Emmanuel and forcing him up against the closed passenger door, a bucket of red paint tumbling from his grasp and out of shot.

'I've also got fifteen witnesses who saw that arsehole use unnecessary force. He'll be hearing from me.'

Erin felt conscious of Emmanuel's lean body next to her, his tightly coiled rage. He had demonstrated a viciousness for the police and a love for Amma that left her feeling suspicious. If he had discovered Mark was following her, she could imagine him deciding to take matters into his own hands. Could it have been him who Amma had fought with that night?

'What was it you wanted to tell me?' she asked.

Emmanuel looked at her. His eyes narrowed.

'You haven't played this game before, but I have. If they were watching her, it wasn't because they were scared of what she might do. They were scared of what she might find. They wanted to be one step ahead of her at all times. And they wanted to have the material to demoralise her, undermine her, discredit her. Which is exactly what they did.

'Which means whatever it is they're trying to hide, it's bad. Who knows, maybe they killed Isaac that day.

'I came here to warn you. Because they're going to do the same thing to you now. Any dirty washing you have, they'll find it.'

51

Tuesday

ERIN RANG THE DOORBELL FOR Flat 4 and waited. Somewhere in the building, a dog started barking.

The journey this morning had taken her two hours in total. Rory, Isaac's closest friend growing up, had moved to Stockwell in South London. She'd gotten his contact details from Amma and arranged to see him in person.

Eventually she heard the sound of footsteps barrelling down the stairs and a lanky, red-headed man opened the door.

'Erin?' he said. 'Good to talk inside?'

'That'd be great.'

She followed him up the narrow stairwell and into his flat. The small living room was dominated by a bike leaning on the wall.

'Mind if I record this?'

He waved a hand. 'Go for it.'

Erin opened the recorder app and placed her phone on the coffee table between them.

'So what do you want to know?' he said.

'Isaac's death,' she said. 'Do you believe it was an accident?'

Immediately, Rory shook his head. 'No. Not at all.'

'Why's that?'

'I mean, someone who's not a confident swimmer – who's basically afraid of the water, not that they'd ever admit it – decides to go for a late-night swim in the river all by themselves? It's mental.'

'Were many people aware of that? That he was scared of the water?'

'He wasn't going to shout about it. But there was an incident everyone knew about, yeah.'

'An incident?'

'When we were kids, maybe nine, we went on this school trip, one where parents come along. We had to build a raft and take it across a lake. Isaac was pissing about and fell in. One of the parents had to dive in after him and save him. He was fine, but he never got over it.'

'Say there was foul play,' said Erin. 'You'd known Isaac since you were kids. Was there anyone who might have had a reason to kill him?'

Rory looked uncomfortable. He glanced apprehensively at the recorder app open on her phone.

'Can you maybe not tell the family I said this?'

Erin nodded.

'When someone dies like that, at that age,' he said, 'no one wants to be the one to say they were a knob.'

'And was he?'

'Oh yeah. A huge knob. I would never say this to Amma or his parents but someone almost certainly killed him, you know what I mean?'

'Right,' said Erin. 'That's very… honest of you.'

'Look, Amma, no disrespect to her, she's lovely… but she's deified him just as much as her parents have. I understand. She lost her brother when she was just a kid. But she doesn't really remember what he was like. I do. And let me tell you, Isaac was annoying.'

'Annoying how?'

'Look, at the end of the day I was his friend, right? But Isaac always had to be right. He was super competitive. Judgemental. Gobby. He created drama.'

'Like what?'

'Teenage stuff. He'd upset friends over the most minor argument, which he should have dropped. He'd insult the wrong person. He didn't treat girls well. He was young, you know, but—' Rory shrugged.

'You re-evaluate these friendships when you get older, don't you? I look back on things that happened and I don't think you can write off his behaviour as that of a teenage boy with a lot of testosterone who's just going through a phase. I think he fundamentally didn't care if he hurt someone. And I think he made that very clear to the people he hurt.'

'What do you mean?'

'You know, this guy in our group, Jack, he was nice but he was quiet and nerdy, right. A bit of a hanger-on. We were always taking the piss out of him for being clumsy or whatever. But affectionately, you know? But Isaac, he just – he just acted like he was our underling or something.'

Jack. Erin felt a spark of recognition. He'd been one of the boys who was there that night.

'I remember one time Jack opened a Coke bottle at lunch and it exploded everywhere. Some of it sprayed over Isaac's bag. We thought it was hilarious. But Isaac lost his mind. We're all laughing and Isaac's there going, "you fucking idiot, Jack". And he picks up his bag and pushes it out to Jack, like, "clean it up". And no one's laughing any more and Jack's staring at him, trying to work out if he's being serious. And Isaac says "clean it up" again til Jack actually goes and takes it to the boys' toilets and wipes it down. It was just weird, right? I should have said something.' Rory paused, running a hand through his hair. 'And then girls… he was a real dick to girls. He was pretty successful, you know, good-looking guy. He'd be really nice to them to start with. And then just – well, you know the sort of thing. Showing us nudes they'd sent him. Ditching them without saying anything when he got bored.'

He chewed his lips, remembering. 'See what I mean when I say he was a knob? It's funny because I am saying it now and I'm missing him, you know. That's messed up, isn't it?'

'You were friends for years.'

'It's not even that, though. He had this charisma. I think it was why he managed to get away with all this and why he's still remembered so fondly now. He managed to make you feel like if you were on his side, you were one of the winners. You know, there was something really appealing about how he just did whatever he wanted without ever worrying about the consequences. I guess maybe it caught up with him in the end. Sorry, I don't know if I mean that.'

'Is there anyone who he really upset?'

'There was this one girl. She got really, really into him. And it ended because, well—'

'What?'

'Because he showed everyone photos she'd sent him of her tits. And this was Aaron's sister, so they obviously fell out.'

'Aaron's another friend of yours? And when did that happen?'

'About two weeks before he died, I guess. That night, drinking at The Hollies, it was the first time they'd hung out after school. You could cut the tension with a knife.'

Erin remembered something she'd read in the case file. 'Is that why Isaac left early?'

Rory nodded. 'He didn't admit it but yeah, one hundred per cent.' He realised what she was implying and added, 'Not gonna lie though, Aaron was quite wet. Big guy but not aggressive or anything. I don't think he'd have done it. Personally.'

'These boys, Jack and Aaron,' she said. 'Have you stayed in touch with them?'

'Yeah, Aaron's still about. Not Jack though.'

'Why's that?'

'Jack's been missing for years now.'

'Are you serious?'

He got out his phone and showed Erin a news story. *Missing person appeal as Jack Riley last seen on Friday*, the headline read. It was three-years-old. The accompanying picture showed an anxious-looking man in his twenties squinting at the camera.

'He left school before sixth form, went to London. I don't think he had much family. Really sad. I don't know for certain, but some people think it was drugs-related.'

Erin's mind was whirring. Isaac had relentlessly teased a boy who went missing several years after his death. Was there a connection? Had the police never looked into it?

Rory pocketed his phone. 'You could speak to Aaron though, for sure.'

'Have you got his number?'

'Yeah, I'll give it to you. I mean, I'm not saying – I really don't know if one of them was responsible. They know the family. Aaron's been on marches as well, you know.'

Erin nodded. But really she was grinding her teeth. It hadn't escaped her that going on those marches would give someone like Aaron a very good cover.

52

ERIN HIT 'RECORD' AND PLACED her phone on the table between her and Aaron, who glanced nervously from the device to her face.

'Look, I understand why you're coming to me. But I did already go through this with the police.'

Aaron had an angular face and pointed ears that twisted a little at the top. He was bald, which only made his ears seem to stick out more.

'Well, sorry to make you repeat yourself. Not a problem, is it?'

Aaron shook his head forcefully. 'Obviously not. No.'

'When did you last see Isaac?'

'At the bonfire. He left early. Never was one to stay late.'

'Did you see him leave?'

'No. We all went looking for him when we realised he was gone.'

'And how did he seem before then?'

'Low-ebb, yeah. I thought he was just tired. Feels shit that, you know – that I didn't notice anything.'

The trouble with interviewing beefcakes like Aaron who spent three hours a day in the gym was Erin found it hard to tell whether they were genuinely emotionally disconnected from others, or just bad at articulating themselves after years of isolation.

'So what time did you leave?'

'About half past ten. This is why the police only questioned me once.'

'I've heard that Isaac had a short… relationship with your sister, is that right?'

He scoffed. 'I'm not sure you can call it that.'

'It sounds like Isaac didn't treat her well.'

Aaron stuck out his jaw. 'No, he didn't.'

'Did you confront him about it?'

'Not that evening, no. A couple of weeks before.'

'But the tension was still there?'

'You're asking, did I drown him in a river because he went around showing people pictures of my sister's tits?'

'You must have been upset.'

He shuffled awkwardly. 'I'm not like that. Ask anyone who knows me. I'm not going to lash out if someone makes me angry. You know, he was a prick for doing that but… I would never do something like that.'

'So you walked home?'

'Yes. With Jack, he stayed over with me.'

'What route did you take?'

He blinked at her as if to say: *really*?

'Okay. I walked back from the village green. Went down the high street. Cut through the park. And then I was home. Probably just before eleven o'clock.'

Aaron was pink in the face now. Perhaps he had only just realised she was serious.

Erin resisted the urge to let out a deep breath through her nose in frustration. The motive was there. But he had remembered his alibi perfectly. And after so many years, she couldn't think of a way to find out whether he really had been walking home alone that night, that night, after Isaac had already drowned to death.

She was about to stop the recording when she realised there was something neither of them had mentioned yet.

'You've heard about what's happened to Jack since?' she asked.

A darkness crept into Aaron's face. 'Yeah. That was really sad.'

'Do you think he's alive?'

'He was a troubled guy. I don't know. I'm not sure.'

Erin felt her mistrust for Aaron building again. 'So you'll march for Isaac,' she said, 'but you won't look for your other friend who never came home?'

*

Before driving back to Wakestead, she searched online for Jack Riley and found him listed on a missing persons website. She wrote to the email on the page, saying that while she didn't have any new information she would like to find out more about the case. By the time she'd arrived back at the flat, a Met police officer had emailed back agreeing to speak with her. She answered his call at her desk while uploading the conversations with Rory and Aaron to her laptop.

'He was known to us already,' he said. 'He'd never been arrested for anything but he'd been involved in various neighbourhood disturbances. House parties going on into the small hours and that kind of thing. Hanging out with people in possession.

'So, yeah, it was a sad case. He walked out of his house share one day and then nobody ever saw him again. We traced him as far as Brent Cross and then, nothing. He was wearing a blue hoodie and tracksuit bottoms. Small bag with him, nothing else.

'He was never the cause of the trouble. But he seemed to attract it. Got in with the wrong sort of people.'

'Did his housemates tell you anything about those last few days?'

'The only thing they said was it seemed like something was eating him up inside. They said he was zoning out, going quiet, crying on nights out. He said something about how no one really knew him. You know what I think?'

'What?'

'I think that day he may have gone to end his own life. I hope it's that, anyway. I hope it's that and not that some bastard's out there who's gotten away with it.'

53

Wednesday

ERIN PLAYED THROUGH YESTERDAY'S CONVERSATIONS in her head as she walked through the village of Bexmere. She was beginning to think that Aaron had killed Isaac that night. But if so, then where did Jack fit into all this? The missing man had sounded extremely troubled. Supposing he really had taken his own life, as the officer suspected, then that implied a guilty conscience. Had he helped Aaron murder Isaac? Or had he acted alone – and was any chance of a guilty verdict for the family gone?

Mark Stormont's cottage was coming up on her left. While Isaac's case had become clearer, Mark's remained just as murky as before. Erin's only theory there at the moment was that the detective may have revisited Isaac's case with the hope of solving it and redeeming himself to Amma, in the process discovering the killer (perhaps Aaron) who then murdered him before he could reveal his identity. It was possible. But right now she had no evidence pointing that way. She needed to go back to square one.

Unless they were the friends and family of the victim, people usually didn't take kindly to a private investigator turning up on their doorstep. So Erin was surprised when she knocked on the Stormonts' neighbours' doors and the one who answered seemed only too delighted to usher her inside.

Mrs Higgins was dressed in a blue-and-white flowery blouse, over which she wore a long woollen cardigan. She was so excited to voice her opinions on the case that she neglected to offer a cup of tea or coffee to Erin, who felt a sense of dread come over her as she sank into the sofa in the living room that smelled strongly of cat litter. *This is going to be a long one*, she thought.

'They were such a lovely couple,' said Mrs Higgins. 'Quiet, but then this whole road is quiet so they fit right in. It's a tragedy what's happened.'

'Do you remember seeing anyone visit Mr and Mrs Stormont in the weeks before he died?'

'Visiting? No, not at all. I don't think they had many visitors. Very private. And certainly *she* never dared turn up here.'

Erin guessed she was referring to Amma.

'Oh really?' said Erin, gritting her teeth.

'That family. You couldn't miss them,' said Mrs Higgins, bursting with an air of self-importance. 'I would go to the school gates to pick up my grandson Charlie. And those siblings were so *loud*. Always shouting at each other. You'd be stood there thinking, "if I can't hear myself think right now, how on earth are any of their classmates able to concentrate?"'

'What does your grandson remember about Isaac?'

'I would never want to speak disrespectfully of the dead,' she said. Erin wanted for the inevitable 'but'. She continued: 'But he was a very badly behaved child. Loud. Arrogant. Very aggressive on the sports field, I heard. When a child has that much anger inside them, it's a sign the parents aren't disciplining them enough. By the sounds of things, the boy drank himself into oblivion that night.

'And after all that, to keep banging on about it like that family. They've caused so much trouble for themselves. All that publicity.'

'And Amma? What's your opinion of her?'

'She wants the attention. So much so that she's gone and killed a police officer. I'm certain she must have done it. Although the police obviously aren't too sure.'

'What do you mean?'

'Well, they've searched that house so many times now, they must not have much evidence.'

Erin glanced out of the window, where the edge of Mark and Olivia's cottage was just visible.

'Mrs Stormont's house? How many times have they searched it?'

'Let me think now. Since he died, I think they've had forensics here four times. Maybe five?'

Four or five searches. That was definitely strange. There was only one explanation Erin could think of.

Gregory was looking for something.

As she walked back from Mrs Higgins', she rang Olivia's number.

Please, she thought to herself, listening to the dial tone ringing out.

She breathed a sigh of relief when Olivia answered. 'I told you not to contact me.'

'Olivia, please don't hang up on me, I just want to ask you something.'

'What is it?'

She got the question out as quickly as she could: 'How many times have police searched the house?'

Down the other end of the line, Olivia was silent for a few moments.

'Where have you heard about this?' she asked suspiciously.

So it was true. 'How many times?'

'Perhaps five now. I don't understand. They did the initial – whatever you call it – full search of the house just after he was found. But since then they've been coming back, just a few each time, saying they want to make sure they've got everything. Going through desks and drawers. Feeling the back of wardrobes. They keep asking me if he had any hiding places.'

54

SHE TOLD THE RECEPTIONIST IN the station that Gregory was expecting her – even though he wasn't – and took off in search of the senior detective, eventually finding him working at his computer in the main office. Exasperation filled his face when she came into his line of vision.

'I suppose you'll want to speak with Jennings?' he said in a disapproving tone.

'Actually, I was hoping to speak to you.'

Before he could say anything, she pulled out a chair and sat down beside him. Grey eyes, greying hair, an old suit that didn't fit very well. She found it hard to see the man in front of her as a malicious person bent on harming Amma and her family.

'We'd better keep this brief,' he said.

'Amma's family has asked me to look into Isaac's death,' she said.

Erin thought she saw a muscle in Gregory's jaw twitch. He directed an exasperated sigh at the table, opened his palm and closed it.

'Big fans of yours, aren't they?' he said. 'Okay. Well, as you know, Erin, there's only so much we can do to help you with your own investigations.'

'I'm not asking for help,' she said. 'I want to talk to you about what I've seen so far.'

Gregory held her gaze steadily. Erin never got the impression anything she was saying was phasing him.

'There are some details in the case that stood out to me,' she said.

'Such as?'

'The injuries Isaac sustained before his death. A dislocated shoulder and bruising around the wrist. How do you explain them?'

'It was suggested to us by the pathologist that Isaac may have weighed himself down with something that was attached to his wrist. Or that he hit something when he fell.'

'So it could have been suicide or an accident, is what you're saying?' asked Erin.

'Either's possible, yes.'

'You weren't concerned that the pathologist never ruled out third-party involvement?'

Gregory narrowed his eyes. Erin could tell he had realised she must have been speaking to Cecilie.

'As you know, sometimes you can't rule it out completely with a suicide or accidental death.'

'Well, it may interest you to know that one of the boys who was with him that evening went missing several years ago. Jack Riley. Remember him?'

For a second Erin thought she saw fear flash in Gregory's stone-grey eyes. But then he blinked and it was gone.

'I can't sit here and tell you I remember the names of every friend Isaac Reynolds ever had, Erin,' he said.

'The officer who investigated his disappearance said his mental health was suffering. That it could have been suicide. That doesn't change anything for you?'

Erin saw Gregory clench his fist on the table. 'Look, this is a family who didn't get the answer they wanted. I understand they lost their child. I completely see that they want someone to blame for that. But for years now, by obsessing over the details of a case that was carried out properly – despite what they say – these people have not only wasted police time, they've even driven their other child to commit a horrendous crime against this force.'

He shook his head.

'I'm done indulging this, Erin. If that family has a complaint against this police force, tell them to make one formally, all right? Now, if you'll excuse me, I have a meeting.'

He was already getting up, pushing his chair under the table with an unpleasant screech. On his desk, Erin noticed a framed photo of a younger Gregory embracing a woman whose hair was tangled in the wind. His wife perhaps? It was strange seeing him look so happy and relaxed.

He was passing her chair when Erin asked, 'Why all the searches at Mark Stormont's house?'

Gregory stopped. He turned around. 'Excuse me?'

'Olivia told me the police have been round there four or five times recently.'

'What we have to do to get a case ready for trial is none of your business, Erin. I'm surprised you're still troubling yourself with that case when a suspect's already been charged.'

Looking for the first time a little rattled, Gregory turned around and left in the direction of Warren's office.

On her way out, fists balled in her jacket pockets, Erin mulled over what Gregory had said. Could those searches really be precautionary, ahead of the trial? She was so lost in her own thoughts that walking down the corridor she nearly collided with an officer coming the opposite way.

It was Lewis. 'What are you doing here?' he said.

She noticed his eyes were avoiding hers.

'Do you know what he's looking for?' she asked.

'What?'

'Gregory. Why's he organised so many searches of Mark's house?'

Lewis frowned. 'Has he?'

'Jesus. Exactly who is in charge of this investigation, Lewis?'

'I don't know what you're talking about, Erin.'

She could see there was no point going into this now. She brushed past him, calling over her shoulder: 'Just ask him about the searches. And give me a ring if you ever want to talk.'

She pushed through the door, aware that Lewis's eyes were boring into her back.

So whatever Gregory was looking for, he clearly didn't want the other detectives to find it.

55

Thursday

THE VISITORS' ROOM OF THE women's prison was large and brightly lit, with two vending machines against one wall. Pairs of blue chairs were dotted around the hall at a carefully measured distance. Over the watchful eyes of the prison guards, families huddled together, meeting their loved ones across a vast but invisible divide. First-timers were easy to spot. While others had adjusted to this unusual place and settled into a natural rhythm, newcomers processed their loved one's uniform and bleak surroundings with visible alarm, wide eyes focused on their face as if it had changed in some fundamental way since they saw them last. Daylight slanted in through barred windows at the top of one wall of the room. Opposite her, Amma sat wearing joggers and a hoodie. This was only her second day here, and she still looked shellshocked to find herself in prison, on remand, while she awaited the trial. Noises made her jumpy – at the sound of a door opening, she winced, retreating back into her hoodie.

'I'm going to get you out of here, Amma,' said Erin.

'What are you doing visiting me? You can't help me. I've told you everything I know. That's it.'

'There's more I need to ask you. I think there's still more we could find out. About Mark.'

At the sound of his name, Amma flinched.

'You were right,' she said. 'He was recording me. Without me knowing. It wasn't real.'

'I don't know if I was right—'

'What do you mean you don't know? You heard that recording. You were there.'

'Everything you told me,' she said, 'made me think that Mark really loved you.'

'Well, I was wrong, wasn't I? I was fucking wrong.'

'Someone killed Mark that day and it wasn't you. But he died on the hill not far from your house. Why's that?'

'Because they framed me.'

'Maybe. Or maybe he was coming to see you, Amma. Like he promised.'

Amma cradled her head in her hands, as if her words were physically hurting her.

'Shut up,' she said. 'Why are you doing this?'

Erin's heart squeezed with sympathy. 'Listen, the police keep searching Mark's house. They're looking for something. Whatever it is, they must think it's important. They still haven't found Mark's phone. It's possible the killer took it. But you've got to ask why they would do that. Presumably he had both phones with him so he could text you. Why take one and not the other? And if they were trying to frame you, why not leave the phone there, since it points directly to you?

'So another possibility is maybe Mark hid it. And maybe that was to protect himself. Or maybe it was to protect you, Amma. And if that's true, then maybe he hid other things. Maybe he worked on a laptop no one else knew about. Unless the killer got hold of it, it must be somewhere. So think, Amma. Did Mark give you some kind of message, even if you didn't realise it at the time? Did he say anything strange that could have been his way of telling you about a safe space where he would hide his findings?'

Amma shook her head frantically.

'I don't know. I can't think.'

'Was there anywhere of importance to Mark where he might have kept it? Somewhere it would be safe, somewhere you both knew about?'

Amma held her head between her hands.

'I don't know, it's all just, you know… parks and…'

Slowly, she looked up.

'Wait. I think… I think there is a place.'

*

Erin zipped up her jacket as a cold wind rolled over Crays Hill, rattling the leaves on their branches. In the distance, a huge wall of cloud loomed ominously, its belly burned orange by the setting sun.

It was difficult to imagine this place as Amma and Mark must have found it in the height of summer. Bleached grass and blue skies and couples picnicking. Erin followed the directions Amma had given her, heading up the incline, in the direction of the trees, bent forwards to protect herself from the assailing wind.

Eventually the monument emerged into view. A miniature castle on the hillside. Erin walked with effort over the uneven ground until she came directly in front of it. She knelt down and ran her palm over each brick. After a few tries she touched one that rocked gently in its place, having dislodged from the others. Erin felt a wave of excitement and relief. With both hands, she carefully pulled the brick free, revealing the dark, tiny cavern inside.

There was nothing there.

56

LEWIS PACED BACK AND FORTH in one of the smaller meeting rooms, thinking. Why would Gregory search Mark's house without him knowing? He almost wanted to believe it was just a sign of the older detective's arrogance. But deep down he knew it could be something far worse. Gregory was keeping secrets from him. He needed to find out why.

He crossed his arms over his chest. What hadn't he looked at so far? What had he missed? He stared up at the ceiling as if under the intensity of his gaze it might reveal to him. After a few moments, his eyes were drawn to something in the corner. It was the black plastic hood of a small CCTV camera watching him.

He couldn't believe he hadn't thought about it before. Mark's final hours. They'd been recorded right here inside the office. The team had combed through his emails, read his messages and tracked the movements of his car but no one – as far as he was aware – had ever checked to see how the man had behaved when he was actually at work.

He opened the footage of the main office on the day before Mark's murder – Friday 20 August. Officers began trickling in as early as seven o'clock. Then at eight came the main wave of people filtering in and heading for their desks. Lewis's heart jumped when he spotted Mark among them. But instead of sitting at his computer, the detective headed straight towards another bank of desks. He seemed to be speaking to someone who was just out of sight behind their screen. After a moment, the person got up and followed him out of shot.

Lewis switched cameras, searching for one closer to the action. Eventually he found one that gave an almost bird's eye view of Mark and his companion walking down the corridor. He bit his lip, almost drawing blood. It was Gregory. The camera showed them walking together for a few seconds before they disappeared.

His fingers were so jittery with nerves he struggled to hit the buttons on the keyboard as he flicked through cameras, trying to find where the pair had gone to next. Finally, there they were. Mark and Gregory talking one-on-one in an empty room. There was no audio and no way of zooming in. Lewis squinted at the screen. Gregory had his back to the camera so he could only see Mark's face. The man looked more serious than he'd ever seen him. He was talking to Gregory in an urgent manner. As the time passed – the whole conversation couldn't have been longer than several minutes – Mark became more and more agitated, gesticulating aggressively, until he turned around and stormed out of the room. Gregory followed.

There was no doubt about it. They'd had an argument.

He took in a deep breath, then emailed Gregory, asking him if he was free to meet in fifteen minutes' time.

When Gregory appeared, he looked disgruntled, as though he had far better things to be doing than speaking with Lewis.

'What is it?' he said, closing the door behind him.

'I was checking the office CCTV. It looks like you had an argument with Mark on the twentieth of August.'

Gregory blinked at him in surprise.

'What?' he said.

'An argument,' Lewis repeated. 'Do you remember that?'

Gregory's eyes flitted between each of his.

'I wouldn't say we had an *argument*,' he replied.

'Do you remember what you were talking about?'

Gregory smiled slightly. 'Are you interviewing me, Jennings?'

Lewis tried to keep his face expressionless, but inside he was burning. He needed to keep this under control. 'I'm sure you agree we all need to think carefully about the last conversations we had with Mark. In case he said anything that could help us.'

'Yes. Of course. Well, yes, he came to talk to me in quite an agitated state because I had suggested taking officers off his burglary case and onto my investigation. He wasn't happy about it.'

'Right,' said Lewis cautiously.

'Obvious why now, isn't it.'

'How'd you mean?'

'Well, fewer officers on his case, more work for him. Less time to spend with Amma Reynolds.'

'Didn't you think Mark was breaking up with Amma? And that's why she killed him?'

Gregory was silent for a moment.

'Well, maybe it had nothing to do with Amma. Anyway, I don't know what it looks like on the CCTV but it wasn't a big deal, Jennings. Not relevant to the case.' He smiled but his eyes were narrowed with suspicion. 'Why were you looking at the office CCTV anyway? We've done all we can do on the Mark Stormont case now, Lewis.'

Lewis felt a stab of anger.

'Have we?' he said, straightening up. 'Then why are you still sending officers to his house?'

For a moment, shock filled Gregory's face but quickly it shifted into contempt.

'Of course. Her again.'

Lewis felt heat spread up his neck.

'I'm just making sure we have absolutely everything, Lewis,' said Gregory.

'Why wouldn't you tell me something like that? We're working together on this.'

'Maybe because my co-workers keep conspiring with PIs we can't trust?' Gregory shook his head. 'I think you ought to drop this now, Jennings. Save your energy for the trial.' He stormed out of the room, slamming the door shut behind him.

Lewis put a hand on the nearby desk to steady himself. He felt faintly sick. Could that be true? Had Gregory really just kept that a secret because of his friendship with Erin? He tried to shake away the thought.

He needed to call Erin. Tell her what he'd found.

*

Erin scanned the road outside the kitchen window, holding the phone to her ear.

'And Gregory hasn't mentioned this argument to anyone?'

'No. What do you think?' said Lewis.

'You know what I think. I think he's hiding something.'

'Yeah, I was worried you'd say that.' He paused. 'I've been thinking about what Tom said. What is it he would know?'

Erin pinched the bridge of her nose in frustration. 'He doesn't know anything, Lewis. Forget about him.'

'I know what you think. But just listen for a second. Tom was here before either of us. He knew Gregory in the early days. What if he had suspicions about Isaac's case as well?'

Erin filled up the kettle and slammed it aggressively onto its base, hitting the switch.

'I feel like you have to see him.'

Erin returned to the sink and stared out the window, bracing her hands against the edge of the kitchen sink. 'No. That's a line I won't cross.'

'Erin, if I could do this for you I would but he's said it has to be you.'

The roar of the kettle filled the kitchen.

'You care about Amma, right?'

'Obviously.'

'Then do it for her.'

57

Friday

THE FOLLOWING DAY, ERIN LIFTED her arms up to shoulder-height so the prison guard could search her, suppressing a shiver of discomfort as his hands skimmed her sides, feeling for contraband.

While the guard patted her down, she stared over his shoulder through the white-painted bars into the airless corridor with cream-coloured walls, and felt as though she were staring down the barrel of a gun.

There was no sound in the corridor apart from the jangle of the prison guard's keys at his waist and that of their footsteps clicking over the linoleum. He took her to the visitors' room. It was largely empty. The prison guard led her to a pair of empty chairs in the middle of the room.

He turned to her.

'You can touch him at the beginning and the end,' he said. 'But not during.'

Erin blinked at him in surprise. The prospect made her feel slightly sick. She nodded.

She sat herself down and waited. The room was poorly ventilated and the stuffiness only added to her sense of nausea. Somewhere in the room, someone's wife or girlfriend was crying quietly.

Out of the corner of her eye, she saw the door to the hall open. A figure she half-recognised entered, accompanied by a prison guard. Together they started walking towards her. The side of her facing the oncomers started burning.

Erin stared at the floor as the man took a seat opposite her. She let her gaze rise up.

For the first time in two years, Tom Radley locked eyes with her.

58

HE LOOKED NOTHING LIKE THE man of her nightmares, nor her dreams. He was thinner, paler. But his eyes ate her up hungrily. Just being in the same room as him made every muscle in Erin's body feel tense. Already she wanted nothing more than to get away.

'Just tell me what you know,' she said.

'I think, after everything, you at least owe me a "hello".'

'You weren't part of the investigation into Isaac Reynolds' death. So why would you know any more about it than I do?'

'Because I was there early on. I remember his poor mum coming in every week. Asking for updates. Asking them to reopen the case. I remember how she was treated like an irritant. Detectives rolling their eyes every time she came in. They just couldn't wait to bat her off, send her on her way.

'When Amma started her campaign, they were intimidated. They literally sent out uniforms to watch those protests. There were concerns about emotions running high, as though it was all going to boil over. Which it inevitably did when Amma clashed with that police officer.'

'None of that surprises me. What do you actually know?'

Her dismissive tone didn't register well with him. His mouth twitched slightly.

'He was watching her, wasn't he?' he said.

She hadn't expected him to say that. Her pulse quickened.

'Yes.'

She waited for him to say more, but he just stared at her without blinking.

'I'm not going to just tell you, Erin.'

She clenched her teeth.

'What do you want?'

'I want a reduced sentence.'

Erin thought she'd misheard him.

'What?'

'I want several years off my current sentence in exchange for information.'

Rage burned hot underneath her skin.

She tried to keep her voice controlled. 'I can't do anything about your sentence. You know I can't. I'm not even in the police any more.'

'You're obviously still in contact with them all. You'll need to persuade them to make the arrangement with me. If they act on the information I have, then the court can decide if they want to uphold it and grant me a reduction.'

'What if you're lying?'

'If the police don't act, and the court doesn't allow it, then there's no reduction. Nothing changes.'

A reduction. Usually if a criminal wanted one, they would apply before the sentencing. She had no idea what the process was now that he was in prison. How many years could be taken off? She imagined Tom strolling out of here in a matter of years, smug and content, and felt panic flood her mind. No, she couldn't allow that. Not after everything Sophie Madson had been through. Everything she'd been through.

She knew now why he'd wanted her here and not Lewis. To hurt her. He had no power any more. He was going to use anything he had over her as best as he could.

She continued: 'You made a real mistake thinking I would help you.'

'I fucked up. I took someone's life. But I'm not a predator. I'm not a danger to society. A shorter sentence is fair. It's proportionate.'

'I'm not playing your games any more.'

Tom looked confused.

'I'm not playing a game. This is a gift. I could have chosen to say nothing. Instead I'm helping you.' After a pause he added, 'There is something else I want as well. You're allowed two visits a month, in case you were wondering. You can write as many letters as you want though. You can't call me but I can call you.'

Her hand clenched in her lap. 'Are you serious?'

He held her gaze steadily.

'You really think I want to see you?'

'There are things holding us together, Erin. Always will be. You can't deny that.'

Erin was stunned. She leant forward.

'If I come here, then all you are ever going to get is a woman who hates you staring at you like the worthless piece of shit you are. Is that really what you want?'

Tom's upper lip twitched.

She'd had enough of this. It was time to go.

But before she'd even stood up, Tom said, 'I'm asking you, Erin, because you're the one who can't afford to say no.'

Erin felt her blood run cold. 'What are you talking about?'

Tom smiled. 'Two visits per month. I'll save the next one for you.'

59

Erin let out a single deep breath as she slammed the car door shut behind her, grateful to be out of the prison. Glancing out of the window, she took one final look at its threatening exterior. Even now, she had the horrible sensation that Tom was still watching her, as if his gaze could penetrate through brick and mortar. Their encounter had left her feeling unclean, like there was a coating over her skin that she needed to scrub away as soon as she got to the flat.

Desperate to hear a comforting voice, she called Lewis.

'You saw him? Well, what did he say?' he asked cautiously.

'Arrogant bastard wants a sentence reduction in exchange for information about Isaac's death,' she said through gritted teeth.

'What if he's telling the truth and he does know something? That could be huge.'

The excitement in Lewis's voice only added to her anger. With her free hand she nursed her overheated forehead.

'He's just trying his luck, Lewis. I guarantee.'

'I have to approach the super about this. We can't afford to ignore it.'

'He's lying, Lewis.' She swallowed. 'He did say something strange though.'

'What?'

'He knew Mark Stormont was watching Amma.'

'Really? How would we know that? There's no way he could have found that out while he was inside.'

'I know,' said Erin, chewing the inside of her mouth. She shook her head. 'What could he possibly share with us that will help, though? He's not going to have anything concrete for us.'

'He could have a lead. Come on, we have to find out what he knows.'

'You can if you want,' Erin snapped. 'I'm not doing that again.'

'Erin, can you take a good look at your priorities right now? If Isaac was murdered, then whoever did it is still out there. They could be reoffending right now. A couple of years off Tom's sentence isn't going to make much difference. Being completely honest, I don't think…'

He trailed off. But Erin could sense what he'd been about to say. Anger pulsed through her.

'Say it.'

'I don't think he's a danger to the public.'

'Are you serious?'

'I just don't think he would reoffend.'

'You sure about that? Don't think he'd feel tempted to come after us and smash our heads in with a hammer?'

'He's not going to *kill us*, Erin, Jesus Christ.'

'How do you know?'

She knew she was being hyperbolic but she hated how easily Lewis had bought into Tom's game. This whole ordeal – her being here right now in a prison car park – felt like a total distraction from the investigation.

'I know it's hard,' said Lewis, 'but keep thinking about Amma. Surely it's worth meeting him again just in case?'

After they'd said their goodbyes she looked out the window and ran her fingers through her hair in frustration, processing the possibility of having to revisit Tom and put herself through this all over again. Deep down, she knew Lewis was right.

Perhaps Tom was lying. But right now they had few options other than to do what he said.

60

SHE GOT BACK LATER THAN expected. The evening light cast the street in a deep blue wash. She pushed open the front door and placed the keys on the side, pleased to be back in this place that had become her home for the last fortnight. But she was running late. Amma was supposed to call her this evening. She checked her phone and saw it was just past 6 p.m. She already had a missed call. She cursed under her breath. Hopefully Amma would call again.

Taking off her shoes, she went through to the kitchen and started cooking dinner. It was as the onions were frying on the stove that her phone rang for a second time. She switched off the hob, abandoned the pan and picked up.

An automated message said: 'This call is from a person currently in a prison in England/Wales. All calls are logged and recorded and may be listened to by a member of Prison staff. If you do not wish to accept this call, please hang up now.'

Then Amma answered. 'Erin,' she said, her voice breathless with desperation.

'What's wrong?'

'I remember,' said Amma. 'I remember who I saw that night. I remember what they said.'

Earlier that day

Sitting at the small desk inside her cell, Amma pressed her fingers to her temples, trying to think. Each of the three days she'd spent in prison had passed her by in a heavy fog. But Erin's visit yesterday had jolted her awake. She had to try and remember what had happened that night, before Mark was killed.

Erin was right. Someone had tried to frame her. Someone who knew where she lived and who had possibly even spiked her drink the night before. She recalled shuffling along in the club's queue next to Neil and June, hovering on the edge of their conversation, too wrapped up in thoughts of Mark to fully engage with either of them. She remembered the bouncer stamping the back of her hand. The fumes emanating from the smoke machine, disguising the smell of sweat. The figures dancing in the half-darkness.

And then it hit her.

*

Amma ran her fingernails through her hair, over her scalp. The music swelled through her. Mark's eyes found hers. The blue light illuminated half of his body and face. The other side was cast in shadow. Longing yawned inside her. She blinked and he was gone.

She bent her head to June's ear.

'I'm going to get some air.'

'I'll come with you.'

'No, I need a second.'

June frowned. 'Okay. We'll meet you at the bar in ten minutes.'

Amma nodded and slipped away. She drifted through the smiling, dancing people towards the exit. It was strange how unfathomably lonely this space full of people had suddenly become. The lights in the bar cast lurid green shapes over people's faces. As she squeezed through the crowd, Amma felt the unbridled stares of the bug-eyed men she passed boring into her skin. A heavy-set bouncer stayed deliberately and rigidly still beside the doorway so she had to brush past him on her way back into the club. A shiver of discomfort crept over her shoulders.

Finally she emerged into the smoking area, where she hugged her bare arms and took in several deep breaths. A couple nearby were entangled in a deep kiss, eyes closed, oblivious to the world around them. Amma ducked back inside.

The club was even more crowded now. Smoke gathered over the heads of the dancers, moving in a demonic red light that pulsed in time with a hypnotic dance track. Amma pushed into the crowd. Dancers spun around, raised elbows over heads, turned their backs to her, crouched low to the ground. They had to be here. She'd looked almost everywhere by this point. There was nowhere else they could be. An especially drunk man with a tattoo of a dreamcatcher on his neck stepped backwards, directly onto her foot. Gritting her teeth, she moved deeper into the crowd, ignoring the apology he shouted at her, towards the DJ at the front, and checked her phone. 00:36. If she couldn't find them in the next ten minutes, she was going home.

Then she saw Aaron. She spotted him, six foot three, looming over the other dancers close to the stage, his bald head rocking in time with the music. She hadn't seen him in months, not since the last London march. Relief washed over her. She wove her way through to him. Still rocking from side to side, he smiled calmly down at her.

'I'm so glad you're here,' she shouted.

'You too.'

'I've lost Neil and June.'

'What?'

'I've lost Neil and June.'

'What?'

'Never mind.'

Aaron said something back that she didn't hear.

'What?'

He spoke again.

'I'm sorry, I can't hear!'

They started dancing side by side. Amma let herself ease into the rhythm. She needed this. Music, movement and someone she knew. She needed this to calm down and shake off everything, forget about Mark completely.

Aaron gently danced closer. Then he stopped dancing altogether. He stood right in front of her, barely an inch between them. Amma smiled politely, dialling down the energy of her dancing. Panic rose in her stomach. Not now. She was too worked up to deal with this. If he made a move she was worried what she might say, and what it would take to undo in the morning.

He said something that was lost in the noise of the dance floor.

'I can't hear you.'

He leant in.

This time Amma heard what he said.

'It was over quickly,' he said. His words were slurred.

'What?'

'It was over quickly.'

His eyes were cloudy with drink and desperately sad.

She pulled back sharply. Then she screamed. She pushed him hard in the chest. Aaron took a step back but otherwise gave no sign he had felt a thing. She lunged forward again, this time gripping him by the front of his hoodie. Someone behind him dropped their drink and droplets of the cold liquid splattered across her bare legs.

'What the fuck did you say? What the fuck did you just say?'

In that moment a hand appeared on Aaron's shoulder. Two more landed on Amma's arms. She continued to scream as they were pulled apart from each other.

Neil spun her around. His eyes were wide with fear. Still grabbing one of Amma's arms, he led her out of the crowd. Amma watched as tall Aaron, tended by the rest of his group, became a smaller and smaller figure, his red hoody and bald head distinguishing him from the rest of the clubbers, who continued to dance in their self-absorbed shuffles until they eventually swallowed him up.

The cool air hit her in the face when they emerged into the smoking area. Amma gulped it in, tears streaming down her cheeks.

What did Aaron mean? All she could think about was Isaac.

Neil led her to the black-painted brick wall of the club, which Amma pressed her back against, shivering uncontrollably.

'It was him. It was him.'

A lanky man with incredibly large pupils wandered over. 'Is she okay?' he asked Neil.

'We're fine, we're fine,' said Neil, waving him away.

Amma rocked back and forth, hugging herself.

'I'm going to get June out here, okay, Amma? Then we'll get you a taxi.'

'It was him! It was Aaron. I could see it. I could see it in his face.'

'I don't know what you mean, Amma.'

'Believe me! Please.'

Neil stared at her helplessly, not understanding.

'We'll get you home,' he said.

He opened his arms. Amma fell into them, sinking into his embrace, hiding her face in her friend's shoulder. But her eyes remained fully open.

She knew what she'd heard.

61

Saturday

'WHAT DID YOU MEAN WHEN you told Amma, "It was over quickly"?'

Erin had texted Aaron first thing the next day and driven to London, meeting him that afternoon in a café not far from his office.

Aaron shrugged. 'I don't know.'

'You don't remember what you said that made her push you and scream at you?'

'No.'

'I think I'd remember that. I think I'd be racking my brains after something like that, trying to work out what made my friend lose it.'

Aaron rolled his neck to one side dismissively. He wasn't scared. That was what angered Erin the most. He looked bored.

'Maybe I'm thicker than you think,' he said.

'Go on then.'

'What?'

'Rack your brains now. What might you have meant by "It was over quickly"?'

Aaron scratched his right shoulder nonchalantly. 'She was saying she hadn't seen me in ages. Since the last march. So I suppose I might have said that the march was over quickly. As in, we didn't get to see much of each other.'

Erin allowed a few moments of silence to pass before she spoke again.

'So you remember exactly what she said to you, but you can't remember for sure how you responded?'

'I'd had about five pints by then, bear in mind.'

'Do you care that you upset Amma?'

'Of course. Just, you know, I haven't done anything, have I?'

It was late by the time she headed back to Wakestead. She'd gotten the train to the station and rather than bus to the Airbnb, she'd decided to take a shortcut through the park. But the gate was locked. Probably the council closed it for the night. There was no getting in any other way; the brick wall surrounding the park was tall enough that most people would need a stepladder to have any chance of scaling it.

She turned away and walked only a few steps before coming to a stop, because a chill had spread over her entire body.

The following morning, she dialled the council the moment their phone lines opened.

The man on the other end of the council's telephone line sounded bemused.

'The park?' he said.

She couldn't hide the urgency in her voice.

'Yes,' she said, breathing fast. 'What time do you open and close it?'

'Let me find out for you. One moment.'

Erin waited in agony, pacing the kitchen, as the council's cheery hold-music played for the second time.

After half a minute or so, the voice returned. 'Sorry for the wait. We open it at seven o'clock every morning, and we close it at ten at night.'

'Ten at night?' she said. 'Has it always been that time?'

'Yes,' he replied. 'As far as I know, it's never changed.'

'Thank you,' Erin breathed. 'Thank you so much.'

'You're welcome,' said the man, sounding confused.

As soon as she hung up, she called Lewis.
'What's up?' said Lewis.
'Lewis. It's Aaron. He lied.'

62

'NO COMMENT.'

Jesus Christ. Not this again.

Aaron sat opposite Lewis with his arms firmly crossed, in a huge white hoodie that against the bleak backdrop of the interview room almost resembled a straitjacket. They had brought him in as soon as they could after Erin's phone call. The tightness in his body language was the only sign of his discomfort. Otherwise, he looked unfazed – his eyebrows arched in arrogant disdain.

'Why did you say you walked across the park on the night of Isaac's disappearance, when the park closes at ten o'clock?' said Lewis.

'I must have mis-remembered.'

'That was the account you gave not just to Erin Crane, but also to police investigators after he went missing. So, within days, you had forgotten how you walked home that night?'

'I'd had a couple of drinks.'

'Enough drinks to forget the route you take home?'

'I go round the park when it's shut.'

Lewis's hand clenched under the table.

'Did you misremember,' he said, 'or did you in fact go through the park? Did you leave the bonfire before ten o'clock?'

'No.'

'Here's what I think. I think you left at the same time Isaac left.'

'That's not what happened.'

'Then what happened?'

'I went home with Jack. We didn't see Isaac. Not once.'

Lewis stepped out into the corridor for a breather. His mind was racing. If Amma was telling Erin the truth and Aaron really had said that to her the night before Mark died, then that seemed like a confession in itself. And now it turned out he'd lied about, or 'misremembered', the time he got home on the night Isaac died. On top of this, the story about his sister's photos gave him a motive. Was it enough to get him charged? He feared not. But he was now convinced Aaron must have had something to do with the teenager's death.

He pushed into the observation room where he'd left a flask of tea. His heart jolted when he saw Gregory waiting there, watching Aaron through the one-way mirror. The older detective jumped when Lewis came in.

'Good work, Jennings,' he said quickly.

'Do you know how that got missed?'

Gregory shook his head. 'Jesus, no. No, I asked the officers to check out the boys' timelines. Whoever checked Aaron's obviously didn't do a good job.'

His voice sounded strained.

'There was nothing about Aaron that seemed suspicious at the time?'

Gregory shook his head. There was a faraway look in his eyes and his mouth was closed tightly.

'I'll ask the team to go through everything they have on him again,' said Lewis.

'Yes,' Gregory said. 'Yes, I'll do that now, in fact.' He shook himself out of his trance, slipping past Lewis and out of the room.

As soon as he was alone, Lewis rolled his shoulders, shaking out the tension that had built up in his body. He checked his phone. Almost time.

At one o'clock, his phone started ringing. He took a deep breath before he picked up.

'Hi Lewis,' came a voice.

'Tom,' said Lewis. 'The CPS has agreed to grant you a four-year reduction in your sentence, provided the information helps us convict someone for Isaac's murder.'

Down the other end of the line, Tom let out a quiet sigh of relief.

'Thanks, mate.'

Lewis's skin prickled with discomfort.

'I really hope it helps you find the person responsible,' Tom added.

Lewis cleared his throat. 'So, what can you tell us?'

'There was another condition to this, if that's all right, Lewis.'

63

THIS TIME TOM WAS ALREADY waiting for her in the visitors' room. He seemed more energetic than he had during her first visit two days ago. He leant forward in his plastic seat as if he was ready to spring up at any moment. Erin hated the small smile he gave her as she sat down opposite him.

'Four years,' she said. 'This better be good.'

Tom's eyes narrowed. 'You really think four years will make a huge difference to me?'

Erin ignored him. The sooner she got this over with, the better. 'So let's have it then.'

'You know I always put in the hours with the seniors on the team. Sometimes they told me things they shouldn't have done. Things they didn't tell anyone else.

'It must have been several months before the start of the Madson case. A few of us were in the pub til late. Peters had had a few. You know he wasn't usually much of a talker. But this time he was talking.

'After the assault, the superintendent signed off on a heightened police presence at any protests associated with the justice campaign. They agreed it was necessary to carry out covert surveillance of Amma Reynolds. They were concerned she and her peers were using these protests to incite violence against the police.'

Erin chewed her lip. 'Covert surveillance,' she repeated. 'What does that mean? In practice?'

'I don't know. Something like this would have had to get sign-off from the very top. It depends where they drew the line. It could mean covert recording, phone tapping, going undercover.'

'That's why Mark came across from the Met. Specifically for this job.'

'It's possible. That's what I was thinking. As soon as I saw his background and heard who the suspect was.'

'Why would they hide this?'

'You know why. They can't afford another scandal. It's reputation management.'

Erin's eyes searched the floor. 'But… but this changes everything. Amma's defence is entitled to that information. If she or someone she knew killed him then this could count as mitigating circumstances. He was stalking her.' She looked up at Tom. 'You'd say this in court then?'

'Yes,' he replied. 'As long as all my conditions are met.'

'All your conditions? What do you—'

Erin had almost forgotten. Then she remembered.

'Those visits? Not happening. No way.'

Tom clenched his jaw. He wiped his hands over his face, restless.

'Do you realise how long it's taken for me to forgive you?' he snarled.

Erin couldn't believe what she was hearing.

'For the past two years, I couldn't believe what you'd done to me. And finally I decide that it would be better to just help you, to be involved in your life in some way. And this is how you repay me? You owe it to me—'

'You think you could scare me into seeing me every fortnight for the next however many years?' Erin snapped. 'After this, you'll never see me again.'

Tom bared his teeth. Rage filled his eyes. 'You don't get to hide from me. You don't get to ignore me. You don't get to just forget and move on.'

'Never again. That's enough.'

'That's your final decision? Don't want time to think about it?'

Erin shook her head.

Tom sat back. He relaxed his shoulders.

'I just want you to know, when you realise,' he said, 'that this is what you've chosen. It didn't have to be this way.' He studied the ceiling. 'But hopefully the people in your life can forgive you for it, right? Hopefully Amma's parents will understand.'

His words hung in the air. A spike of terror went through her.

'What have you done?'

'Someone's been asking about you, Erin.'

'Who has?'

'You took everything from me. It's only right I take something from you now. You're never going to get away from me.'

64

ERIN'S MIND RACED ALL THE way back to the flat. Once inside, she dropped her bag beside the front door and dived into the bathroom, where she bent over the sink and splashed cold water on her face. Tom's words repeated in her mind.

Someone's been asking about you, Erin.

Who? Who could have been asking about her? Was it a bluff?

She looked down at her pale hands holding the sink basin, her fingers trembling slightly, her veins gleaming blue under the delicate skin. Why hadn't she been more careful? Tom knew things she'd never admitted to anyone else. Things that could definitely harm her. She thought of Lewis and felt a jolt of anger. All along she'd insisted meeting him was too big a risk. She should never have ingored her better judgement.

For a long moment she stayed there in the cool room, trying to steady her breathing.

Then her phone buzzed.

She took it out of her pocket and checked the screen. It was a news alert. A story that had been published just an hour ago.

Her heart plunged into her stomach.

This was it. This was what Tom had meant.

Private investigator concealed romantic relationship with Sophie Madson's killer

Erin Crane, the private investigator known for solving the murder of teenager Sophie Madson, concealed a romantic relationship with former partner and convicted murderer Tom Radley.

A source told the Examiner *that Ms Crane and Mr Radley hid their relationship from the force during the investigation and continued to see each other privately following Mr Radley's arrest.*

Text messages shared with the Examiner *show that while Mr Radley was on bail conditions he met with Erin Crane, who at the time was investigating Ms Madson's murder.*

Photographs and letters confirm that Mr Radley and Ms Crane have remained in contact since he was charged two years ago. He is currently serving a twenty-two year sentence in Bullingdon Prison.

65

THE SOUND OF THE CAFÉ door opening signalled Alex's arrival. From the corner of the room came the familiar sound of the barista bashing coffee grinds into the disposal unit. Erin looked up as Alex sat down opposite her, sliding off his dark coat. There was a look of strange apprehension in his face that told Erin he knew what was about to come. That only made her angrier. He knew what he had done.

'How did you get that story?'

'An anonymous tip-off,' he said.

'Then how do you know it's true?'

'Because they gave us photographs of you visiting the prison. Letters.'

'Those are private.'

He shrugged. 'You're working on a high-profile murder case. We decided it's in the public interest.'

'I don't care. Who told you?'

'I can't tell you.'

His evasive response didn't surprise her. But his cold tone did. She felt as though it was an entirely different man sat in front of her to the person she'd met before.

'This is a murder investigation. And you know something that could help solve it. So help me. Did you approach them or did they approach you?'

'They approached me.'

'Did they identify themselves?'

'No. It was sent in a letter.'

'And who do you think it was who sent this? Who would have been close enough to me to know about—'

'A friend.'

'You think one of my close friends has betrayed me and gone to the press, that's what you're saying? You're an intelligent person. Don't lie to me. Who do you think sent this to you?'

Alex was grey in the face. In a low voice he said, 'It could have been a police officer.'

'And that didn't concern you?'

'Of course it's concerning. But I had no way of proving it. It might not even be true.'

Erin narrowed her eyes. 'Are you lying? Do you know this person? Do you have a relationship with them?'

'No. I don't know who it is.'

Erin's blood ran red-hot through her body. 'Did it ever occur to you,' she said, 'that it might be in the interest of the killer to discredit me like this?'

Alex said nothing.

Erin leant forward. 'Here's a scoop for you. I think Amma's being framed. And I think the police know about it. Possibly even orchestrated it. How about you print that?' She got to her feet. 'Only you won't, will you? Because that's not such an easy win, is it?'

'It wasn't my choice to cover this story.'

'You could've said no. So yes, it was.'

Her shaky legs carried her out of the café and into the busy street, towards her car. She tugged up her scarf to cover the lower part of her face, suddenly covinced that every passer-by was staring at her, recognising her from the story.

Her phone started ringing. The street pulled in and out of focus as she read the name on the screen. She took in a deep breath before answering.

'Vicky.'

'Erin,' she said. 'I've seen the story.' Her usually warm voice was filled with reproach. 'It's your private life, and this must be hard for you,' she continued, 'but something like this… we can't ignore it.'

'Look, it's true,' said Erin breathlessly. 'I didn't know. I didn't know what he was. If I had known, I never would have gotten involved with him.'

Down the other end of the line, she heard Vicky take in a deep, shaky breath. Erin dug her nails into her palm. *Please no*, she thought.

'I just don't know what to make of this. It's made us question your judgement. And your honesty. I mean… you never told anyone. During the whole trial over Sophie Madson's murder, you didn't say a thing.'

The incredulity in her voice made Erin flinch.

'We're going to need to step back.'

'Think about why this is coming out now. I made a mistake. But Tom Radley's getting it out there in order to punish me. And he didn't do that on his own. He had help. Help from someone who wants to discredit me. Who wants me off this case.'

'Don't bring my daughter into this.'

'I can work this out,' she said. 'Please. I can save her. I'm close.'

'I'm sorry, Erin. Please don't talk to our daughter again.'

Vicky hung up.

Her phone rang a second time when she was walking along the river, back to the Airbnb. Erin felt faintly sick seeing Maia Andrei's name on the screen. Maia, one of the survivors in the Madson case. Who'd encountered Sophie's abuser in her past life as a sex worker, nearly dying by his hands. Ever since the case had finished, she and Erin had maintained a close relationship. Not you too, thought Erin.

'Hey Maia,' she said, coming to a stop beside the water, rubbing her forehead in agitation. 'Is this about the story?'

'It is,' said Maia. 'I'm very confused.'

There it was again. That same mistrust that had run through Vicky's voice.

'Why didn't you tell me?'

A couple of waterbirds were drifting slowly out from the reeds, creating a dark bend in the river. Erin felt tears well in her eyes.

'I – I was ashamed,' she said. She had never fully grasped this idea until now but she realised as soon as she said it how true it was.

'Did you know?' Maia asked.

Horror flooded Erin's chest. She bent forward. 'No,' she said desperately. 'I swear, no, no, I didn't know what he did, Maia.'

For several long excruciating moments Maia said nothing.

Then she said, 'I'm sorry. This must be horrible for you. But I'm finding it hard to comprehend this. I just don't understand how you couldn't see what he really was.'

The shudder of a suppressed sob went through Erin. She wanted to cry. But she couldn't bear the thought of Maia having to listen to her self-pitying tears, after all this.

'I don't know either,' she said. 'I don't know.'

'Even after he was arrested,' she said. 'Is that true? That's what the story said. You went to him.'

Erin swallowed. Her throat hurt. 'I got it wrong.'

'And after all that, you still see him,' she said.

'I had to see him for this case,' said Erin. 'I swear. I hate him now. But I – I had to see him because he knows something about the case I'm working on. I didn't want to, I promise.'

It sounded ridiculous. It sounded like she was lying.

Maia didn't say anything.

'Maia?'

She looked at her phone screen. Maia had hung up.

Erin held her hand to her mouth and now released the sob she'd been holding in, feeling all the humiliation and fear spill out of her. Only once it was out did she feel her breathing begin to slow. She listened to the quiet sounds of the river and the birds. And slowly she felt her sorrow turn to anger.

She'd been on her way home. But there was somewhere else she decided she needed to be.

*

Lewis, looking unfamiliar in his casual clothes, opened the door. His mouth opened slightly in surprise as he registered who it was.

Erin stepped forward and punched him in the face. Her knuckle hummed with pain as it connected with the bridge of his nose. She had lashed out clumsily but the blow was strong enough to daze him. She watched his eyes swim as he stumbled back, raising a hand to his face. She advanced into the house.

'It was you. It could only have been you.'

'What the fuck is wrong with you?'

'You knew what that would do to me.'

'It wasn't me, Erin!'

'That story couldn't have just come from Tom. Alex Spencer had other sources. It could only have been you.'

'I didn't speak to Alex Spencer!'

'Then who did?'

Lewis squinted at her, still clutching his nose. 'Some of the force know.'

She bared her teeth. 'Oh, yeah, things have changed so much, haven't they? Still all you lot can think about is who's shagging who. And you were only too happy to finally have some gossip so you could rub shoulders with the other detectives.'

'That isn't what it was like – people asked, and I just – it wasn't deliberate – I'm sorry, Erin.'

'Do you realise what this has done? No one will see past this.'

'Well, maybe people need to know the truth. They're right. You trusted him. You got it wrong.'

'We both trusted him. It was your idea I see him. You who went and visited him in the first place.'

She grabbed him by the front of his t-shirt and pushed him up against the wall. His body felt slim and limp. He wasn't going to fight back. Eyes wide with shock, Lewis breathed heavily in her face.

'You're weak,' she hissed. 'You always were.'

She released him and swung out of the house.

66

'AMMA. YOU HAVE A VISITOR.'

Amma pulled on her shoes and followed the warden out of the cell. The sound of their footsteps alerted one of her louder neighbours. From her cell the woman started shouting incoherently, as she always did when there was noise, as she did sometimes at two in the morning, as if to remind herself and others that she was here, still here and alive.

Amma hadn't yet adjusted to the sounds that drifted out of each cell and down the corridor. The metallic clang of barred doors opening and closing. The shouting. The crying.

The warden led her to the visitors' room. Her mum came by as often as she could and it was her she'd expected to find waiting there. Her heart jumped when she saw Olivia sat like a pale ghost in the unlit room.

She looked hilariously out of place in an expensive-looking cardigan with a beautiful green scarf wrapped around her neck.

Amma imagined she must have stopped here on her way to work. She slowly lowered herself into the opposite seat.

'Hello,' she said.

Something about Olivia was different. She'd only ever seen the woman's eyes filled with hatred and grief. Now she just looked tired.

'I came here to give you something.'

Olivia unfurled the scarf from her neck and held it out to her.

Amma blinked at her in confusion, trying to work out what was going on.

'Please take it,' said Olivia.

Cautiously, Amma took the scarf. As she did, Olivia's hand touched hers, placing in it something small that was concealed inside the material. Amma tried very hard to stop her face betraying any emotion. Bringing the scarf into her lap, she glanced down and felt a rush of adrenaline when she saw what was inside the green folds. It was a Dictaphone.

'When Erin asked about hiding places, I remembered seeing you two at that monument,' said Olivia, speaking quietly now. 'I went back and found this there. I knew I should have left it there and called the police. But I couldn't help myself. I wanted to hear his voice. The last message – the one I heard – is for you.'

Amma felt her heart swell with longing. His voice. Captured here on this device. She suddenly felt his presence in the room, a fleeting impression of vitality.

Olivia was staring at the scarf in her lap with a pained expression.

'I knew it was too soon for him,' she murmured. 'We were young and I wanted to get married and he wanted to wait. But I didn't care. I couldn't stand to think he wasn't feeling what I was feeling. And I think it continued that way for a while, looking back. I ignored his unhappiness.

'I didn't know him in those final months. You did. I don't think I'll ever forgive him for what he did to me. But I will accept that what we had was over. I should have let him go a long time ago.

'I'm sorry I didn't believe you,' she said calmly. 'I wish I'd been strong enough to. But I wasn't. I wanted to hold on to him forever if I could.'

The cold seeped through the prison walls.

'I lost everything I had come to rely upon very quickly. That's all I can say in my defence.'

Amma shook her head. 'I understand.' And she did. Noticing the guilty tears in the other woman's eyes, she said, 'It's not your fault.'

Olivia blinked away her tears. To Amma's surprise, the woman suddenly reached out and gripped her arm.

'Get yourself out of here.'

It was quiet in the prison library. There were just two tables in the middle of the room, one of them occupied by a woman sat reading, fully immersed, with her unwashed hair falling in curtains down onto the pages of the open book. Desperate for some privacy, Amma went behind one of the bookshelves. Without thinking, she allowed her body to slump down against the shelf until she was sat on the floor. She cradled the Dictaphone in one hand, running a thumb over its buttons. Then she pushed her headphones into her ears. She wanted to listen to the recording in as quiet a space as she could, with the volume up high, so his voice could ring aloud, as it would if he were right there speaking with her.

She pressed the play button. For a few seconds nothing happened.

Then he said, 'Amma.'

The world outside faded to white.

'I'd better keep this quick. I'll limit it to three things.'

She had almost forgotten what he sounded like. Specific phrases had stayed lodged in her mind – the way he said hello, the precious things that she had decided as soon as he uttered them to commit to memory – but she had never been able to conjure the natural cadence of his voice. She clutched the device in her hand, willing this past version of Mark to speak for hours and hours.

'The first thing. I'm sorry. I'm so, so sorry.

'The second thing. I think I know who did it.

'The third. They are watching you. The police. They've always been watching.'

67

THERE WAS A SOFT CRACKLING noise in the background. Wind. Amma imagined Mark circling the field, speaking into the Dictaphone, which he would afterwards place in its hiding spot inside the monument.

'I want to say all of this to your face. But I don't know if that's going to happen now. So here goes… I made a mistake, Amma. I – I fucked up from the very first moment I first met you. That night wasn't a coincidence. I didn't just happen to be out the same night as you. I was following you. I'm a police officer.'

Amma put her head in her hands.

'I used to work for the Met. There I sometimes carried out surveillance operations. When I came here, they put me in charge of monitoring—'

Here he stopped. There was no sound other than the wind whistling in the background while he gathered his breath.

'Monitoring the justice campaign you and your family set up.'

It was true. Amma started to rock back and forth on the balls of her feet.

'We put a tracking device in your car. We put a recording device in your house and in your parents' house. And when we saw you were meeting Emmanuel or any other member of the group, we followed you.

'That night I followed you. I was never supposed to make contact. I told my manager, DCI Martyn Gregory, thinking I would be dropped from the surveillance team. But he – he said I should get to know you. Record conversations. Find out more about the campaign group. About you.

'I should have told you everything from the start. But I lied. And I told myself the lie was harmless because every time… every time I saw you, I thought it would be the last time. It wasn't supposed to ever get this far.

'There's no excuse for what I've done. It was despicable what I did to you. But I want you to understand what was going through my head at that time. And honestly, I was – I was so disconnected from myself. I was waking up every day next to a woman I no longer loved. I was turning up at work and doing this surveillance job just because they told me to. Even though I knew none of you posed a threat to anyone. Lying had become second nature.

'You were right, Amma. There's something not right about your brother's case. They're hiding something. To get covert surveillance signed off, the most senior staff need to be on board. The case for monitoring the justice group was made before I came in. But I know they argued it was necessary because of the clash you had with officers in London. They argued the group was trying to incite violence against the police.

'Even if you hate me forever, the one thing I can do is help you expose what they've been doing to your family. There's a file before this one. Listen to it. Listen to it and then get it to a lawyer or a journalist or an investigator. Someone not in the police. It should answer some questions.'

Amma could hear her blood roaring in her ears.

'It's up to you if you want to involve me, Amma. I leave it entirely in your hands.'

Amma clicked through to the next file and hit play.

It took a few moments for her to realise what she was listening to.

This was it. This was the thing that would make it all blow up.

68

Tuesday

For the next two days, Erin hardly left the Airbnb. She couldn't bear the idea of seeing anyone she knew. The shock of the news story had left her feeling ill – heavy-limbed and foggy-brained. She moved as slowly and as infrequently as she could, leaving her bed only to force down some food or make a cup of tea, before returning to Isaac's case file, scrolling over the documents she'd read a million times in the hope something new would emerge, something that could help her strengthen the case against Aaron. But the words in the documents had dissolved into a meaningless sea.

When she heard someone knocking on the front door, before answering she went to the living room and peered through the window, trying to catch a glimpse of the visitor. Realising who it was, she drew in a sharp, anxious breath.

The letterbox squeaked as Alex pushed it open to call into the house: 'Erin. I understand you ignoring me. But please. It's important.'

'Fuck off,' Erin muttered to herself, stepping back into the middle of the living room.

She was planning to wait there until she heard Alex turn around and depart down the garden path. But then a nagging thought occurred to her.

What if he'd received another letter? One that could help them implicate one of the police officers.

She forced herself to go into the corridor and open the door.

He looked as shocked as she felt to find herself there. Erin could tell he was trying to conceal his delight.

'I'm a knob,' he said.

Erin felt her eyebrow arch up in disdain.

He continued, 'I'm an absolute piece of shit. I'm the dirt underneath your shoe.'

She mentally prepared herself to shut the door.

'Look, I am here to apologise. But I'm also here because I have an idea.'

'They won't like this,' said Erin. 'I'll be burning bridges with them completely.'

'Fuck them. If you're right, then that bridge is going to get burnt eventually.'

Alex watched the display on the camera, instructing her to shift slightly this way, turn her head slightly that way.

Eventually, still watching the miniature version of herself on screen, he said with deep appreciation, 'That's perfect. The way the light's hitting you. Beautiful.'

Erin glanced uncomfortably around the room. Alex blinked rapidly and coughed, straightening up. 'So yeah, anyway, good to go.'

Erin made Alex a cup of tea and watched while he edited the clip. In under an hour they had a finished product. She felt slightly self-conscious as she watched herself reel out the message she'd prepared:

'The police have always said that Isaac Reynolds' death was an accident. But in my investigation I've found evidence the police ignored, which suggests a third-party was involved. If you are aware of anyone who owned a boat in the Wakestead area thirteen years ago, please come forward. They may have since sold it or gotten rid of it. But either way your evidence could prove instrumental in solving this case and helping Isaac's family find out who killed him.'

Alex pressed pause.

'Do you think many people will watch it?' she asked.

'Most of our readers are older people who've been in the area for ages, right. I'm hopeful you'll get something out of this.'

'I don't understand why you did it,' she said.

'It's my job. I thought another paper would get the scoop if we didn't publish.'

'That's not what I mean. I mean I don't understand why you did it to me.'

Alex looked away, out through the window.

'What you said, that first night we had a drink together, about not publishing stories about people you liked. I guess that was just bullshit?'

He winced.

'It's okay. You say what you need to say to get a story. I get it. I just want to know.'

'It wasn't bullshit,' said Alex quietly. 'I just read it wrong.'

He opened something on his phone, and placed the device on the table in front of her. Then he edged away from her in his seat, retreating, embarrassed.

Erin stared at the image on the screen. It was a photograph of herself heading into the prison where Tom was kept. She felt first a rush of disgust at the idea of someone photographing that shameful, private moment. And then another realisation slowly sank in.

She looked up at Alex. His cheeks were flushed. He blinked and in his eyes there was a flicker of envy and bitterness – emotions she had seen on his face only once before, when she confronted him about the newspaper article. She hadn't understood then, but now she did. It must have been the first time she'd seen him since he was sent this photo.

Alex said, 'I believed it. I thought you were still... you know...'

Erin tried to think of something to say.

He bit his lip, then inhaled sharply and, emboldened, asked her: 'Do you – do you actually… do you still have feelings for him?'

Erin fought the urge to burst out laughing.

'Because, can I just say, I reckon you could do better.'

69

Wednesday

Following the map on her phone, Erin pushed deeper into the wood. The last of the evening sunlight probed through the canopy, forming long shadows on the forest floor.

The phone call had come in earlier that day, from a man named Robin. 'I'm a member of the local rambling society,' he'd said. 'I do a lot of walks around the Wakestead area. I think I've seen the kind of thing you're looking for.'

She was close now. A tiny animated pin marked the spot Robin had identified for her.

Eventually, she reached it. Beneath her feet, a crevice opened up, its sloping walls lined with moss-covered rocks and dark, gnarled tree roots. The wreck of an abandoned motorboat was lying on its side in the dusty gully, almost resembling a beached white whale.

Brambles caught on Erin's jacket as she moved with urgency down into the passage. Twice she almost lost her footing and fell. But she managed to fight her way through the undergrowth until the boat was looming over her. Years of rainfall had stripped away the white paint so the metal underneath was exposed in rusty patches. A dusting of green mould coated the underside as well as the railing that had once protected its former owners from going overboard.

Erin was trembling now with excitement. This had to be it. The boat where Isaac was killed. But this discovery was almost meaningless unless she could find out who had owned it. There would be no hope of any DNA surviving this many years outside, exposed to the elements.

She edged around the wreck, taking pictures on her phone and studying it for any signs that could help identify an owner. Eventually she reached the back, where its name was printed in beautiful looping cursive.

Her heart stopped.

The Hollies.

70

LEWIS NURSED THE BRIDGE OF his nose, wincing at the pain as his fingertips grazed the bruise where Erin had hit him. He was working late in the office again, scouring through Isaac's case file. So far the incorrect timeline was the only evidence suggesting Aaron had had something to do with Isaac's murder. There had to be more. There had to be something in the interviews, something someone had seen, that would give a stronger indication of what had happened that night.

He finally came across an interview with one of the girls, a peer of Isaac's, that made the hairs along his arms stand on end:

'Jack and Aaron kind of do everything Neil tells them to.'

*

Night was drawing in by the time Erin walked up to the front door of The Hollies. A floor lamp glowing through the large bay window told her someone was home. Her heart thudded painfully in her ribcage as she knocked.

Neil poked his curly-haired head around the door. His large, naive eyes went wide with surprise.

'Erin? Everything okay?'

'Is June in?' she asked.

'No, she's at a family thing.'

Good, thought Erin. 'I need to speak with you.'

'Sure,' he said, sounding unsure.

He edged the front door open. Erin followed him, noticing how silent it was inside the big empty house. Yet still she couldn't even begin to feel intimidated at being alone with Neil. Once they were in the living room, the sight of him standing there in his joggers, wide-eyed and quizzical, instantly made Erin doubt herself. Could she have got this wrong?

'So what's up?' he asked.

'Why did you get rid of the boat?'

'Huh?'

'Your family's boat. Why did you get rid of it?'

'Oh yeah, that thing. It was my mum's. We sold it ages ago. Reminded me too much of her. Why?'

Erin opened her phone and showed him the photo of the wreck.

She studied Neil's expression carefully. But his dark eyes were hard to read.

'You might have sold it, if you were older. But you were seventeen, weren't you? And you'd never done anything like that before. So instead you took it out to the woods and you dumped it there where you hoped no one would ever realise it was yours.'

She pocketed her phone. 'Why did you say you'd sold it?'

Neil sighed. 'Look, I just didn't want my dad knowing I'd abandoned it like that, okay? I told him I'd take care of it.'

'Or,' said Erin, 'did you not want anyone knowing you'd abandoned it so no one would ever take a look at it? And find possible evidence connecting you with Isaac's death?'

Neil raised his hands defensively. 'What? You're saying this is about *Isaac*?'

She said, 'A witness heard a motorboat that night, Neil. I imagine few teenagers knew how to drive something like that. So I'm almost certain you were on that boat that night. What I don't understand is why you did it. It seems like Isaac got on everyone's bad side. But you? As far as I can see he did nothing to you. You were friends. So why?'

Neil ran his ringed fingers through his hair in frustration. She waited patiently for him to gather his thoughts. He looked like he was going to deny it. Pass the buck on to Aaron.

When he met her gaze, there was an impish gleam in his eyes.

'I always did want to tell someone.'

71

LEWIS COULD FEEL THE EYES of Gregory and the other detectives burning into him through the glass of the one-way mirror.

'Right now, we know you've lied, Aaron,' he said. 'You also have a motive. But I'll be honest, I don't think you're the main culprit here. So you need to help us help you. You need to tell us if Neil had anything to do with this.'

'Neither of us had anything to do with this,' Aaron said.

'And what about your friend? What about Jack?'

'We don't know what happened to Jack. It has nothing to do with Isaac.'

'You're absolutely sure about that?'

Aaron nodded.

'Two people you knew as teenagers just so happened to go missing or die in strange circumstances? You're unlucky.'

Aaron said nothing.

He stared up at the white haze shining through the narrow windows at the top of the room. Raindrops crawled down the glass. He was tired. So tired. By comparison, this person lounging in front of him seemed well-rested, almost content, utterly impervious to everything he was saying.

Then something switched.

'I can't help feeling,' he said, 'that you aren't quite paying attention, Aaron.'

Aaron stared at him. In his blank expression, there was a flicker of surprise.

'Maybe you think that if you stay quiet – if you keep saying "no comment" – then you will drift through this event, untouched. It will just be an inconsequential moment, and you'll be able to carry on as before. But I have to tell you the truth. Because I would hate for you to fail to grasp what is happening right now. This is the most decisive moment of your life. And the last thing I would want is for you to underestimate the sheer, monumental pile of shit you are in.'

Aaron continued to stare at him. Now his eyes were wide.

'Defending someone who hasn't been your friend for years. Who doesn't give a shit about you. And for what? How do you think the Crown Prosecution Service will interpret your silence? How do you think it will go down with a jury?'

Aaron looked like a young boy again.

'He told us we were only going to scare him,' he said.

72

SHE STARED AT NEIL IN disbelief. As she held his gaze, that look of inappropriate mischief continued to play at the corners of his mouth.

He exaggerated breathing out deeply.

'It's a relief, you know, it really is. It's hard keeping it to yourself for that long, you know? At school the next day, that was the hardest bit.' He held his hands to his face in fake shock. 'Isaac's missing? Oh my god, who saw him last?'

Then he stopped, lifting a hand. 'Actually, no, you know what was the hardest bit? Seeing everyone treat him like a fucking saint. I knew I needed to stay close to that family, to keep them off the scent. But Jesus Christ. It's nauseating how they talk about him. I mean you know by now, right, that wasn't what he was like?'

Erin realised she was shaking slightly. She gritted her teeth. 'Did you start a relationship with June,' she said, 'so you could keep an eye on Amma?'

At June's name, the mischief left Neil's face. 'Did I stay in a relationship with her because of Amma? No. Did I start one because of her? Yeah. I did.'

'Does she know?'

'Of course not. And she's not going to find out. Everyone's made their minds up about you. No one's on your side right now. They think you have a vendetta. You ring up your friend Detective Jennings right now and he won't believe you.'

The words flowed out of him. His eyes were bright with excitement.

'No one touched me then,' he said. 'You can't touch me now.'

'You're deluded,' Erin snarled. 'You killed Isaac. And Jack Riley too.'

'No one cares about Jack.'

'I care,' she said. 'You did it because he couldn't handle the guilt, right? He was going to say something.'

He nodded. 'Jack was going to say something.'

'Where is he?'

'There's only one way you're ever going to find out.'

'What's that?'

'Take me to the station and I'll never say a word. But come with me now and I'll take you to where he's buried. The closer we get, the more I'll tell you. You turn away, I'll never tell you or anyone else the rest of the story. The family will never find his body. You come all the way, and I'll tell you everything.'

The living room was ice-cold. Erin could feel nothing except her own lungs taking in deep, slow breaths.

'On one condition,' he added. 'No phones.'

He smirked and reached out his hand.

Erin gritted her teeth.

Then, reluctantly, she reached into her pocket, pulled out her phone and placed it in Neil's open palm.

73

BRANCHES SNAPPED UNDERFOOT AS ERIN followed Neil into the woods. It was so dark that all she could see was a triangle of the forest floor illuminated by her torch, strewn with leaves and fallen branches, and in front of that, Neil's solemnly marching figure. Occasionally, a car drove past on the hill beside the forest. Headlights swept like UFOs through the trees.

'You get three questions,' said Neil. 'First question.'

'Why? Why kill Isaac?'

'My mum was never there for me. And then she was gone forever. But Isaac, Isaac she treated like her own kid. As if, because he was badly behaved, he was some project she needed to work on.'

'Did the other two know what was going to happen that night?'

'They knew something was going to happen. They're not innocent in this.'

'Mark Stormont. Why did you kill him?'

'So many questions, Erin. You need to spread these out. Don't you get how this works?'

'Whoever killed Mark Stormont knew they could blame it on Amma,' she said. 'They knew she didn't have an alibi. They made sure she was out of it the night before so she'd be lying in bed the next morning, doing nothing, with no one to say for certain where she was. It was you.'

Finally he came to a stop. He lowered his torch, lighting up one small section of the forest floor.

'Here?'

Neil nodded.

'I need proof. I need to know.'

He dropped his holdall and unzipped it, pulling out two garden spades. He placed one on the ground in front of her.

He couldn't be serious. Was he really going to arm her? At any point she could swing round and hit him. But he held her gaze with disdainful amusement. And this was why: he knew she wouldn't. If no one was buried here, and she swung out at him, then there would be no evidence linking Neil to the murders, no evidence she had lashed out in self-defence, nothing to prove her attack was anything other than a cold-blooded killing.

She stared down at the miserable patch of grass. There was no turning back now. She had to know. Even if it meant digging her own grave.

She crouched down to pick up the spade. Lifting it off the ground, she was struck by the weight of it. She wondered how deep the grave was, how long it might take her to reach the body – and whether she would even be strong enough to make it that far. Suppressing those thoughts, she sank the spade into the ground, pushed it down with her boot and wrenched free the first scoop of clumpy earth.

Time dragged by. Scoop by scoop, they shifted the dirt, pushing through the minute roots of neighbouring plants, freeing insects from their hiding places, exposing wriggling worms to the cruel night air. Very soon sweat started running down the back of her neck. Her sides began to ache. As a mound of earth piled higher up on her right, she kept half of her attention constantly fixed on Neil, his head bowed as he dug on the opposite side of the six-foot hole. What if there was nothing here and he knew it? What if, while she was digging, he made the first move?

The hole deepened until they had to jump inside to keep digging.

It was an hour before her spade hit something.

74

AARON SPOKE WITH HIS HEAD bowed, fingers interlocked together against his forehead.

'He hated Isaac. He convinced himself that Isaac had taken his mum from him.'

'What do you mean, taken his mum from him?'

'His mum took a real shine to Isaac. You could see they had this bond. His mum literally saved Isaac from drowning once on a school trip. And Neil, you know, he wanted it but I don't know if he ever had that with his mum. She annoyed him, I think. They fought a lot. So when she died, all that anger at not having had a good relationship with her… he took it out on Isaac.

'He became obsessed with needing to get Isaac somehow. He was endlessly coming up with little plans. Saying we should follow him and attack him.

'So we take the boat out. And we drive along for a while, and then we stop and Neil's like, right, we're getting in. And Isaac's saying he can't swim that well. But all Neil needs to do is call him a pussy and within a couple of minutes he's stripped down to his boxers and he's the first one in, doing that little doggy paddle people do when they've never properly learnt.

'And I start taking off my shoes, getting ready to jump in too. But Neil says, "no, no one else get in. Isaac needs to learn by himself." And Isaac's pissed off now, trying to tread water, calling Neil a wanker, saying he's going to get back on. Only it's easier to jump in than it is to board from the water, right? And Neil says "fine" then throws a rope out to haul him back on. And he's laughing while Isaac swims up to get hold of the rope. But instead of pulling him up, quick as anything, he grabs Isaac's wrist. The rope has a – what do you call it, a loop knot? – at the end. Neil slips the loop over his wrist and pulls it tight. I think Isaac was so shocked from the cold he didn't realise what was happening. And Neil lets go of his hand, leaving him in the water, while Isaac's saying, "the fuck, man?" Then he goes to the wheel of the boat. And accelerates. The engine starts roaring. This tiny boat is crashing down the river in the almost pitch dark. I could hear Neil howling and laughing. I looked to the back of the boat. There's this huge white froth. And I couldn't see Isaac any more. Just these churning waves swallowing him.

'I realised it could get bad. I said to Neil, "we need to slow down. Isaac keeps going under." And it was like I hadn't said anything. Neil's just staring straight ahead with his hand on the throttle. Then he goes to the back of the boat, and I think, "thank god, he's gonna untie him". Only he doesn't. He just stays there. He – he just wanted to hold the rope and watch.

'I swear to you, I swear,' Aaron pleaded, 'I tried to stop the boat. But it was pitch-black and I had no idea what I was doing. Finally I pressed the right thing and it slowly stopped.

'I pushed past Neil and ran to the back of the boat. In the darkness you could see all this white where the froth's passing over the water. And then I see Isaac. He's just floating there. Face down.

'I looked at Neil. I thought he was crying. But it was just the wind. Making his eyes water. And then we asked for help.'

'Help? What do you mean, you asked for help?'

Suddenly a voice cut in over the speaker. Chris's.

'Jennings, we need you in the observation room right now.'

Not now, thought Lewis. He was so close. He couldn't afford to interrupt Aaron, give him time to reflect, gather his thoughts, decide maybe confessing to everything wasn't such a bright idea after all. But if Chris was calling him out at a time like this, it had to be important.

He rushed into the observation room. Chris was hunched over his laptop with an officer by his side. Both of them were pale as ghosts.

'We sent officers to Neil's house. He's not there. But his vehicle has shown up in the ANPR just forty-five minutes ago. He's with Erin.'

A jolt of electricity shot through Lewis.

Barely a second passed before he was back in the interview room, slamming the door shut behind him.

'Where has he taken her?'

Aaron stared up at him, eyes wide with shock.

'What?'

'Neil was last seen forty-five minutes ago driving my friend. Where are they going?'

'I – I don't know.'

'Yes, you do. Tell me.'

Aaron shook his head frantically. 'I don't know! How would I know?'

Lewis slammed his palm down on the table. 'They're on Bexmere Road. Where could they be going? It could be a scene connected with Isaac's death. With Jack's death. Think, Aaron.'

Aaron blurted out, quietly and quickly, as though the words had been on the tip of his tongue the whole time, 'The woods. South of the car park. I don't know where exactly. Near an oak tree.'

Immediately, Lewis got up and stormed out of the room, his body flooding with adrenaline.

He burst into the observation room, where Chris and the other officer gawped at him without restraint.

'*Lewis*,' Chris exclaimed with breathless approval. 'When did you get so *forceful*?'

'Are we going?' Lewis snapped, and swept down the corridor.

75

EXHAUSTED, ERIN BENT FORWARD, RESTING her free hand on the soft wall of the open grave, gasping until the cold night air burned in her throat. All she wanted was to sit down. But she couldn't afford to – not with Neil barely a metre away, still clutching his own potential weapon. Also panting, he wiped the sweat off his brow, stepped back, and aimed the torchlight down between them.

'See for yourself,' he said.

Beneath their feet, reaching up through the dirt, were the first few fingers of a skeleton hand. Erin experienced a wave of nausea so strong she felt momentarily faint. She took a deep breath and crouched down inside the grave. Using her bare hands, she clawed at the thick earth surrounding the bones, until she had carved out a small dip that revealed the sleeve of the boy's hoodie.

Blue. Just like the officer had told her.

She rose to her feet. 'Jack,' she said.

'Yes.'

She knew exactly where this was going. She needed to buy herself time.

'You said three questions. You haven't answered my third.'

'What was it again?'

'Why did you kill Mark Stormont?'

'Are you sure you want to ask that?'

She turned the torch in Neil's direction so it illuminated the spade, which looked suddenly huge, held upright in his hand. The light touched his face, exposing a faint smirk that made all her muscles clench with fear.

'Yes,' she replied.

'I didn't kill Mark Stormont.'

Erin felt her legs go numb. Her mind raced. How could that be? Was he lying?

'Who did?'

'Three questions, Erin.'

'Fine. We've played your game. I'm going back.'

She started backing away, aware that her legs were shaking.

Neil's voice carried over in the darkness, slow and steady: 'We never agreed we were going back.'

76

A RUSH OF AIR BLEW THE hair off her face as Neil's spade arced past, narrowly missing. In the darkness and confusion, Erin lunged for the wall of the newly dug grave. She tried to pull herself up, kicking against the wall, but her feet kept slipping in the loose dirt and without her toes inside she couldn't get a foothold. Her fingers clawed at the thick earth. The torch left her grasp and rolled down the gentle slope, sending an erratic beam of light shooting up to reveal the ghostly canopy.

Her muscles were screaming but with one final effort she managed to haul herself over the lip and onto the forest floor. As quickly as she could she flipped onto her back, knowing Neil would be right behind her. She could just make out his dark form moving quickly against the moonlit wood, coming towards her.

Where was her spade? She'd abandoned it in the grave. She threw herself forwards, crawling back towards the rift in the ground. Her hand flailed blindly inside. Finally the handle touched her palm. She gripped it and pulled back.

She swung the spade round and felt it connect with Neil's cheekbone. There was the horribly blunt sound of metal smacking against flesh. Immediately he stopped and, swaying, tried to stop himself from falling forwards. Erin kicked his legs out from under him. His barely decipherable figure crumpled away in a spidery motion.

In the gloom she heard Neil hit the bottom of the grave with a sickening thud.

Erin dropped to her knees. Her breath came out in ragged gasps.

She fumbled around the forest floor for the torch and shone its beam into the hole. The light reflected off of Neil's face, mottled with dirt and jagged cuts. He was out cold.

Not long later she saw a cluster of light sources in the distance. They grew larger until eventually she made out torch beams and the fluorescent jackets of four officers. Seeing her, they broke into a jog. Erin felt relief flood over her when she recognised Lewis among them.

She winced as he shone a torch light directly into her eyes.

He stumbled towards her, eyes wide with alarm as he registered the dirt and cuts on her face. 'Erin, are you hurt?'

'You took your time,' she coughed. 'You need to call an ambulance.'

'Are you alright?'

'Not for me. For him.'

She gestured to Neil. It was a miracle Lewis had not fallen into the grave in his urgency to get to her. The other officers' torch beams darted over the opening. 'Jesus,' one of them said when they spotted the body.

'It's Neil,' she said. 'Along with Jack Riley.'

'What the—'

'He did it, Lewis. He just told me. Killed Isaac. Killed Jack as well.'

'Aaron told us,' he said.

'It was his mum,' she gasped. 'That was why Neil did it. He was jealous because she took a shine to Isaac.'

'We know. We've got them, Erin.'

He pushed his hands under her armpits and half-lifted her up onto her feet. Erin swayed on the spot. She'd been running on adrenaline for so long. Now there was finally an end in sight, she could feel her body starting to crash.

Chris was typing into his phone.

'This her, I'm guessing?'

Chris showed her an article on his screen. ***Tributes for beloved mother.***

Beneath the headline was a photograph of a woman in her early forties, who the article named Helen Starling, with her young son – clearly Neil – perched on her knee.

Erin's feelings of tiredness disappeared. In her ears she heard a faint ringing noise.

She'd seen a picture of this woman before.

In the framed photo Gregory kept on his desk.

77

Thursday

AT EIGHT O'CLOCK THE NEXT day, Erin, Lewis and Chris watched the police officers file into the main office one by one. Erin had barely slept last night but adrenaline kept her wide awake as she searched for Gregory's face among the crowd.

'Here we go,' said Lewis, spotting him.

The senior detective must not have been told yet about last night's events. He looked strangely calm as he strode across the office in the direction of the kitchen unit, where he opened a cupboard to fetch his mug and began making a cup of tea.

Erin and the two detectives advanced towards him.

'Gregory!' she called.

He spun round. 'What's going on?' Hardly looking at Erin, he said, 'She needs permission to be here.'

'Last night, we arrested Neil Starling for the murder of Isaac Reynolds and Jack, and the attempted murder of Erin. He's in the hospital.'

Gregory looked as though a wave of nausea had just swept through him.

He cleared his throat. 'Jennings, Baldwin – it sounds like we need to discuss this in my office.'

'Do you have any familial connection with Neil, Gregory?' Erin asked. 'One you didn't disclose at the start of the investigation?'

Gregory's face drained of colour.

'If you don't feel like talking, don't worry, because I know someone who does.'

She opened her phone and pressed the number. Then, out of the speakers in the main office – usually reserved for fire alarm tests – came a woman's voice.

'Is he there?'

Erin heard the voice twice – once in her ear and also ringing out into the office, out of the speaker linked to the Bluetooth on her phone.

Around the room officers were looking up from their desktops with the same bewildered expressions.

'He's here,' she said into the phone. 'We're all here, Amma.'

Gregory's eyes widened.

'Gregory, hi,' said Amma. 'There were a few more recordings, weren't there? Besides the one you played to me. And you managed to get rid of those. Only Mark kept copies, it turns out. Olivia was kind enough to share them with me. I'm going to play one for you now.'

Amma's voice cut out, to be replaced by another that was deeper, gruffer, older.

'Are you all right? You look dreadful,' it said.

Recognising his own voice, Gregory frowned in confusion.

Another voice, a younger one, came in next on the recording, spilling out into the main office: 'I need to speak with you.'

Around the room, eyebrows furrowed. Officers turned to their partners to check if they'd heard that correctly. Could that really be…?

Mark Stormont's voice.

Gregory's eyes widened as he realised what he was listening to.

'Turn it off,' he said.

'Why should I? You didn't turn it off for Amma, did you, Gregory.'

'Stop playing it,' he hissed.

Holding his gaze, Erin pocketed her phone, signalling that that wasn't going to happen.

'Where were you on the morning of the twenty-first, Gregory?'

Gregory suddenly looked very unwell. His skin had turned waxy.

'Wait,' he said, holding his hands up. 'Just give me a chance to explain.'

Then it all happened very quickly. Gregory lashed out with one arm, hurling the recently boiled kettle towards them. Instinctively, Erin flinched away, covering her face. In that moment of darkness she heard a scream. Opening her eyes she saw Chris almost doubled over in pain, hot water dripping off his body. Lewis yelled for a medic.

Within seconds they were engulfed in a swarm of officers. Not knowing what else to do, Erin threw herself into the kitchen unit and scrambled around in a cupboard until she found a bowl then filled it with cold water from the tap. One of the officers took it from her and poured it over Chris' scalded collarbones and forearms. The detective screwed up his eyes as the water splashed over his exposed skin, already red and blistering.

Erin forced herself to look round the group, convinced she'd find Gregory on the floor, having been tackled by one of the officers. But he was nowhere to be seen.

'Gregory,' Erin shouted. Looking past the officers, she realised with horror that the door to the stairwell was slightly ajar, as though someone had just escaped through it. He was gone.

Lewis reached out and grabbed her.

'Go,' he said. 'Just go. I'll stay here and help Chris.'

She nodded and launched herself across the office, pushing through the open door and clattering down the stairwell. The sound of her footsteps echoed around the tall, narrow space as Erin descended as fast as she could, leaving the audio recording still playing out into the chaos of the office.

78

Friday, 20th August

GREGORY FELT A GROWING SENSE of unease as Mark stared at him. The younger detective had a stern expression he'd never seen on his face before and he stood squarely in front of the door as if to block Gregory from leaving.

'Did you read my report?' he asked.

So that's what this is about, he said.

'Yes. It was very interesting, thank you.'

'So you agree?'

'Agree with what?'

'That we need to end the surveillance of Amma Reynolds. And anyone else who's part of the Justice for Isaac campaign.'

'That's not your call to make, Stormont.'

Mark's voice rose with anger. 'Every protest I attended was non-violent. And there's nothing Amma's done that suggests she's conspiring to commit violence either.'

'Well, I might suggest you just haven't looked hard enough. You've only been talking to her for a couple of months.'

'Did you share my report with the super?'

'I don't think it's ready yet.'

'We only allow covert surveillance in extreme circumstances. I'm the officer on this. If I'm questioning why we're doing this, that needs to be shared with the super immediately.'

'Now, there's no need to get so worked up over this.'

'You wanted me to find something,' he said. 'From the very

moment you got the force to sign off on this, you wanted me to find something that you could use against Amma.'

'Why on earth would I do that?'

'When Amma clashed with that police officer, you saw an opportunity and you took it. You knew you could use this to gather as much information as possible about Amma and her family.'

'What?'

Mark shook his head. 'I don't know what you plan on doing with what I've gathered for you. All I know is you have something against that family. We have no justification for watching Amma. None whatsoever. I'm ashamed I played a part in this. I'm not doing this any more.'

Gregory could tell he meant it.

'Where's this come from? Why are you saying this now? After you've been following that woman around for months?'

'Just leave her alone, all right. Never, ever go near her or send anyone else after her ever again.'

His voice almost trembled with rage.

It was only then that Gregory understood. Only one thing could have prompted such a sudden change of heart.

'Jesus Christ, Mark. You know, I thought she must like you, but I never thought…'

Mark was silent. But his expression told Gregory everything he needed to know.

He still didn't understand. Why was he about to lose everything? Just for this girl?

He leant in, hissing through his teeth: 'You think you have a leg to stand on here? If you drag this down, you're going down with it.'

'I don't care. I know I'll lose my job. But I don't care any more. She deserves to know what we've been doing. And if you won't tell her, then I will.'

Before Gregory could stop him, the younger detective had turned around and left, slamming the door shut behind him.

The room seemed to swim in front of his eyes. Gregory swayed on the spot and placed his hand flat on the desk to steady himself. With that one conversation, everything had changed.

He could not allow Mark to take this any further. Not under any circumstances.

He pushed through the door and rushed after the detective.

'Mark!'

Mark turned around.

Gregory came to a stop in front of him. 'You're right,' he said. 'She deserves to know. And she deserves to hear it from the person who put you both in this situation.'

Mark's eyebrows lifted in surprise.

'Really?'

'God knows what'll happen to us now. But I can see your mind's made up. It's time to do the right thing. We'll tell her. Together. But I want to be careful about how we approach this. Let's discuss, but not here. Meet me tomorrow, near hers, at Crays Hill.'

79

Now

IT TOOK ALL OF GREGORY'S willpower not to propel himself forward at full speed in the direction of the Emergency Department. He'd been lucky to reach his car before any of the officers could follow. Now he rushed through the hospital corridors, invisible among the stream of anxious and grieving relatives. Finally he recognised the correct door number coming up and, panting, turned into the ward where Neil was kept.

His son was lying prostrate in a bed at the far end of the room.

Gregory swept over. His heart nearly burst out of his chest at the sight of Neil's face. His right eye had swollen up like a plum beneath a shining red dent where it looked like something hard had connected with his temple.

'Police, yes?'

Gregory turned around. A middle-aged nurse with a wide gait shuffled across the room towards him.

'He can't be discharged yet,' she said with a weary shake of her head. 'We'll contact the custody suite when he's ready.'

Her condescending tone shot through Gregory.

'I'm not here to discharge him. I just need to ask Mr Starling a couple of questions.'

'He's only just woken up. I should think he's not fit to answer any.'

Did she suspect something? He tried to hide his distress. But he knew the underarms of his shirt were damp with ice-cold sweat.

'It's urgent. If you don't mind?'

The nurse arched an eyebrow at him before leaving the ward with obvious reluctance.

He turned back to his son.

Fear and hope shone in Neil's good eye as he watched the detective, waiting to see what he would do next.

'I'm going to get you out of here,' Gregory whispered.

Neil stayed silent like an obedient dog.

'You're going to change into these,' he said, dumping his satchel, which contained his gym kit – a clean pair of joggers and a t-shirt – on top of the bed. 'And I'm going to cuff you until we're in the car.'

That, he thought, was their best chance of getting out undetected, provided none of Neil's carers saw them. It was risky. He knew they might not make it. But they had to try.

Slowly, Neil nodded. Then, more hastily, as if roused by a sudden shot of adrenaline, he sat upright and began shamelessly untying his hospital gown, discarding it on the bed and changing into the new clothes.

'Where are we going to go?' he said, jumping up to wriggle into his trousers.

'Far away as we can,' said Gregory.

'What about you?' said Neil. 'Are you going to stay?'

'No,' he said. 'I'll come with you. It's over for me here. We'll travel south. Go to Europe.'

Neil nodded again, his left eye wide with amazement.

As he lied to his son, Gregory imagined Helen. He saw in Neil the same bright-eyed naivety that she had always had. Her ability to float through life unhurt and unconcerned had been frustrating yet endearing, somehow part of her irresistible charm. But in Neil, the same trait was utterly toxic. And he had been too late to realise it.

In his jacket pocket, he closed his fist around the packet of sleeping pills he'd been taking ever since Mark Stormont's death – no, murder.

Forgive me, Helen, he thought.

Then he let his mind flash back to where this had all begun, thirteen years earlier.

*

Gregory thanked the Starlings for their time and forced down the rest of his coffee. What a grim day. A dead teenager and no obvious witnesses.

Ian, Neil's father, said goodbye to him in the doorway, arms folded.

'I should've given him a lift back,' he said, shaking his head. 'Before they all left here, I offered to drive them there and then home after. He was a strapping young lad; when he said he could walk back, I just thought—'

Gregory winced. He had never learned to become comfortable in Ian's presence. He kept expecting to see hatred lurking behind the other man's eyes. Even now he was desperate to move on to the next household, afraid that if he stayed here for much longer he would somehow betray the affair he'd concealed successfully for all this time.

'It's not your fault,' said Gregory. 'He didn't live far away. I can see why you'd think he'd be all right. Don't blame yourself.'

'Well, does it look suspicious?'

'It's just too early to say,' he replied.

They'd only found the body several hours ago. There were no obvious signs of a fight but it was hard to believe a strong young man had just stumbled into a river and drowned on his way home. Gregory felt dread stirring in the pit of his stomach as he walked down the garden path. Already he was afraid of where this investigation might lead him.

Suddenly he heard footsteps and turned around to find Neil lingering there with his hands in his pockets.

'Martyn? Can I talk to you for a second?' His face was hard to read.

Emotion swelled inside Gregory's chest. Neil would never know how much it meant to him – to be asked for help.

'Of course.'

Not far from them was the family's garden shed, its wooden walls stained green with moss. Before Gregory could protest, Neil pushed open the squeaking door and disappeared inside.

Gregory grimaced. 'Really? Christ.'

Reluctantly he ducked under the rotting door frame, following Neil into the cramped, dank space. It was filled with garden equipment that was swathed in cobwebs. Gregory caught the earthy smell of cannabis soaked into the walls.

'I'm going to pretend I can't smell that,' he muttered, shutting the door behind them. 'So what is it? Did you see something on Bonfire Night?'

'I'm really sorry.'

The words left his mouth automatically. Neil's style of apologising had always concerned Gregory. As a child, he had been constantly in and out of trouble, and yet the moment he broke a plate or made his playmate cry, there it was, 'I'm sorry', reeled off in the most unsorry manner Gregory had ever heard. It seemed to be an almost knee-jerk reaction. Gregory had blamed Helen for focusing too much on her son's good manners and not enough on actually disciplining him. He remembered arguing with her about it: 'You can make your kid as polite as you like – it doesn't mean he's well-behaved.'

But this apology, this apology unnerved him more than all the others before it. Why was he saying sorry to him inside a dirty shed? What did he know? And why couldn't he have said it back there – in front of the other officers?

'Has one of your friends had something to do with this?' he asked.

There was one small window in the wall of the shed. It lit half of Neil's face in a cold light.

'Neil, I really need you to tell me if you know anything about this.'

'I don't know what to do,' he said.

'What do you mean? What is it?'

Neil looked at his feet.

'Do they… do they think it looks suspicious?'

'What? Why are you asking me that?'

Gregory hated his silence. He could feel himself starting to panic, his chest rising up and down, faster and faster.

'Do you know who did it, Neil?'

Neil's eyes pleaded with him.

'You're such a good friend to my family,' he whispered. 'Can you help me?'

Gregory felt a shudder go through his whole body. Suddenly the shed became airless. He bent forwards and placed his hands on his knees to steady himself.

'Oh my god,' he said.

The floor came in and out of focus. He took a moment to breathe deeply. Then he reached out and grabbed Neil's arm.

'Was it an accident? Was it an accident, Neil? Is that what you're telling me?'

Neil stood motionless.

'I wanted to teach him a lesson. It got out of hand.'

Gregory tightened his grip on Neil's arm. Then he grabbed the collar of his hoodie and jerked down until they were almost eye-to-eye.

'How. Tell me right now how it happened. This is the most important thing you will ever say in your life.'

Neil swallowed. 'He was in the water. I tied him to the boat. I drove the boat faster until—'

Until he stopped moving.

Not manslaughter. Not manslaughter at all.

Gregory released Neil as his hands went numb. A wave of sickness rolled up from the bottom of his stomach. He managed to stifle it. He'd never cried in front of Neil, not even at his mother's funeral. But now, covering his mouth with his hand, he allowed himself one short, wretched sob. Through his tears, he looked at the blurred colours of his son's trainers. This stupid boy. His lack of urgency. His shamelessness. His empty apology. Please get me out of trouble.

He straightened up and slapped Neil hard across the face. Hot pain fizzed across his palm.

Neil stared back at him in shock, his hair slightly dishevelled, his cheek inflamed where Gregory's hand had landed. Tears filled his eyes.

'Do you have any idea what you've done?'

Neil said nothing. The slap had shocked him and his breath came out in shallow gasps. The more distressed he became, the more childlike he looked.

The more like his mother.

Neil flung his arms around him. At first Gregory's rage stopped him from moving. But then he felt Neil's thin, lanky body trembling as he cried. He fastened his arms around the teenager's middle.

'I don't want to go to prison,' Neil sobbed.

Stupid boy. Stupid, stupid boy. Gregory felt the fabric of his son's hoodie brush against his chin and stared at the back wall where a pitchfork loomed ominously. He knew. He hated that he knew, but he knew there was only one thing more unbearable than this moment. And that was watching Neil leave the dock after a guilty verdict, heavy-footed, in handcuffs and still too young to fully comprehend how much he'd ruined his own life.

He had made a promise to Helen. Helen, who was good and kind and gone. Whatever Neil had done, some vestige of that goodness had to be in him somewhere, even if it took them years to find it.

'Who knows?'

'Aaron and Jack. They were there.'

'Who saw you?'

'Nobody. It was just us.'

'Listen to me very carefully.'

80

ERIN SLAMMED THE CAR DOOR shut and hobbled towards the hospital entrance, sensing with panic that she'd strained something in her right ankle. She scanned the sea of glinting car bonnets. She'd been too late to get out of the police station and follow Gregory's car. But she was certain this was where he must have been heading – to the hospital where Neil was currently staying.

She lurched to a stop. Her lungs were burning. Gregory's car was nowhere to be seen. Nor had she spotted him among the trickle of patients leaving the hospital. Perhaps she was already too late. Managing a groan of frustration and pain, she threaded her fingers together behind her head. 'Shit, shit shit.'

Just as despair was starting to sink in, two figures emerged through the automatic doors of the hospital entrance. Even from this distance Erin immediately recognised Gregory escorting Neil – bruised and hunching – across the hospital car park. The pain in her lungs and ankle vanished in an instant. She was too far away to catch them in time. But she could follow them from here. As quickly as she could, she rushed back to the car.

*

Erin trampled through the forest, wincing at the pain in her right ankle. It was late morning and the birds were singing. The cheerful sound filled Erin with fear that time was running out. The ground was dark and slippery with leaf litter. The scent of decay filled the air.

The sound of running water grew steadily louder until she reached the top of the river bank. In the blue she could make out the white flash of a shirt collar and sleeves. Gregory was sat on the other side of the river. Between his legs he clutched Neil's unconscious body, half-submerged in the water, a disturbed baptism. The young man's pale, clammy face looked strangely restful as the opaque grey waves lapped at his waist.

'Don't do it, Gregory.'

Gregory's face was red and inflamed. Erin could see he'd been crying.

'This is the place, Erin. The place where it started. And this is where it's going to end.'

'I know why you did it, Gregory. Neil's your son.'

Shame and relief glistened in Gregory's eyes all at once. 'Kids are a second chance, aren't they? We think they'll redeem us.'

'Just take Neil out of the water. We can talk.'

Gregory buried his head in his son's neck for a few moments. When he next showed his face, it was glistening with fresh tears.

'We were only together for a few months. Me and Helen,' he said. 'But sometimes in my head it feels like years.

'She'd never leave Ian, I knew that. But they'd been trying for years to have a kid and never managed it. So when she got pregnant, she told me she wanted to keep it. And we decided it was best if no one ever knew.'

'Does Neil know?' asked Erin.

'No. A family friend, that's what I am to him. Uncle, he used to call me.'

He sniffed tearfully. 'You know what happened to Helen,' he said, 'so you must see what position I was in. Before she died, she made me promise to look after her son. Our son. What would you have done, Erin? After making a promise like that? If your own child came to you saying they needed help, or they'd go to prison? They were just kids, Erin. It was an accident.'

'It wasn't an accident. You know that and I know that.'

Gregory was shaking his head, eyes squeezed shut, as though in pain. 'I didn't know about Jack.'

'Jack was going to tell the truth. And Neil killed him. Because of your decision to protect them, Jack is dead. And he's not the only one, is he? How long were you spying on Amma for?'

'She should've stopped,' he said. 'She should've let it go.'

'How long?'

'Years,' he said. 'I needed to know what she found out about the case.'

'Why did you kill Mark?'

'He was going to tell her.'

'Except you needed to make it look like it was Amma. You needed to make sure she didn't have an alibi. That she'd be home all day. So you got your son involved again, didn't you?'

A tear rolled down Gregory's cheek.

He said: 'He invited them all out. Then he spiked her. Not enough she'd be harmed. But enough that she'd sleep in. Stay at home while… I promised I would look after him. I can't let him go to prison.'

Gregory started climbing onto his knees and slowly sliding Neil into the water. Neil's head flopped down to his chest. The current passed by, slow and steady.

'Don't!'

'What do you care if he dies?'

'Isaac's family deserves to see him in court. Please.'

Gregory's mouth hung open as he cried.

'Please,' called Erin, 'think of Helen. Think of what you promised her.'

Gregory pushed Neil's body down into the water. Then he stopped. Sobbing, he heaved his son out and onto the bank, resting his head against his.

81

Monday

A SQUARE OF SUNLIGHT GLOWED ON her thin mattress as Amma packed up her small selection of belongings – the few things she'd been allowed to bring into the prison. Before she left, she took one final glance into the room that had been her cage for over a month. Good riddance, she thought.

Her parents, along with June, came to take her home. On the drive, June rested her head on Amma's shoulder and held her outstretched hand. After weeks with no physical contact, Amma treasured the gesture of sisterly affection.

She rolled her head back and looked out the window. Through the bug-slicked window the rolling hills were turned yellow by the gently setting sun. For one painful moment she imagined the miniature figures of herself and Mark scaling the incline. She looked away, dismissing the image, and rested her head on top of June's.

She had almost given up her life looking for answers. Now she finally had them, she could start living it.

82

Three Months Later

THEY ALL ROSE TO HEAR the judge's verdict. Inside the dock, Tom lifted himself off his uncomfortable seat and stood up straight. The handcuffs felt cold against his wrists. The judge's booming voice filled the echoey space of the courtroom.

'While the information given by Mr Radley aided in the detection of Isaac Reynolds' killer, it was not instrumental in finding the person responsible. Moreover, the information was given under conditions that I believe were intended to humiliate and control his former partner Ms Crane. His insistence that it was her who should receive this information and that she should, in exchange, continue to pay him visits against her clear preference and wishes strongly suggests that his vindictive and manipulative character is unreformed. I believe there is not sufficient justification to shorten the sentence for what was and remains a hideous and brutal crime.'

Tom dug his nails into his palms until he felt close to drawing blood. For one last time that day, he searched the heads and faces of the crowds below.

But the woman he was looking for was nowhere to be seen. As soon as she had given her testimony in the witness box, she had left without returning to the public gallery, having never once looked at him.

*

Erin very nearly didn't recognise Amma when she stepped into the café. Dressed in a thick winter coat, the exonerated woman looked almost completely different. Her eyes were bright and all the pain had left her face. Crossing the room and sitting down opposite her, peeling off her coat, she moved gracefully, free from the emotional weight she'd been carrying for so long.

'Mum told me about what happened. How Gregory almost killed Neil. But you talked him out of it. Thank you.'

Erin felt reluctant to accept much gratitude after everything Amma had been through. 'I just kept thinking about what your mum said. How your family deserved to see the killer behind bars.'

'It's good it was you there and not me. I'd have been tempted to let him drown.' Amma shook her head. 'That whole time. He was right there. Hiding in plain sight. But you found him.'

She continued: 'One day my brother never came home and even though they found a body, we never knew why. Now we know why. You brought him home.'

Erin blushed. She asked, 'What are you going to do now?'

'I have plans.'

Amma opened her phone and turned the screen towards Erin. On it was an email saying her application for a DHEP had been accepted.

Erin looked up in surprise. 'You're going to be a police officer?'

Amma held her gaze as she slid her phone back into her pocket. She looked almost defiant, as though she was expecting Erin to object.

'When do you start training?'

'In a couple of weeks.' She shrugged, pocketing her phone. 'June thought it was the worst idea in the world. And for a while I did too. And then I realised I couldn't imagine doing anything else.'

'You'll be amazing,' she said.

Amma half-smiled. She looked at her feet. When she looked up again, her face was filled with discomfort.

'There was something I wanted to ask you. From the start.'

Erin waited.

Amma blinked. She swallowed.

'How did you get over it?'

That vulnerability Erin had become familiar with had slipped back into her voice.

Erin's throat tightened.

'It wasn't the same. What you had was different. Completely different. I'm sorry I didn't see that at the time.'

Despite Amma's calm demeanour there was a silent desperation in her eyes. 'Still. How did you?'

'Slowly. And maybe not completely.'

It wasn't the answer she'd wanted to hear. Amma furrowed her eyebrows and nodded. Then she looked out of the misted-up windows of the café, onto a stretch of green where the grass had frosted over.

'I'm scared of what that means.'

'It will get easier,' Erin replied. 'I promise it will.'

83

SHE WENT FOR A DRINK with Lewis on the day of her train back to London. One pint turned into three and they ranted non-stop as they weaved a path down to the station. The sun had just set and the sky was a deep dark blue. The platform was empty. The five o'clock train was not due for fourteen minutes. They waited, shivering in their coats.

'Don't feel you have to wait for me,' said Erin.

Lewis pulled her into a hug.

'You sure you don't want to stay a bit longer?' he said. 'You can stay in my second bedroom.'

'Absolutely not,' she replied. 'I'm not coming back for a long time.'

'Fair.'

Lewis chewed his lips and studied the train tracks. He looked strangely pensive.

'You'll be fine,' she said.

'I don't know. I don't think I can do it any more,' he said.

'You're one of their best detectives, Lewis. Don't let them get you down.'

He tapped his shoe against the brick floor. 'One of their *best* detectives? You've changed your tune.'

His tone was playful but guilt rose inside Erin's throat. 'I should apologise.'

'Don't worry about it.'

'No, I'm sorry. I really am. I shouldn't have called you weak; that was wrong.'

'No, I was. I was weak. Anyway, I don't mean I *can't* do it. I mean maybe I'm done. I was wondering, if you needed a partner…'

Erin hadn't seen it coming at all. She was surprised by how delighted she felt at the prospect.

At the start of this investigation, she had been determined to do everything alone. Now, looking back, she thought how much easier it would have been if she'd had someone else there from the start.

But she swallowed back her emotions. She needed to be sure Lewis knew what he'd be getting into.

'It's tough,' she said. 'The money's unpredictable.'

He nodded. 'I know that. I'm all right with that.'

'Sleep on it,' she said. 'Call me in a couple days. And then we'll talk.'

They hugged again and said goodbye. She watched Lewis's gangly figure cross the bridge over the tracks, waving goodbye in too-large gloves.

At the far end of the platform, where the railway shelter stopped, snow was falling. The yellow lighting revealed it drifting down in a steady stream. Erin walked towards it until she was standing underneath the snowfall, silent and miraculous.

About the Author

Photo Credit © Charlotte Langley

Charlotte Langley works as a personal finance reporter at the *Telegraph* and is a fresh, breakout voice in gripping psychological police dramas.

𝕏 **@c_langley_**

@charlottelangleyauthor